My Heart Knows . . .

by
Ethel Cook

Published by:
Empire Publishing, Inc.

3130 US Highway 220
Madison, NC 27025-8306
Phone: 336-427-5850 • Fax: 336-427-7372
www.empirepublishinginc.com

Library of Congress Control Number: 2009922182
ISBN Number: 978-0-944019-56-6

Published and printed in United States of America
1 2 3 4 5 6 7 8 9 10

When Wild Geese Fly

The geese flew south tonight
    and I was fascinated
By the steady rhythm of their
    beating wings.

I could not think of other things
    But rather was transported,
        and I found myself
High in the majestic blue so wild
    and free,
And then I thought, this cannot be,
    For I am earthbound . . .

Yet I know some spirit in me soars
    with them on high,
Whenever wild geese set their pattern
    in the sky.

                  —Johanna Ter Wee

... Where the Wild Goose Goes

A wise man wrote many years ago "Of making many books there is no end" (Ecclesiastes 12:12). This volume is sent forth not as the last word on the struggles of a young family in hard times (times sandwiched between two World Wars and a "Great Depression"). The struggle to survive and to succeed is a story that could be repeated many times over. Harley and Effie were my parents, and eight of their nine children were my sisters and brothers, myself being the ninth and oldest. Other characters were relatives, and neighbors, many who were enduring the hardships of days past. Names have been changed so that no one could be embarrassed or offended by the revelation of the hardships endured.

My Heart Knows is basically my story and what I remember, and have been told, especially the early childhood days. The flight of the geese, facing the severity of the northern winter and fleeing to the warmer southern climate is my flight from the hardship of the farm, to the more favorable environment of public work and independence. Unlike the geese who knew their destiny—I did not understand at the beginning that a wise and all-knowing providence was steering my life, not just from the trials of the farm, but to a life of peace and eternal life through Jesus Christ my Lord. My family would never have believed that I would marry a minister, matriculate in six colleges and universities, serve with my husband in five states (travel in all but three) and travel in twelve countries of Europe and the Middle East. I attribute my flight solely to my Lord and Savior.

Many things I write about in my story are things unknown by many people today, and especially young people. I have included

5

many things and emphasized expressions which belong exclusively to the life and language of days past.

God has not only favored me with the things written above, but I am the mother of three lovely daughters, two grand-daughters, four grandsons and seven great-grandchildren.

Before concluding this introduction, let me proudly say, all of the children of Harley and Effie have succeeded in life with good families, beautiful homes and success in their flight from the past trials and troubles. Harley and Effie lived to be in their eighties, and of the nine children they raised, eight of them are still living, and none of them have come to shame or have divorced or brought any measure of reproach upon their parents.

Acknowledgments

For many years, my inner voice prompted me to put in writing the experiences, trials, and tribulations of families struggling to survive during troublesome times. The ability to endure and eventually succeed required hard work, primitive tools, patience and faith.

That still, small voice was put to silence until an educational goal had been reached, then marriage, children, grandchildren and even great-grandchildren arrived. Then I yielded to that pent-up desire and began writing of my own personal journey describing my childhood, youth and the rigors of farm life, and my flight to the city and to faith in Christ. To get from there to here required long hours and even months. I was not alone in this endeavor. Dear friends were on hand and frequently called upon for advice, counsel, and from them came also much encouragement.

In particular are Marilyn Swinson, teacher, counselor and poet who read my story, gave suggestions, and edited the manuscript. Dana and Wade Rorrer had the difficult task of transferring the written manuscript to a CD format. Thanks, too, to Robert Aheron, friend and fellow church member, who introduced me to his publisher and also encouraged me to proceed. He, too, had taken a difficult journey that is described in his book, *Hope for the Hopeless.* The cover of this book was painted by Wesley Priddy, Rockingham County's recent Artist of the Month. None of this could have been accomplished without the oversight and direction of Rhonda Lemons at Empire Publishing. Thank you all for your good help.

One

The wild geese were on the wing, that cool, crisp Wednesday night in the latter part of November 1927. The lead gander honked hoarsely as he veered his beak to the right, into the south wind. The V-shaped formation, followed close behind, consenting in low, grunting notes. The combined instincts of the brantians knew that the mighty river, the Mississippi, was somewhere beneath the haze of the lunar light.

From a farmhouse in Western Tennessee came a shriek of pain. A young woman of nineteen summers was bursting with child. The calls of the migratory creatures from above and the cries from the pangs of pain down below mingled in the frosty air as surreal. Momentarily, the atmosphere was punctured by a primal scream. The final contraction heaved forth, a hefty pulsating baby girl dripping with rosy-red dew, as of the morning. The tender lungs grabbed for large gulps of air. The squall ended nine months of incubation and darkness.

The country doctor gently, but firmly, snipped the umbilical cord and passed the slippery neonate to the strong hands of the ample neighbor, Mrs. Jones. From the edge of the kerosene light appeared the tiny figure of the grandmother, "Ma-Bett." She set the lamp on a nearby table and pushed forward a pan of warm water for the initial cleansing. A bushy head of hair was matted with a yellow, waxy substance. A hard rub of the towel revealed a mop of fire-red hair that came down over the baby's eyes.

The doctor leered with amusement as he reached for the

smoldering cigar on the window ledge. Most definitely the husband, who had dark hair, had impregnated this shy, dark-haired young woman. But had the doctor not known this pristine maiden, he could have surmised there were genes from another pool present.

The whiffs of ether were wearing off. The exhausted new mother craned her short neck to see her first-born. The sight of the red hair shocked her sedated senses. The deep inhaling pulled her back into ether-land.

On a bright Sunday morning in early June, she and her new husband's mother were loping along in the Sunday buggy on their way to the Methodist Church. The country road led around a large semi-circle of timberland, down a steep hill and across a bridge dividing two counties, up another hill onto another bridge of the same winding creek. As the horse's hooves began their clip-clop on the timbers of the bridge, his foot caught in a crack between the planks. The horse began rocking back and forth, becoming more frantic by the moment.

The two women, the young and the old, froze with fear as they tried to constrain the frightened animal by tightening the reins. For long moments they expected the buggy to overturn, tossing them onto the rocky bed of the creek below.

Down the sloping grade where the road led on to the bridge came a young man on his way to church. He responded to the women in distress, his shiny red hair glowing in the warm Sunday sunshine. After calming the nervous horse, he carefully twisted the entrapped hoof from the crack. The young woman, three months pregnant, still sat, paralyzed with fear—her eyes fastened on the brilliant head of red hair. Being assured by the young man's presence and help, the older woman loosened the reins, clucked a "giddy-up," and once again, they were on their way to the church, just up another slight hill and a short distance beyond.

As the days passed into weeks and weeks into months, the incident at the bridge was put in the back of the young woman's mind. The child growing inside her abdomen kept her wondering and pondering about the day that was to surely come.

The ether had done its job. From her twilight zone, she became fully aware of the new little stranger squirming and whimpering nearby. The two older women had finished bathing and powdering the rosy red cherub with the brilliant red hair. They fashioned a Birdseye diaper into a three-cornered swing and placed the baby inside. Next, they hooked the diaper on to a household scale. With the fragile load suspended in air, the spring pulled down to number four, on to number six, and stopped at seven and one-half pounds. Proudly they removed the Birdseye contraption from off the grunting little one. MaBett reached out her hands and took her new little granddaughter to herself for a short moment. Mrs. Jones tidied up the birth bed and fluffed the pillow of the new mother.

A fresh pan of warm water, along with soap and towel, was brought out to the doctor. He washed and dried his Hippocratic hands and closed his little black bag.

From the shadow of the other front room stepped Harley, the new father, speechless, smiling as he learned he was the parent of a seven and one-half pound baby girl.

The doctor sauntered out through the front hall to the front porch, feeling his way in the dark to his faithful T-Model Ford. He would be home by midnight. He rode away down the rutted lane to the primary road, taking his cigar with him.

Reluctantly, MaBett surrendered the infant, who was already snuggled close to her heart. Woman and child had bonded forever.

The baby was put to the mother's breast. The eager infant soon perfected the sucking process, rolling its little pink tongue around the spout of the mammary gland. It was a beautiful moment. The new mother was radiant, satisfied with the labor of this day. Her newborn was feasting on the warm milk of her bountiful body.

When everything seemed just right, mother glanced

11

again at the new baby. "Red hair. Red hair." Never in her wildest imagination had she dreamed of having a red-headed baby. Now the ether memories began to make sense—the young man with the flaming red hair who rescued them on the bridge. Her baby had been marked by that frightening experience.

Harley entered the room. Although the young doctor was gone, his presence and smell penetrated the room. Mrs. Jones was tired, but glad for having had a part in this important event. MaBett was quiet but joyful. She began mechanically jabbing in the simmering coals in the fireplace. With so much attention focused on more demanding matters, the last spark had faded. As she poked in the ashes, her youngest son, the new father, hurried to help. He had felt so useless the last few hours. At least he could build a new fire to keep the room warm. Bringing a shovel of coals from the fireplace in the other front room, and adding some strips of kindling, he soon had a fire going.

Mother and the baby had fallen asleep. Mrs. Jones pulled the covers up around their shoulders as MaBett lowered the wick in the coal-oil lamp. Reaching for her shawl and head covering, Mrs. Jones reckoned that she should be on her way home. The tired father awkwardly expressed a sincere "much obliged." MaBett, not accustomed to being confined for so many hours, took this opportunity to get some fresh air. She ran to her room, grabbed a sweater and a kerosene lantern from the side room, and offered to walk with her friend at least part of the way home. Most women were not brave enough to leave the perimeters of their yards after dark. She would go with her neighbor at least to the top of the hollow that led down into the deep ravine and up another hill to her home. The "Nightingale of the Night" could continue on with the lantern. MaBett could find her way back in the dark with the aid of the dim moonlight shining on the worn path. Her feet knew every bump, rock, and dip.

The gentle glow of the flickering flames sent a warm light across the room. Harley was exhausted. He took his eyeglasses from his face and laid them on the mantel. Then he removed his outerwear and shoes, brushing the bottom of his feet for any clinging grit, and climbed into the other bed in his union suit. Under a heavy homemade quilt, his head resting on a thick feather pillow, he tossed for a few minutes, reliving the events of the day.

Reality settled in: he was now a father and had a father's responsibilities. He could not always live with his folks. His growing family would need their own house and farm. The house would need furniture; the farm would need its own tools and implements, work animals, and a cow or two for milk and butter. The weight of these thoughts took their toll. His brain closed down and he sank into a deep sleep.

At daybreak, the rooster began his familiar call. Everyone was still in deep sleep. Why did this loud fowl have to be so eager to break the bounds of darkness and light? MaBett was the first one to hear and heed the rooster reveille. "All right." She swung her slender legs from under the cover to the edge of the bed and plunked her feet down on the cold floor. Then it dawned upon her—she really did have reason to rise and began this new day. There was that new grandchild waiting for her.

Reaching for her long cotton dress that hung from the foot of the bed, she hastily pulled it over her head and pushed the long bottom part all the way to her ankles. Then she pulled lisle stockings up and over her knees, securing them with elastic bands. From under the bed she yanked her high-top everyday shoes, stuck her tiny feet in them, and pulled the laces tight. Grabbing her long white apron from the back of a nearby straight-back cane-bottom chair, she tied its strings snugly around her tiny waist.

By this time, Grandfather, occupying the other bed, had awakened. He mumbled something about fixing the fire.

MaBett scurried to the cold kitchen. She fumbled to open the firebox of the cast-iron cook stove. After filling the fire space with skinny pieces of kindling, she doused the tinder with some coal oil from a gallon can stored behind the stove. She scratched a match across its box and started a crackling fire. She reached for the dipper in the water bucket to fill the coffee percolator. The tin bowl was setting on the almost dry bottom of the bucket. The birthing process had used up almost all the water. Grasping the empty bucket with the bail over the palm of her hand, she bounded out the back door, her feet barely touching the one step to the ground.

Behind the pear tree, the sky was aglow with orange-red hues of the rising sun. She inhaled the fresh morning air. The day was dawning, and so were her thoughts of the past few hours. She was coming alive. New spurts of energy were invigorating her stiff joints.

As she set the water pail on the wooden stand by the well, she caught a glimpse of a pointed object near the base of the pear tree. Coming closer, she saw that it was a gray feather, standing almost erect, the quill precariously stuck in the ground. She picked it up and twirled the vane. Still slightly mesmerized from last night's happenings, she wondered, "Could it be from the wing of an angel?" She no longer had geese to provide the down for pillows and feather beds, though the fowls had insisted on staying on the pond the past year. With little rain, the water in the pond became goose soup, so she had dispensed of the source of the goop. Besides, the feathers of her geese were whiter than this one. Puzzled, she laid the feather upon the ledge under the eave of the well shelter. Instinctively, she allowed the slender metal bucket to descend to the bottom of the well. The water filled the vacuum. By the turning of the windlass, she brought the full bucket back to the top of the well. With the pull of the valve lever, the narrow bucket was emptied and the round one was full.

With the weight of the water pulling on the fingers of one hand and the waft of the feather lodged between the fingers of the other hand, she hurried back up the step into the kitchen where the fire was hot. She put the water on the table beside the window and laid the feather on the ledge of the same window.

She filled the coffee pot with the fresh water. Then she added the coarsely ground coffee beans to the top basket. Soon the hot, bubbling water was doing its job. On the other eye of the stove she placed the iron teakettle with water to heat water for purposes other than cooking and washing dishes demand.

Afterwards, she found herself pondering the meaning of the strange feather that had fallen from the sky.

MaBett reached into the flour barrel and drew out the wooden dough bowl and metal sifter. Filling the sieve with flour, she turned the handle a few turns and then slapped its sides with the palm of her hand. This threshing caught all the lumps of dried dough and other particles from the flour; the waste was then dumped into the slop bucket sitting under the window near the stove. To the sifted flour she added a pinch of salt from the brown-brindled saltcellar, some Arm-and-Hammer baking soda, and then a fist full of lard. After squishing this together she added a cup of buttermilk, making a puddle in the center of the flour mixture. Gradually, she worked the liquid into the dry ingredients. The mixture became malleable. The lump of dough was kneaded, slapped, and patted, then shaped into flattened rolls. No dough board or rolling pin was needed. Onto a greased cast iron griddle went the raw biscuits and then into the hot oven.

MaBett then sliced the last hunk of fatback from the smokehouse into thin strips. This was a nice piece of middling meat with strips of lean to enhance the taste and appearance. The smokehouse was empty. She remembered that this was Thanksgiving Day, the usual time to kill the hogs. But with the impending arrival of the baby this job had been postponed until at least next week.

The strips of meat began to sizzle as the fire forced the oil from the fat fibers. Soon the pieces were golden brown. MaBett pierced each piece with the tines of a fork and lifted them onto a platter. The hot grease was left in the hot skillet. A fistful of flour was added to the melted fat and stirred quickly with a large spoon. A dash of salt and a sprinkle of black pepper were added while stirring continued. The combined flour and grease became the thickening for the gravy. Grabbing a handful of apron tail, she lifted the teakettle and poured about three cupsful of boiling water into the lightly browned flour mixture and stirring furiously until it was of the right consistency.

By now the biscuits had browned to perfection. The menfolk were making their way to the kitchen. The aroma of the perking coffee was arousing their hunger buds.

The son, Harley, came in first, trying to appear calm and unaffected. His mother pointed out that the hen house door should be opened to allow the flock to fly down from the roost and stretch their wings to the morning sun before the beginning of their pecking and scratching for nuggets of grit and gravel.

As the weather had cooled, so had the roosters' fervor for fertilizing the eggs of the dames of the chicken crowd. The hens were not laying well. This was the time of the year when egg-laying slackened noticeably. During the year the average hen laid only about one hundred eggs. Just when the "egg money" was most needed, the supply was curtailed by nature's way. With Christmas not far away, MaBett harvested and managed the eggs. She needed the proceeds not only for cooking needs such as sugar, coffee, and nutmeg, but also for her own pet vice and pleasure, that of snuff dipping.

During this time, breakfast usually consisted of biscuits, thickenin' gravy and sometimes fried fatback, with a side dressing of homemade jelly or jam or some store bought corn syrup.

This morning she took six eggs from the egg basket to scramble. She felt these were all she could spare until the hens started laying again. After the new mother's long hours of labor, she knew that she must be hungry.

Harley came in from feeding the chickens. MaBett would feed them cracked corn later. She prepared a wash pan of warm water, soap, and a towel and sent the new father to his wife's bedside for her morning wash-up. From the pie-safe she took out a jar of her prized pear preserves. She twisted off the zinc lid and wiped green mold from the neck. She then scooped the golden preserves into a small dish and split two biscuits into halves and covered the four parts with light golden brown gravy. A third hot biscuit was left intact, along with a lump of fresh butter for mixing with the preserves. She

16

placed about half of the scrambled eggs on the plate, alongside the warm bread. She put this, with a cup of hot coffee, already sugared and creamed, on a tray and made her way from the kitchen, across the side room, up the one step into the front room, through the front hall and into the other front room that had been the young couple's abode since their marriage a year ago.

The daughter-in-law, accepted the bountiful breakfast, showing her gratitude with a quick smile. She was hungry. MaBett accepted the silent thanks and hurried back to the kitchen where the menfolk were waiting.

The grandfather seemed impatient and hungry. After all, this had been a long night for all of them. They dragged the straight-back, cane-bottom chairs up to their usual places at the table. Quickly, the biscuits were split and spattered with the gravy. The remaining portion of the scrambled eggs was mixed in with the gravy-biscuit on the grandfather's and Harley's plates. They crunched down on the crispy strips of fried fatback. Bits of biscuits were used to sop up straying gravy. Hot coffee was poured into saucers and blown. Then mouthfuls of the filling food were washed down with the cooled liquid.

Finally, MaBett wiped her hands on her apron and filled her plate with two biscuits and gravy, and, of course, some of the pear preserves. She pretended that she did not care for eggs anyway.

The family ate in silence, each deep in thought. Soon, Grandfather finished his meal, scrubbed his chair from the table, and allowed that he would feed the stock. The son, always a slow chewer, labored with his food, piling used meat skins on the edge of the plate. He slathered the fourth biscuit with the sweet syrupy cane juice and sopped up every bite. Then he pushed his chair back, stood up, and stretched his slight body. Instinctively, he stepped over to the slop bucket, grasped its greasy bail and stomped out the door toward the hog pen.

MaBett's gaze wandered to the window and the feather resting there. She stood to her feet, mentally noting that she was going to keep this single goose feather. She remembered a prized patent medicine bottle with an ornate shape that she had treasured for years. She did not know exactly where it came from, but she'd had it since she was a girl. She did know its original contents were a cure for malaria, because on its side were the words, **SURE CURE FOR MALARIA**. She took the bottle from its hiding place, removed the stopper, and inserted the quill in its neck. Not knowing exactly why the curious interest, she stood on her tip toes and placed the plume on top of the pie safe.

Most of Thanksgiving Day had come and gone without special notice. The hearts of this home were lighter, warmer this day. MaBett was humming, singing, and whistling on the inside. Grandfather—usually scowling and gruff—was on the edge of a grin through his long smokey-gray whiskers. He did not talk to himself quite so much. Harley tried to suppress his delight, but everyone knew he was excited about his little daughter.

Taking care of the new mother and the new baby gave MaBett numerous reasons to tiptoe in and out of the front bedroom. The little girl had settled in nicely to the comforting arms of her mother, the lavish affections of her dad, and the anxious heart of her doting grandmother.

As the day neared sunset, the jangle of harnesses and rumble of a rolling farm wagon was heard from up the rutted road leading to the homeplace. When the wooden-steel vehicle came into view, MaBett looked out the backdoor and saw it was Maudie, one of her older daughters, her husband, and three of her six children, coming to see the new baby. They had killed hogs and were bringing fresh meat. MaBett proudly showed her daughter and granddaughters the new baby. Meanwhile, Harley had joined the other menfolk down at the barn. Men and boys just did not take an interest in woman-things such as new babies.

MaBett stoked up the fire in the cook stove, washed the fresh ribs and backbone, and sprinkled the meat with salt and pepper. Barely covering the meat with water in the heavy pot, she lowered the kettle with the iron pegs into the opening of the stove eye. The meat would need to cook slowly for about two hours. Leftover biscuits from breakfast and half of the pone of cornbread from the midday meal became the main ingredients for a pan of dressing. With broth from the simmering pot, a beaten egg and a smidgen of dried sage, she made a crunchy side dish for the fresh meat. There was half of a kettle of long simmered green beans left from the former meal. While the dressing was browning in the oven, she hurriedly brought out a quart of canned blackberries from storage in the side room. She put these together with a dough crust, to fashion a cobbler that would go into the oven as soon as the dressing was browned.

After eating, Maudie and family soon 'lowed it was time for them to head home before dark.

By dusk, the eggs had been gathered and the chicken house locked up for the night, the cows milked and the stock fed. The hogs' bellies were full and satisfied. Ring, the faithful dog, had feasted and gnawed on the pork bones and gristles that had been thrown out the back door to him.

MaBett's sumptuous meal was a perfect ending for the day. She was pleased; everything had turned out just right. She relaxed by backing up to the open fire, pulling up her long skirt, and rubbing her legs and rump. Standing on one foot and then the other, she became lost in contemplation. Only she knew her thoughts, but her countenance revealed perfect calm.

As Harley passed by her on his way to see his wife and baby, MaBett remembered that the child had not been named. Doctor Thomas would need the name by Monday to finish the birth records that would be sent to Nashville for permanent recording. She joined her son at the foot of his wife's bed. Harley felt like someone on the outside looking in, but he did want to be a closer part of this intimate circle. MaBett's presence broke up the silent communication. The three agreed that the baby needed a name. After some hesitation, Effie, the new mother shyly stated that she had always liked the name Catherine. Harley overrode her suggestion, remembering fondly the name of his first girlfriend in Kentucky. His mother and he had made yearly trips to see her sister Mollie at Mayfield, and her children were his favorite cousins. During his adolescent years, when he was becoming aware of girls, he had met an attractive young lady, Carmelene, who more than piqued his interest. The distance between them, however, had prevented any romantic notions from developing. She had sent him a picture of herself standing on a bridge. The picture is still among the family photos.

Why not name his first girl-child after this special memory; Effie sensed Harley's delight in even speaking of her, and whatever made her husband happy made her happy. The name Carmelene was repeated three or four times, then accepted. MaBett did not offer her approval or disapproval of the name.

Carmelene seemed to lend itself as a middle name. MaBett suggested they think about a first name for a day or two to see what might come to mind. The young couple shook their heads in agreement.

The eyes of the night were heavy. Soon the coal-oil lamps were extinguished, except one with a low flame by the baby's side of the bed.

Friday and Saturday came and went with regular routine of chores and fixing meals. The baby's needs, warm milk and a dry bottom, were readily met. Effie was quickly regaining her strength.

A bright Sunday sun awakened the family. Soon the coffee pot was perking, and the oven was hot for biscuits. This morning, they would have one of Effie's favorite breakfasts, salmon cakes and gravy over biscuits.

Even though it was Sunday, chores had to be done. Preaching day was the first Sunday of the month, so there would be no church today, this being the fourth Sunday. Sunday dinners were always prepared with care. It was customary for some of the children and their families to drop in around dinner time. MaBett was always ready with a full table. In fact, she would be hurt if no one came, especially today with the arrival of the new baby.

Sure enough, some of the nearby family members, along

with their families, came for a short visit. MaBett insisted that they stay for a spell and eat dinner with them; they gladly obliged.

After the Sunday meal, the leftovers were placed in the pie safe until supper. The womenfolk remained in the kitchen for chit-chat and the washing of greasy dishes in a pan containing lukewarm water, a bar of yellow, Fels Naptha soap and a dishtowel made from a flour sack.

Each female felt obligated to take part in this operation. While MaBett washed, the others dried. To do less would imply that they were lazy or considered themselves above such a menial task. Only Effie was excused. She sat on a pillow on a straight-back cane-bottomed chair with her arms wrapped around her baby, who was sore from being passed from one woman to another. The smaller children had pulled on her arms and legs and stroked her red hair. Soon the wee one was asleep. MaBett took the baby from her mother's protective arms and laid her on the foot of her bed for a long nap.

The shuffling of feet and the sound of familiar voices were heard from the front door. It was Mrs. Jones and her two daughters. She was eager for her girls to see the red-haired baby. Also she wanted to make sure that Effie was making a normal recovery from childbirth. MaBett shared with Mrs. Jones the choice of the name for the baby. So far, they had not come up with a second name to go with Carmelene. When the source of the name was revealed, Mrs. Jones was amused and shocked. Only Effie would allow a husband to attach his old girlfriend's name to their firstborn. Thoughts began to click. She had always thought that Golda was a beautiful name, and with the child's golden-red hair, this would be a perfect match. MaBett thought so too. That night after all the company was gone, MaBett shared this potential name with the parents. They readily accepted and Golda Carmelene became the baby's name.

As MaBett went about her work in the kitchen, her eyes would momentarily take note of the goose feather resting on top of the pie safe. Knowing that curious eyes could see and question the reason for such a silly thing, she took it down;

she questioned her own fascination with such a frivolous object. Taking it from the blue bottle, she swirled the pale gray vane between her fingers. What would make a secure place for such a delicate little thing? Of course, a pillow filled with other like feathers. She tiptoed to her bed and grasped her favorite plump pillow. With scissors, she snipped the seam of one end and tucked the weightless object inside. With chagrin, she chided herself for such an unexplainable obsession. But it was done and she was glad.

Two

The colder days of December served as impetus to complete the remaining jobs of the fading year. First on the docket was killing the hogs. After butchering, the carcasses were cut into hams, shoulders, and middlings and placed in the saltbox. The fat from the intestines was rendered into leaf lard by frying down the scrap fat remnants in the large iron kettle wash pot and placing it into 5-gallon lard cans. The crackling, the browned fat pieces, was stored in sugar sacks to be used later in cornbread.

The basic food supply secured, the matter of creature comfort was addressed. This involved the gathering of wood for the fireplaces and the cook stove. Some wood, now seasoned, had been strewn around the edges of the fields after clearing had occurred. More trees had to be cut down and sawed into sections, then split by wedge and sledgehammer. Two or more wagonloads were brought to the front yard and tossed near a large tree. There was never enough time to stack the wood.

By now the increasing rains had made the fields soft. But the remnants of a field of late corn, mostly nubbins, must be gathered. Pulling the wagon over the rows with the tongue straddling dry rough corn stalks, the team of mules straining with the load waded through the middle of dried cockle burrs. The gruff commands of the wagon masters drove the animals on in merciless labor.

The wagon bed, filled with ears of shuck, grain, and cob, was drawn into the hall of the cavernous barn. With a large corn scoop the load was shoveled into the corncrib.

The corn crop was the chief provender for the livestock with the exception of the cows, which fed mostly on dry hay. The corn would also be used as an invaluable source of food for the family. Select ears would be shelled and taken to the gristmill for cornmeal. There was always at least one large skillet of cornbread made each day. It was the bread for dinner and supper.

Once or twice during each winter, choice white corn would be shelled to make a batch of hominy. To about one gallon of shelled kernels, four or five cups of ashes taken from the back of the fireplace where it was free from ambeer or other human contaminants. Covered with water, the corn and ashes would soak for several hours. Then the mixture would be boiled for about three hours or until the hulls loosened. With fresh water, the corn was washed and rubbed vigorously until all hulls were removed. The skinned corn was cooked with some butter or meat drippings, and became a good and substantial meal that stuck to the ribs.

Early in the month of December, MaBett found herself looking forward to Christmas. This would be a very special one with a new baby in the house. She had saved some money from her own cotton patch. Usually she would hold on to this meager amount for possible hard times. But she felt especially warm and generous. She, like most women in rural areas, very seldom had opportunity to go into town to Woolworth's for shopping. The men would venture out maybe once or twice a year to sell farm products. Growing their own food and making their own clothes, sheets, pillowcases, and towels satisfied most of their needs. Things not grown—such as flour, salt, pepper, baking soda, and vanilla flavoring—were bartered for at the store, using country-cured hams, fresh eggs and butter. Even live hens were taken in and sold by the pound.

MaBett began to pore over the Sears catalog for the items to meet needs of each family member. First she found a chick-in-egg rattler made of white rubber with whistle and teething ring, only fifteen cents for the baby. Next, she saw two pairs of tiny socks, made of white mercerized cotton, size 4 ½, one pair with sky blue tops and the other pair with yellow tops, each pair twenty-five cents.

For her menfolk, a pair of union suits in cream color of elastic ribbed cotton with long sleeves for $1.25 a pair. Also a package of twelve white hem-stitched handkerchiefs for sixty-nine cents. She would give them two each for now and save the others for later on. Harley went through so many, sneezing and blowing his nose incessantly.

For Effie, she chose a union suit with buttons down the front and a sure-lap flap seat in white striped madras in large size for ninety-eight cents For both of them she ordered some stockings of fine-combed cotton yarns, hers in black and Effie's in dark brown.

For herself, she found a leather coin purse in the catalogue with nickel-plated metal frame with two pockets for only thirty-five cents. All these years she had carried her money in a tobacco sack with a drawstring top. She met the rural mail carrier at the store and gave him $8.00 for a money order plus the money order fee. This was the largest order she had ever sent to Sears Roebuck. She felt very good about herself.

Christmas was only a few days away. The last picking, actual pulling, of the cotton was finished. The cotton burrs had been snatched from the dead stiff stalks with the locks of cotton still clinging inside. Dried leaves and fragments of twigs clung to the fluffy locks. Handfuls of the whole bit, soft and rough were crammed into the well-worn canvas cotton sacks. The gathered roughage was of cheap quality and would bring only a cheap price. The remnants of the harvest were stashed into the bed of the farm wagon until the next trip to the store and the nearby gin. At least there would be enough from its sale for the Christmas treats.

Early Christmas Eve, on a cool, cloudy Saturday morning, the menfolk hitched up their prized, matched mules to the wagon and made another one of their pleasure trips to the store about one and one-half miles away. Other menfolk in the area were doing the same, so they had to wait in line with their Christmas cargo at the gin. They did not mind. The idle moments gave them a welcome chance to mix and mingle with their fellow farmers. Harley and his father sat hunkered on the hard buckboard seat, loose reins in hand, not talking, but listening with great interest. They "chawed" tobacco and gestured about the year's crops, some good and some that failed because of dry weather or too much rain at certain times. Some of them had intended to buy their first car this year, but the price of the Ford T-Model had jumped from $385 to $570. An A-Model had just come out that could go as fast as seventy-one miles per hour and had twice the horsepower of the old Ford. Maybe next year. But according to the *Nashville Banner* there was already a backorder of 50,000. President Hoover claimed that the American worker could expect continuing good wages. The farmers should benefit from the increasing demand for cotton.

Just before dinner time, the men, returned, laden with brown paper sacks of apples, oranges, bananas, a coconut or two, and some chocolate drops. There were also some Brazil nuts in their three- cornered shells. There had been enough money left for a ten pound bag of flour and five pounds of sugar for the Christmas baking and some days ahead.

All day MaBett busied herself in the kitchen. Effie had many Birdseye diapers and other baby things to wash and hang by the fireplace for drying while the menfolk were gone. MaBett killed the fatted hen that had been cooped up for several days for this occasion. She plunged the fowl into a tub of very hot water to loosen the feathers. After much plucking, only the pinfeathers remained to be singed over a low flame. Quickly drawing out the entrails and washing the carcass thoroughly, she cut the fowl into several large pieces and covered them with water in the iron kettle and placed it into one of the eyes on the cook stove to cook slowly for about three hours. Then the tender meat would be removed from the bones and the broth would be used for making a big pan of dressing with lots of sage.

The tasks of the day finished, MaBett hurriedly cleaned up the kitchen after a simple supper meal. The good stuff would have to wait until tomorrow. Earlier, the menfolk had sneaked their Christmas goodies into the front closet by the fireplace. The smell of apples, oranges, and brown paper bags permeated the house. It was a nostalgic aroma of Christmases past.

MaBett brought out the largest of the coconuts, held it to her right ear, shook it hard, listened for gushing sounds that would assure her that it was full of liquid. With a hammer and a sixteen-penny nail, she pierced the hard husk through its soft spots, the eyes. Then she set the coconut upside down on a jar to let the milk drain out. With the oven still hot from baking a pone of cornbread for tomorrow's dressing, she put the whole hull inside the oven for a few minutes. After the heat had loosened the leathery inner skin from the shell, she tapped all over it with the hammer, thus loosening more of the coconut meat from the tough covering. Then she cracked open the hard shell with her hammer and pried out the white meat with the butcher knife. With the help of a metal grater, she soon produced almost four cups of grated fresh coconut.

After sifting together the flour and baking powder, she set them aside. She then blended fresh butter and sugar together and added the three stiff egg whites which she had beaten briskly with a rotary beater. She added some vanilla flavoring to one cup of coconut milk which she alternately mixed with the dry ingredients and creamed mixture. She poured the batter into three greased and floured round cake pans. It would take about thirty minutes for the layers to bake and some time to cool.

Grandpa was already snoozing beside the warm fireplace. But his wife had a job for him. After all, Christmas was a family affair. One of her specialties for this season was making molasses popcorn balls. She had raised her own patch of popcorn for just such an occasion. A metal popcorn popper always hung on the wall left of the fireplace. This tin, plump rectangular box had a sliding top and a long handle. Wiping the inside of any fine ashes of dust, she poured less than a cup of corn grains into the popper. There must be room for the last kernel to explode. Grandpa aroused from his early nap. She placed the handle in his big, rough right hand and he began to shake the tiny metal box back and forth over the highest log with the simmering flames. A non-verbal task for Grandpa. Soon the muffled sounds of the kernels bursting inside the popper turned into a silent thud. A dishpan was placed on the hearth. At least two batches of the popped corn would be needed. After all it was only natural that Grandpa would snitch a few hot grains for his own enjoyment. In the meantime, MaBett was combining about two cups of molasses, some sugar and water, plus a small amount of vinegar, and boiling it to a hardball stage. Then a dash of baking soda would be added. All this would be poured over the popped corn and mixed thoroughly. Then with greased hands, she would shape this grain and goo into baseball-size balls.

The cake layers were now cooled. MaBett combined two cups of sugar with some water and a teaspoon of vinegar into a heavy pan and cooked it over medium heat, stirring constantly. With the rotary beater, she beat three egg whites until stiff. Then she poured the hot syrup over the beaten egg whites and continued beating until the frosting held its shape. One-half teaspoon of vanilla was added for a delicate flavor. Each layer was covered with some of the frosting and then sprinkled with grated coconut. The layers were stacked one on the other with the top and sides lavished with the luscious topping. Then the remaining freshly grated coconut was piled on the top and smeared on the sides. This cake was a snow-white ambrosial sight. The diminishing fire in the cook stove had allowed the kitchen to cool. The cake would be mellowed to perfection by tomorrow.

A stocking for each member of the family was hung on the mantel. Christmas morning would find them filled with hard candy and gum. The brown paper sacks of fruit and chocolate drops were brought from the closet and placed on the hearth. It would soon be time for Old Saint Nick to make his round and scoot down the sooty chimney with his pack on his back. Besides the chick-in-egg rattler and socks, the baby would have a doll. MaBett had found a sack of flour with a preprinted pattern of a gingerbread man. Mrs. Jones had cut out the pieces and sewed them up on her sewing machine, leaving open the top of the head. She had stuffed the doll's arms, legs, and body with soft cotton and sewed up the top of the head with needle and thread. In the catch-it-all drawer she had found two brown buttons for the eyes; these she attached with heavy buttonhole thread. The nose and lips were already printed on the face.

From her secret hiding place, MaBett brought out the union suits, handkerchiefs, stockings, and the leather coin purse — all ordered from Sears Roebuck. Santa Claus had done himself proud this year.

Weary of body, but joyful in heart, MaBett fell into bed. She had taken many steps today, perhaps miles of them, but they were steps of love. Although her body had stopped moving, her brain kept working. She mentally retraced the accomplishments of the day to see if she had left anything undone.

One of the first tasks in the morning would be to bring the prized Christmas churn from the cellar. A week before, when the house was empty, Effie, with the baby, had walked across the hollow for a visit with Mrs. Jones. It was a balmy day and MaBett had encouraged the young mother to get outside for some exercise and sunshine. Meanwhile, she seized this opportunity to prepare her special recipe of eggnog. It would need a few days to mellow in the cool cellar. First she had separated twelve eggs. The whites were beaten until stiff with the rotary beater. Such a batch would take two bowls. Sugar was added and then a half gallon of fresh sweet milk with cream. The secret ingredient came from Grandpa's stoneware jug with cork stopper that always stayed in the closet by the fireplace, supposedly for medicinal purposes. MaBett knew Grandpa took a nip now and then and especially on Christmas. With the wooden-handled corkscrew, she yanked out the stopper. The whiff from within almost took her breath away. Pouring out a quart of the potent elixir was a jarring experience. She shoved the stopper back into the jug and shoved the jug back to its hiding place.

Back in the kitchen, she mixed all the potions together

and beat the concoction until frothy. A gallon-sized crock, used for making cucumber pickles in the summer, became the perfect container for her Christmas specialty. She filled the churn to the brim and covered it tightly with a clean flour sack and the heavy lid. Then into the cellar went the special libation until Christmas morning. After another vigorous beating, it would be dipped out and served in cups, sprinkled with grated nutmeg. Yes, she had remembered to get some fresh whole nutmegs on her last trip to the store. The clock on the mantel was striking midnight. She fell fast asleep...

The bright sunlight heralded that Christmas Day had arrived, Grandpa had awakened early and revived the simmering coals of the fireplace. Even the roosters had reserved their raucous calls. A reverent air seemed to have settled over the home.

The adults, in childlike glee, snatched their stockings from the mantel and unwrapped the simple gifts of practical apparel. All eyes were on the baby as she was brought into the front room by the fireplace. Adoring parents, doting grandmother, and a guarded grandfather surrounded her. Her eyes followed the rustle of the brown paper sacks as Harley pretended surprise at the contents. MaBett placed the chick-in egg rattler into the warm chubby hands of the baby. Her fingers eagerly grasped the handle. Someone tweaked the egg. The baby's arms and legs pummeled the air. Then MaBett put the soft cuddly gingerbread man to her cheek. She gurgled, cooed, and snuggled up to her first doll. Golda Carmelene had made a merry Christmas for all.

The family had enjoyed a cozy and contented winter. The fires never seemed warmer; the home-soul foods never better. January, February, and March gave way to the months of spring. MaBett did the usual outside chores such as milking the two cows, feeding the two sows, plus the one boar left for stock for the coming year. Putting out the laying mash and gathering the eggs from the hen house each day was a pleasure. Cooking the two main meals, breakfast and dinner, set the rhythm of each day. Supper was quite simple. Many times, the leftover cornbread from the noon meal was crumbled into a big glass of sweet milk. Sometimes the women preferred buttermilk. On very cold nights, cornmeal mush was cooked as porridge and eaten with milk and a spoon. The leftover mush solidified overnight in the cold kitchen and was sliced and browned in a skillet the next morning for breakfast. Slabs of fresh butter were smeared on the crisp slices with sorghum molasses for the topping. This became a satisfying fuel to sustain the body until noontime.

Effie tried to find her place in the household, which included a hesitant husband, a strong stringent mother-in-law, and a silent sullen father-in-law. She observed with much interest the mother-in-law's mastery of the kitchen. At present, her part of the housework was washing dishes and putting away food, sweeping the floors that were always gritty with ashes; and other fallout from burning wood for heat and cooking. Much of the water had to be carried from the spring, which was a far piece, since the water supply from the well was weak.

Several times a day, Effie had to come apart and find a quiet place to nurse the baby. This was a pleasant time since her ample breasts were always bursting with the need to release some of the milk from their corpulent reservoirs. It was a time to sit and rest without feeling she was shirking her part of the work. MaBett reserved a special chore for herself; that of churning the soured milk into butter. This task was carried out every other day. The container of milk sat on the hearth for several hours, until the cream rose to the top. Then the cloth covering was removed and the cross-shaped dasher with a long handle was placed inside the large stoneware crock. The top, a circular crock lid with a hole in the middle for the dasher handle, was placed on the top. By pumping her right arm, she activated the dashing, churning, and sloshing of the agitator. It usually took at least thirty minutes for big globs of yellow butter to form on the top, leaving the buttermilk on the bottom.

All this time, MaBett held her grandchild on her lap tucked into the crook of her left arm. The baby was fascinated with the gyrating motion of MaBett's churning arm. Her chubby feet would dangle from the limited lap and kick with glee. The two seemed to be in their own little world. They would rock back and forth, snuggle and giggle, as two children at play. All the while, the churning was being done to the rhythm of some nursery tune of Mother Goose Land. Of course, the baby did not know the meaning of the words, but she enjoyed the lilting sounds. At other times, MaBett would ride the little princess on the top of her foot, singing:

Yankee Doodle went to town, riding on a pony,
Stuck a feather in his cap and called it macaroni.
Yankee Doodle, keep it up, Yankee doodle dandy;
Mind the music and the step, and with the girls be handy.

As good as everything appeared, something was not right with Effie; something about Golda, was not wearing well with her. The baby's hair was growing very fast. Already, she had cut it twice. The first time in the first week of her life when the hair came down over her eyes and grew down her neck. Now it had to be cut again, and it seemed to be getting redder and redder. The name Golda, "Goldie" by almost everyone, was just too much. For once, Effie prevailed, and the child's middle name, Carmelene, became her calling name.

Three

Sounds of spring caught the undiscerning ears of the baby. The songs of the birds seemed to be calling to her. The cackling of the laying hens and the mother's clucking caused the baby to look toward the windows for the source of the delightful noise. MaBett gave the baby her first experience with the farm babies. As soon as the baby chicks had pecked their way out of their egg incubators and began running around the feet of their mothers, she and the baby, with food in her apron pocket, made their way to the backyard. She squatted to the ground holding the baby near the cheep-cheep of the moving yellow balls using food as bait for the fussing mother who came up to eat from her hands, and soon one of the little ones was in tow. MaBett took the baby's hand in her hand and stroked the down soft baby feathers of the chick. Then she brushed its soft body against the infant's cheek. Spreading the baby's fingers apart, she led them over the contour of the head and beak and whole body. The baby girl chuckled and kicked with joy.

Before spring was too far gone, MaBett took little granddaughter on a grand tour of the hog pen. The grunting, blowing sow now had a brood of ten piglets. The new babies were fussing over their rightful place at the teats. MaBett called to her son who was working nearby, to come down to the pen and hold the baby while she scurried over the rail fence to sneak away one of the porcine babies from the unfriendly mother. Its squealing caused the baby to wince, but she stared in fascination. Her heart fluttered excitedly and her feet jabbed the air in rapturous delight.

MaBett remembered with mixed emotions the pet pig she had once owned. The runt of the litter, it had thrived on her cornbread, milk, love, and attention. It had followed her all over the barn lot and the backyard of the house, even trying to follow her up the back steps into the kitchen. She had had baby chicks, baby ducks, and goslings, and sometimes a baby calf that gave her much enjoyment. Now she had a baby granddaughter. She was very happy.

The menfolk used every daylight hour and the good weather to ready the fields for planting. The cotton was planted during the first days of May. Some corn had been planted already, but most of the corn crop would be tended to after the cottonseeds had been carefully buried in the top of the ridge rows.

The womenfolk had planted the garden in late April and were eagerly watching and waiting for spikes of onions, beets, English peas, and beans to push through the ground. They would lovingly till around each row of plants.

By the latter part of May, it was evident that there was a good stand of cotton. None would have to be replanted this year. The men did the plowing and planting, and the women did garden work and the chopping of the cotton. That entailed using a flat hoe to thin out the plants and then scrape the ground around the plants to remove the grass that thrived in the freshly tilled soil.

June was a very busy time for the females on the farm. Besides the regular chores and preparing two main meals for two hardworking men and themselves, they went to the field each day to tend the cotton plants.

Carmelene was now almost seven months old and crawling everywhere. Her day bed was the pallet on the floor. For some time she had been sitting up alone with a very straight back. She was taken to the field when the women went to do their work. Donning bonnets and socks for gloves, the women carrying two hoes, a file, and a fruit jar of fresh water, would habitually head for a patch that needed immediate attention. Now with the baby, a pallet, an old quilt, were added. MaBett even took along an old horse collar with which to confine the baby.

There were always tall trees not far from the edge of the rows to provide shade from the summer sun. After finding a level spot, MaBett placed the pallet on the ground with the horse collar in the center. The baby was placed inside the leather rim. She seemed to know that she was supposed to stay and watch as her mother and grandmother chopped down two rows and up the others. They constantly kept their eyes on the little one, not going far away. The baby was fascinated with the great outdoors. Looking upward, she watched the puffs of cottony clouds drifting across the bright blue sky. From her vista, she could see birds fly from the nearby trees and soar out of sight. Pretty yellow and black butterflies would flutter in and out, stopping briefly to sip the nectar from the blossoms of the weeds. Now and then, a dragonfly would flit by, searching for other insects to fill its enormous appetite.

The ground was teeming with moving things — ants, that is. For a few moments, she focused on the scurrying little creatures. Then, out of the fringe of grass and weeds, hopped a friendly toad. It came near the horse collar and the baby reached out over the leather loop to touch the dark green bumpy lumpy thing.

Just as she was crawling over the confining rim, her caretakers became aware of her outside interest and hurried down the rows to the pallet to check on her. MaBett picked up the young naturalist and strolled around the edge of the field, picking some wildflowers. One of her choicest finds, a morning glory, was placed in the baby's chubby hands. By now, Effie had unscrewed the zinc lid from the green water jar and was drinking of the cool-warm water. After MaBett quenched her thirst, she poured some of the water into the jar top and put it to the lips of the little farmerette who was also thirsty.

After a brief rest the women leaned their hoes against one of the trees and filed the cutting edges to razor sharpness. They then resumed their work on the rows of cotton. The sun was almost overhead. Its warm rays brought out the sweat on

their tired bodies. They would hoe four more rows before going to the house for dinner which MaBett had prepared very
early in the morning.

The baby was getting sleepy . . .

By the first of July, the cotton had been hoed three times.
The first time was mainly for thinning out the plants; the last
two times for fighting the battle of the grasses.

In early spring, the stables had been cleaned out and the
rotting, smoking manure was strewn over the fields for fertil-
izer. Animal waste had accumulated over the winter, until
it was several inches deep on the dirt floors. Several times,
the waste mixture would be shoveled to the outside of the
barns and later spread on the fields. This mixture provided a
perfect mix as the soil was turned and harrowed into a mellow medium for the cottonseeds. The spring showers and the
rich nutrients of the manure gave a jump-start to all the seeds
including the hayseeds. Human power was applied to the
handle of the hoe all the way down to the blade. By the third
time around, the grasses had been conquered.

The women's work in the cotton fields was mostly finished. The corn would get one hoeing, but not as meticulous
as that required for cotton.

By this time, the blackberries were ripe for picking.
Someone had to watch the baby. MaBett gladly took the job,
and Effie chose the outside work. She rubbed some kerosene
on her ankles and upper arms to repel the chiggers, those infinitesimal red mites that burrow under the skin and cause intense itching. The little red pests sense the presence of warm
blood and somehow march right off the end of the berry canes
onto the arms of their victims. With her head covered with
a bonnet and her arms covered with a long-sleeve shirt, she
made her way to the bottom land where the blackberries grew
in profusion along the edges of the fields. Two empty water
buckets dangled from one hand and a hoe was clutched tightly in the other. This she carried for defense against the sharp
thorns and possible snakes lurking in the underbrush.

Grandmother and child enjoyed their time together. The
baby crawled from the pallet to the floor around the table,

pulling on the long skirt of grandmother's dress as she prepared the noon meal. MaBett took some warm soft teacakes
from the oven, poured two glasses of sweet milk, and set them
on the table. She picked up the baby and set it on her lap,
and they ate an early lunch. The baby was tired from crawling over so much territory, and now with her tummy full, she
sank deeper into grandmother's arms. MaBett tiptoed to the
rocker that sat near the stove. With a gentle rock, both were
soon fast asleep.

Just before dinner, Effie returned with two heaping buckets of juicy blackberries. They would become a cobbler for
tomorrow, some jam for several breakfasts, and four or five
quarts of canned berries for the coming winter.

By the Fourth of July most of the crops were laid by. The
middles of the rows had been plowed. This accomplished
two things—first, it destroyed the grass; and second, it rolled
up dirt around the bottom of the plants to give them support
for the remainder of the growing season.

It was a relief to finish up the cultivating process. The
weather was becoming quite hot. But an even hotter job await-
ed the menfolk. The hay was ready for cutting. Two mules
pulled the McCormick hay mower with a large-toothed blade
that extended at least four feet with a wide swath over the
green vegetation. The cut grass lay on the ground a few hours
to dry. The fragrance of the new mown hay permeated the air.
The smell of the sweet freshly cut hay can never be forgotten.
Keeping a watch on the skies was important; rain was a large
concern. At the right time, the long cumbersome hayrack was
rolled in, pulled by the team of mules. The driver sat on an
elevated seat in the middle of the machine. He also directed
the work animals, and with a lever, lifted up and down ap-
proximately eight feet of large circular teeth. The long hay
racker pulled the loose cut hay into long mounds. The farm
wagon was then pulled across the field as the men with pitch-
forks gathered the hay into the flat bed. Sometimes the load
was very high, resembling a moving haystack. The driver sat
on the top, looking down on the team with pride. The aroma
of the newly cut hay had a soothing effect on man and ani-

mals. The bracing smell was tantalizing as the load was taken to the barnyard. Some of the hay was tossed into a haystack and some thrown up to the hayloft in the barn. With the hay gathered, the menfolk usually had a few days of leisure.

The garden stuff had been coming in for several days. Already lettuce, radishes, green onions, English peas, and new potatoes had provided the meals. Now the beets were ready for pickling and the beans, crisp and bright green, were just right for stringing and breaking. The first picking would be consumed for the main meals. Fresh green snap beans were, perhaps, the favorite of all vegetables. MaBett took great delight in yanking pods of immature beans and chomping on them raw.

A bright Monday morning found Effie in the garden— two water-buckets in hand. The dew had dried off the bean-laden stalks. Under the bottom leaves were clusters of tender pods filled with immature beans just right for canning. She relished the touch and smell of the crispy green pods as she bent over each row, pulling handfuls and filling the buckets that sat on the ground nearby. In a short time, the pails were full and running over. Back in the kitchen, grandmother and grandchild were communicating in their own special way, the elder, cooking victuals for the day, and the younger one, basking in the love and affection she always experienced when just the two of them were together. Effie came in the back door with her bean-load. She pulled up a cane-bottom chair onto which she sat her stocky body. She began to string and break beans for the dinner meal. After a quick, wash the broken pods were put into the iron kettle and covered to the top with water. A piece of slit fatback was dropped into the mixture for seasoning. Setting the kettle down into the eye of the stove; the beans and water were soon boiling. Adjusting the pot's position, she allowed the beans to simmer for about two hours. Three or four hours would be better. Dinner will be a little late today. Everyone agrees that beans swimming in water are not worth eating. The slow cooking would gradually turn the liquid into steam. As the liquid simmered away, the beans soaked up their own juice.

Effie watched with interest, realizing that her own mother never took so much time and effort to prepare green beans. She admitted to herself that her mother-in-law's green beans were the best and determined that from here on she would cook her snaps the same way.

After a dinner of the fresh green beans, cornbread hot from the oven, boiled potatoes, sweet milk, and yesterday's blackberry cobbler for dessert, the family was full and satisfied. The baby had not been overlooked. Breast milk was still her mainstay, but she also enjoyed "table food." Green beans, mashed and mixed with potato broth, were fed to her from a spoon. She also was given a biscuit softened in the sauce of the blackberries.

The dirty dishes were put into the dishpan and the oilcloth on the table was wiped free of crumbs and drippings. The leftover vegetables and bread were pushed to the back of the table and covered with a cloth. This would be supper.

MaBett washed the dishes and put them into another pan. Mama wiped the baby's hands, face, chin and neck and took her to their bedroom to nurse her; she soon fell into a peaceful nap.

Back in the kitchen, the two women strung and broke the remainder of the beans for canning. After being washed in cool water, the broken pieces were put into two large granite pots on the stove, covered with water, and brought to a boil. After a few minutes of a soft boil, vinegar and sugar were added, the amount determined by MaBett. Then, about fifteen minutes of additional boiling was required.

In the meantime, Effie was out by the smokehouse, where the canning jars are stored, washing them in a tub of warm soapy water. With a rag wrapped around the handle of a case knife, she scrubbed dried particles of food left inside the jars when they were last used. The jars were brought inside and scalded. The zinc lids and rubber bands had been simmering on low heat for some time. The hot beans were placed in the clean, hot jars and punched down with the blade of the case knife. The rubber bands were stretched over the neck of the jars, and the zinc lids screwed down tightly. They were then left to stand on their tops until the jars cooled. When they were finished, they had five half-gallons.

There would be more days of picking, stringing, snapping, and breaking pods of beans into two- or three-inch lengths, and preserving them for the coming winter.

Before the canned beans could be served, the vinegar-water would be drained and the beans washed thoroughly in cold water. Then they would be cooked as fresh beans, slowly, for two to three hours with a little pork seasoning.

By the end of the summer, three shelves in the cellar were bulging with jars of the verdant legumes. Besides the garden variety of the low, bushy plants, Kentucky Wonders had been planted in "hills" around the bases of stalks of one field of corn. The corn stalks served as a ready support for the hulking, twining vines. After about two months of growing, the hefty pods were gathered and the coarse strings stripped away. The strong fingers of the two women snapped the frangible pods by the dishpanful. Near the bearing season, the nearly ripening beans became shellies. That is, the pods were shelled before fully mature and hard. Then the beans were mixed with a portion of broken juicy pods, creating a substantial meal.

Four

The hot days of August brought two special joys. The long, humid days and very warm nights produced an abundant crop of fresh, tender corn. The ears were pulled and stripped of the green shucks, brushed of the clinging silks, and cut and scraped from the cob. Then the soft, milky grain was put into an iron skillet and slowly cooked with some fried meat grease. When cooked to doneness, the corn was carefully scraped loose from the bottom of the skillet and turned, having just a tinge of brown, crispy crunch. With a pan of hot biscuits, this became a filling and fortifying breakfast or a delightful part of the dinner meal.

Sometimes for dinner, the ears were broken into portions and dropped into the teakettle of boiling water for a few minutes. Then the pieces were lifted out and smothered in fresh, sweet country butter. One of the men's favorite ways to enjoy the fresh corn was in corn oysters. The corn was cut and scraped from the cob and mixed in a batter made of flour, salt, one egg, and some milk. The battered corn was dropped by tablespoons onto a hot, well-greased griddle and browned on both sides.

The first joy was sustenance for the body; the second was sustenance for the soul. Revival meetings were held the first week of August each year. There were two meetings each day, the first at 11:00 in the morning, the later at 7:30 at night. Usually the visiting preacher was invited to a church member's home for dinner and remained there until the evening service. But he would find opportunities to visit shut-ins, or to call on a wayward sinner—someone whose heart was hardened by a stubborn will, but who still felt guilty for not being in the Lord's House at meeting time. Church was held only on the appointed Sunday of the month. Usually the pastor-preacher lived some distance from the church, so annual revival time was a very important time to reinforce spiritual priorities and to give a clarion call to sinners to repent.

The singing of the old hymns of faith, sometimes a shout from a jubilant soul, rejuvenated saints who had become weary from the burdens of life. As some matron pumped the pedals of the organ, the bellows inhaled and the reeds exhaled, praises to God in such songs as "The Lily of the Valley" and "The Old Rugged Cross." Spirits weighted down with the uncertainties of life, inevitable illnesses and hard times, were consoled and uplifted with "What a Friend We Have in Jesus" and Sweet Hour of Prayer."

> I come to the garden alone,
> While the dew is still on the roses,
> And the voice I hear, falling on my ear,
> The Son of God discloses . . .
> And the joy we share as we tarry there,
> None other has ever known.

Became the "balm of Gilead to make the wounded whole." Untrained voices harmonized from their hearts. Usually there were two or three natural altos and a basso or two to balance out the choir. By the second day of services, the combined voices were sounding out the glories of "Beulah Land." From Jordan's stormy banks they were "casting a wistful eye," wistful of an unfulfilled yearning for Canaan's fair and happy land. They did not want to leave members of their families and friends behind so they pleaded with them to come and go with them.

After the preacher had exhorted saints and warned sinners of the coming judgment day, singers and the congregation entreated wayward ones to heed the Gospel call: "Pass me not, O gentle Savior, Hear my humble cry, and while on others thou art calling, Do not pass me by." If the hearers were reluctant to respond, the preachers and singers would change songs and prayerfully appeal with the supplicant: "Almost persuaded now to believe, Almost persuaded Christ to receive . . . Some more convenient day on Thee I'll call."

Some of the more devout in attendance would leave their seats and walk the aisles, imploring the sinners to come to the altar and give their hearts to the Lord. To some, this prodding was all that was needed; to others it was an embarrassment that hardened their hearts even more. Curious spectators on the outside of the building, usually men and boys on the fringe of light, would cast glances through the open windows to see who was responding to the "altar call."

MaBett and her son attended most of the morning meetings. Effie chose to stay home with the baby. Grandpa did not go to church anytime. Harley even went to some of the night services. Effie was afraid to be home alone at night so MaBett stayed with her. Harley listened attentively to every word of every sermon, but he kept his faith and his feelings to himself. He had always been an honest, upright young man. He abhorred sin in any shape or form. A curse word had never passed his lips. He did not know the taste of alcohol. He would not strike a lick of work on the "Sabbath." This virtuous individual was a puzzle to the leaders of the church. They could not understand why he had never made some movement to affirm his faith. Did he not believe the articles of faith espoused by the church?

Next to Christmas, the week of revival was the highlight of the farmer's year. With the intermission in farm work, it was the nearest thing they had to a vacation or holiday. For a week, the main meals were prepared with more care, and Sunday-best clothes were donned for the meetings.

This time of the year, August, was the hottest period. Funeral home fans with pictures of Christ the "Good Shepherd" beat the hot air, stirring up small breezes across the perspiring faces and bodies. At night, oil lamplights attracted candle moths . . . There were no screens on the open windows so the insects of the night were drawn to the flickering flames, many thereby incinerating themselves. Now and then, a horsefly, having followed the animals to church, would bombard the interior of the sanctuary, going from one light to another until it found an opening through which to escape.

Bats have been known to dart through the windows into the cavernous church building in pursuit of a crunchy bug. This did indeed create an unholy commotion—frightened women ducked and covered their heads as the mini-monster dived from the rafters towards their bonnets. Children shrieked from the invading, flying creature. One or two of the quick-thinking men grabbed a broom from the back corner and swooped down upon and swatted the frightened insectivores out the open door. The parishioners took the interference in stride and soon settled down for a blessing from the Lord.

Another hot August day... The house was like an oven. After the chores and supper were completed, the family sought relief on the front porch. Twilight darkened. A cool, gentle breeze blew around from the eastern side of the house. The sun had set behind the barn, leaving a pink-lavender hue across the western sky. The darkness settled around them; no artificial light attracted wandering insects.

Grandpa sat on his end of the porch nearest the barn. The womenfolk sat at the other end. Effie took this time to shell the small sugar peas for tomorrow's dinner.

MaBett held her granddaughter on her lap, lovingly rocking her in the old worn rocking chair. Mosquitoes love pink and tender skin, so Grandmother covered her with a light blanket and held her close.

Summer's dark shadows were filled with night music. Carmelene heard, but did not understand, the twitters, droves, and winnowing trills. MaBett took great delight in the symphonies of the seasons. Spring had brought out the bellowing bullfrogs at the pond. Early summer nights abounded with the diving, dipping antics of the mockingbird in the cedar tree at the barnyard gate. Its lilting mimicry was endured wearily after long hours in the fields.

Now in the late summer as the sun set, the lively creatures found their night abode in clumps of weeds and hanging branches. MaBett listened intently to the call of the nocturnal bird, the whippoorwill that she had never seen. She repeated the calls to the baby girl, accenting the first and last syllables: "WHIP poor WEEL, WHIP poor WEEL." The little one would chuckle with delight, snuggle down closer, and want to hear more.

As the whippoorwills faded into the night and into the woods, the chirping of the crickets increased in intensity. A steady rhythm of trills came from the nearby trees. Crickets fiddled their music with a scraper on one wing and a rasper on the other. The raspy tune was designed to woo a silent mate. Katydids filled the night air with an ambivalent debating: "Katy-did, Katy-didn't, Katy-did, and Katy-didn't." Tomorrow's light would reveal an oval-shaped grasshopper-like creature of brilliant green much like a leaf caught in a spider web clinging from the outside wall of the house.

MaBett made Carmelene know that bugs high in the trees were sources of the night noises that could be heard, but not seen, in their hiding places in the night. But there was a certain, curious beetle that could be seen by its own light. The "lightning bug" celebrated the joys of life by swooping along near the ground with a lantern in its tail end. Suddenly, there were flashes everywhere. The little girl excitedly pointed her forefinger toward the twinkling lights. The calling of its name by Grandmother made an early impression on the eager learner, and thus was born an avid interest in crawling and flying things.

The biting black gnats soon drove the family inside, including Grandpa, who had been swatting himself and mumbling and grumbling about the pesky little varmints.

Soon, all were asleep on top of the featherbeds, covered with sheets made from feed sacks. The air was now pleasant and balmy. Grandfather snored, Grandmother snoozed, and baby dreamed, but no one knows what—perhaps of reaching out and catching handfuls of the pretty, flashing bugs.

The strident serenade on the outside continued until the wee hours of the morning.

Carmelene's curiosity increased by the day. She was absorbing the outside world like a hungry sponge. Indoors, she was allowed to crawl and explore her world around the feet of the adults. The grandfather was careful to mind his step. She began climbing up the slim legs of her father as he sat in his particular chair, holding on to his knobby knees. She wasn't too sure about Grandpa. As she pulled up to the sides of the counterpane-covered beds, she pulled things from the beds that were in her reach. One of those things in her reach, she discovered, was the Sears Roebuck catalog. As it fell to the floor, she sat down beside the bulky form and began to turn the pages. Carmelene was fascinated with the images on the thin sheets of paper. She realized the likeness of these images to her parents, grandparents, and herself.

As her eager fingers turned the pages, Carmelene saw other mothers' dresses and slippers. There were children like her cousins, and many pairs of overalls and socks for them. She had never seen so many "daddies'" shoes and shirts. Many things she didn't understand, but there were those things that ticked-tocked and made a ringing sound in the early morning. There were beds like she slept on and stoves that warmed her food, and so many pots and pans. There was even a buggy like the one that took her grandmother and father away sometimes.

Looking at this book became her favorite thing to do when not eating or sleeping; she lost interest in pulling up to all those straight and solid things. But after a few days, the urge to walk on her own legs prevailed. By eleven months, she had mastered stiffening her knees and putting one foot in front of the other. She held her arms out for balance. Soon reluctant steps became sure steps, and she was on her own. All the caretakers, parents and grandparents, grinned with satisfaction. The little girl had reached an important stage in her development: her first step of independence.

Summer days blended into early fall. The cotton bolls were cracking open and releasing the dangling locks. The women would do the gathering of the white fibrous money crop. As soon as the dew evaporated, the women, with the baby, made their way to one of the cotton patches. The men had gone earlier and positioned the farm wagon with the slide boards with swinging scales secured at the back. Each filled sack was weighed and recorded in a little black book. The load had to be around 1200 pounds, which would fill up the extended sides and would make a bale of ginned cotton of about 500 pounds.

MaBett had outfitted the junior partner of the cotton-picking team with proper attire: a romper of tiny striped blue denim and a pair of hard-soled shoes. The growing child was becoming more rambunctious and difficult to confine. In the cotton patch, her playpen was the bed of the wagon. From there she watched as her mother and grandmother pulled their seven- to nine-feet sacks up and down the rows, snatching and pulling the white stuff until the sacks were filled. Then they pulled the long bags across the ends of the rows and up to the scales. With great effort they pulled the sacks into the back of the wagon and emptied the packed wide tubes of canvas. The child giggled as the cotton was strewn around her. She flung her whole body with the chubby legs and flailing arms on to the bed of fluffy clouds.

After a depth of about one foot had been reached, it was no longer safe for Carmelene to be in the loose cotton. Grandmother pulled her from the back gate of the wagon, and placing her astraddle her right hip, took her back to the farmhouse to play while the noon meal was being prepared. After dinner, about 12:30, Effie would remain behind to nurse the child and put her down for a nap. MaBett would go back to the cotton patch to resume picking. This was their pattern for the cotton-picking season.

By the first week of November, most of the cotton and corn had been gathered. It had been a good year. The menfolk took the last bale of cotton to the gin on the sixth day. Other farmers had also chosen this day to make their last jaunt to the gin. The air was a buzz with today's Presidential election—Hoover or Smith?? Some of the patriarchs voiced their choice and the consequences for the country if their man didn't win; others, still not sure who was the best man, listened intently for some soul signal.

The debate continued from the gin into the store. Herbert Clark Hoover was running on the Republican ticket. His platform slogan had been "a chicken in every pot, a car in every garage." He had confidently affirmed that, "America was nearer the triumph over poverty than ever before in the land." He also called for rigid enforcement of the Prohibition law, pledging that he would carry out "the ideals of the American people."

The Democratic candidate was a political-pro: Governor Alfred E. Smith, of New York, who had served four terms already. Donning a brown derby and a cigar, he was known as the "happy warrior." In his New York accent, he promised to repeal the Prohibition law. The candidates' distinct stances gave the voters a clear choice. Things were looking great for the country; only last month the stock prices had soared on Wall Street.

The Nashville Banner came to the store each day providing the nail-keg brotherhood the pulse of the state and country. Father and son could not tarry too long. The stimulative atmosphere was what was needed to move them to their civic duty. Their voting precinct was several miles away. They had made sure they paid their poll tax this year. Although their trading and social life was here, they lived near the boundary line of two counties. For government business, they had to backtrack about eight miles to Barter Ridge. To cast their votes for the next President, they had miles to go before night. Their votes were very secretive. Political proclivities were never discussed publicly. What they did in the voting booth was never disclosed even to members of the family. Since they had voted for the next President, they were anxious to hear the results. On Thursday the eighth, two days after the election, Harley found an urgent reason to go to the store for coal oil and chicken mash.

In a couple of hours, Harley was back from the store, happily informing his father that Hoover had been the winner. At suppertime he pretended indifference, but his mother needled from him what she wanted to hear. She felt good about the future. So did her son. They did have a "chicken in the pot" sometimes. Before long, he was going to put a car in his garage.

MaBett's cotton patch had yielded one bale. She was pleased to have this much pocket money. Already she had plans for some of it. She was very much aware that the baby's first birthday was coming up—a year old already. Every little girl must have a doll. With the Sears Roebuck catalog in hand, she searched until she found two pages of dolls. After much consideration she ordered a Dandy Play Doll. The doll had a voice that said "Mama" and was dressed in checkered rompers and hat. She came complete with imitation black leather slipper and white socks.

Pleased with the choice of the doll, MaBett thought that a picture must be made on Carmelene's first birthday. The doll it would make it perfect. She remembered that the child did not have Sunday shoes to dress up the picture. Flipping through the catalog, she found the footwear for young women, girls, and children. In the middle of the page she saw "Mary Jane" patent leather slippers. This became the second item on the list. Then a roll of Kodak film completed the order.

With the order in the mail, MaBett busied herself with the usual household work. About once a week she walked to the store for things like sugar, salt, and baking soda. Most of the time she carried two dozen eggs in a basket and a pound or two of fresh butter for trading. While in the store she could not help but notice the bold headlines across *The Nashville Banner* proclaiming that New York trading wave had swept to new peaks. A few days later, she again learned, from the newspaper laying on the counter, that the New York Stock Exchange had shattered all records. She did not understand all the implications for the country, but somehow it gave her an uneasy feeling.

The order from Sears Roebuck came in a few days. Both items for the baby exceeded expectations. The shiny slippers were fit for a princess. Of course the little girl was a princess and more. The doll deserved such an adoring owner. Carmelene's birthday came. The film was slipped into Effie's small Brownie camera. The two women devised a posing platform. From the topsy-turvy woodpile, they chose several standard-size logs and stacked them in a neat pile waist high. They covered the top of the logs with a quilt. Then they sat the little princess on the top. After some coaxing, she posed with her chubby feet in the shiny "Mary Janes." Effie snapped the camera for two pictures of the child and her doll and then a picture of Grandmother holding her granddaughter in the rocking chair.

When Sunday came, the menfolk washed up and put on some clean clothes. The women insisted that they come outside for a picture also. While the men were reluctantly being photographed, Harley's favorite dog, Ring, got into the picture. The black and white shepherd came up to his master wagging his tail. These moments of mutual affection were caught on film. Pictures were made of mother and father with their first child and of the grandparents in their respective rocking chairs. This had been a perfect day. The shutters of the little brown box captured memories. But the happiness of the day was short-lived. That very night, under mysterious circumstances, Ring left, never to return. The dog had seemed attentive toward family members all day. He had eaten his supper of table scraps with gusto. Harley had sensed a special love toward him; his heart was warmed by the animal's attachment to him.

Harley had gone to the front porch to shake out and smooth the tow sacks that served as the dog's bed. Ring came around the end of the house and looked up at him with appreciation. Then he trotted off into the edge of the woods, his normal routine after eating and before bedding down for the night.

Harley went back inside with the family, assuming that the dog would be home in a short time. The sun went down. Darkness settled around the farm. The coal-oil lamps sent their warm lights across each room. The hearts of the family were also warm tonight. Soon the lights of the lamps were blown out as the family settled down for the night.

Harley thought again of his dog and stepped out to the porch to see if he had returned. He had not; the bed was empty. Harley feared that he was gone. He walked around the house and the outbuildings whistling and calling softly, "Ring, Ring, here Ring." But Ring did not come. He widened his search by walking up the moonlit road for a short distance. Then he heard a dog barking further up the road. What a relief; perhaps he had treed a 'possom. He kept walking toward the barking. He thought this was only natural for a dog to not respond to his call when the strong scent of a wild animal was in his nostrils.

Harley turned around and walked back toward the house, believing the dog would soon tire from barking up a tree at a 'possom. The closer he came to the house, the fainter became the bark of the dog. He stepped up on the porch and glanced again at the empty bed, feeling assured that in the morning Ring would be there to greet him.

Early the next morning, Harley opened the door to the porch and saw the bed was still empty. His heart sank. He was gripped with regret. If only he had gone after the dog to see why he was barking. He clung to the hope that the dog would return. Anxious glances and expectant listening came to naught. The dog did not return. The mystery lingered. Why? Did someone traveling along the main road see this nice animal and take him? If only he knew and was sure that Ring had a good home. If only he had pursued him and brought him back home. Harley cherished the memory of his special pet; no other animal would ever take his place.

The late days of November blended into the early days of December, thus the second Christmas with Carmelene. The child thrived on the love of her parents and grandparents. She was babbling and learning new words each day. Of course "Ma," "Pa," "Mama," and "Daddy" were her favorites.

Each day Carmelene made new discoveries and tried new skills. The adults found it difficult to suppress their pride in the eager little learner. The new year came with all its expectations and promises. But Effie was not feeling well in the mornings. She was having morning sickness, which meant she was probably pregnant with her second child. She was becoming more nauseous each day. She had no choice but to wean the baby. It was time anyway. The child's mouth was filling up with teeth, so it was a welcomed relief. Carmelene's diet was already being augmented with food from the table. Grandma made sure there was always creamy oatmeal for each breakfast. She took more and more responsibility, not only for the child's food, but also for all her care. She even took it on herself to pursue toilet training with a small chamber pot.

Effie spent most of the mornings heaving behind the smokehouse. She was not only nauseous from the early stages of pregnancy, but she was also nervous and ill at ease. She did not really want another baby so soon. Older women had a tendency to look down on young women for having so many babies, especially if they were close together. MaBett did not scold her for this second pregnancy, but she sensed disapproval—or was it her imagination? In reality, this gave MaBett more freedom to be the child's chief caregiver without guilt for assuming so much responsibility.

Spring warmed the winter months. More and more, Carmelene followed her grandmother from chore to chore. Feeding the chickens and gathering the eggs were two of her favorite ways of helping her grandmother. She could toss the chicken feed to the flock. She chuckled with glee when the rooster and hens squawked and scratched over the scattered grain. Grandma would gather the eggs from the straw-cushioned nests into a basket. Then she would let the child pick up each egg, some of them still warm, and they would count them together . . . one, two, three . . . until they were all counted.

The little helper would follow the grandmother to the well, and with fascination, watch the windlass unwind, letting the cyclinder-shaped bucket descend by rope down, down, down into that deep, dark, narrow hole. Carmelene learned quickly to listen for the bump when the bucket hit the water and then the blu-b-b when the water pushed the air from the bucket and rushed into the vacuum, filling it all the way to the top. Then the windlass would turn forward with an iron crank until the bucket came up out of the hole and was suspended in mid-air by the pulley. When the slim bucket was positioned over the wide water bucket, the valve was pulled upward, releasing the liquid. MaBett would then clamp the lid down on the well top, stressing strongly to the toddler that nothing, nothing, was ever dropped into the well.

MaBett would take the dipper and dip a small portion of water for the child to sip from the edge of the dipper. Carmelene smacked her lips and clapped her hands. The water was so refreshing, and the grandmother was so interesting.

With 1929 fast approaching on the New Year's horizon, Harley and his father hitched their team of mules to the farm wagon and headed toward Milan, to scout around for a car. The election of Hoover had pumped up the spirits of these small-time farmers and the whole country. More and more farmers were leaving old Dobbin in the barn and casting a wistful eye on a new Ford flivver. According to the newspapers, Henry Ford had sold 15 million of his "Tin Lizzies" since they first rolled off the assembly line in Detroit in 1908. But this father and son had been impressed by what General Motors had been doing the last few years. After all, they were the first to offer the electric starter. No longer was it necessary to crank the car by hand, taking a chance of suffering a broken arm if the driver lost his grip and the iron crank back-kicked. Only after heavy tugs and turns, and finally the engine turned over once; then the driver had to jump inside the car and open wide the throttle. With the new starter, the ignition key caused an electric spark that ignited the gasoline and the engine was ready to roll.

After several days of pondering the best choice and a second trip to town, Harley and his father chose a Chevrolet complete with closed sides. Both men agreed that the Chevy seemed to be a more substantial car. So in the early days of 1929, with the cooperation of the father and a bank in Milan, Harley became owner of a blue Chevrolet sedan. This purchase added one more sale to the General Motors dividend, now the largest in the nation's history.

A new car demanded a shelter from dust, hail, and rain. Father and son salvaged some rough planks from around the barn. Nothing could be found for the roof, so with froe in hand and using seasoned timber, they split and cleaved shingles for covering the new garage and the new Chevrolet.

Five

Effie was growing heavy with child. Her morning sickness had subsided. She helped in the planting and early work in the garden. By cotton-hoeing time in June, she was not able to help much with the work. Besides, the weather was unseasonably hot.

Maudie's two older girls came down for a few days to give their grandmother a hand with the hoeing. MaBett compensated them by purchasing some pretty floral voile at the store. Maudie was an able seamstress, and in a short time the girls were sporting their new frocks.

The crops were hardly laid by when early on the morning of July 3rd, Effie began to have contractions. After an hour or so, she knew it was the real thing. Harley cranked up his Chevrolet and headed toward the store to find Dr. Thomas. His mother suggested that he stop by Mrs. Jones' and ask her to come over for the day. It would be difficult for Mrs. Jones since she had a little one less than a year old, but she made arrangements. She knew she was needed.

By late afternoon, Effie had delivered her second child. This one had come much more easily. The baby, another girl, was smaller than the first one. This time the baby looked like her, with dark hair and dark blue eyes that would soon turn brown. (This was what she expected the first time.) This time, the new mother chose the name, Hallie Sue . . . She was a beautiful baby, but she was colicky and fretful. She cried a lot at night, which kept the old folks awake. This made Effie very nervous. Her tenseness was sensed by the child, which aggravated the situation. Grandmother stripped leaves from the mullein plant growing near the barn lot and made tea. This usually soothed a crying infant, but for this one, it did not help. The next morning, she walked to the doctor's office near the store for some paregoric, which brought much relief for the little one and the adults.

Since the baby had been crying at night, Grandmother moved the toddler to her bed in the other front room. The big-little girl loved this arrangement. Now both she and her new little sister could each have a mother.

The summer had been very hot. Grandma made her weekly trip to the store soon after breakfast in the cool of the morning. While browsing this Saturday, she noted something in the newspaper that caught her eye and caused her to chuckle. Since July 3rd, President Hoover had announced that he would not be shaking hands any more until September due to the hot weather and a sore hand. How was that for a servant of the people?

Two other colorful characters seemed to be on the front page of the paper these days. "Billy Sunday," a former baseball player who seemed to have descended from the pitcher's mound and ascended to the pulpit as a raging, evangelist warning sinners of the coming judgment of the Lord. His platform antics had caught the attention of the country.

The other character was Al Capone, the Scar face criminal, who was jailed for carrying a gat. MaBett wondered "What is a gat?" She later learned that it was a handgun — short for the Gatling gun. Other new things seemed to surround this unsavory character — bootlegging, booze, and speakeasies.

In that hot summer of '29, the lines tightened around each immediate family within the extended family. Besides serving as sidekick to help with all the chores, Carmelene tagged along on the picking excursions in the fields. Sometimes Grandmother would pick her up and swing her on her hip through the thick briars or rough paths. Early on, the child learned to pull the hulls from the peas and to pick the silks from the corn. But it seemed each time Carmelene was exposed to the weeds growing on the farm, her legs became red with welts and intense itching. Because of her desperate scratching, her legs were soon covered with sores. Grandma tried all her known remedies, but a creamy paste of baking soda seemed to bring the most relief.

The new baby continued to fuss and fret. Of course, the prickly heat didn't help. Effie and the baby seemed to cling to each other as if defending themselves from some invisible enemy. When the baby cried, the mother cringed, shrinking behind her over-sized apron, behaving in an excessively servile manner. Effie became more uptight, causing the baby to cry even more. She felt she wasn't pulling her part of the load with the housework and the outside responsibilities. In desperation, she would let the baby cry, which in turn convinced her that the mother-in-law was thinking that the baby was terribly spoiled. At day's end, when the baby was finally asleep, her husband was not at home with her, but was elsewhere pursuing his own interests. The feeling of neglect and that those other things were more important to him than his wife and small children, bruised her vulnerable spirit.

When Grandmother and Carmelene returned from their outside activities, tired but tingling with the fun of the experience, Effie would literally cower in the grand matron's presence, her head sinking into her shoulders. Each woman was having an adverse effect on the other. MaBett was puzzled, asking herself what she had done to her daughter-in-law. Effie saw her mother-in-law as domineering and oppressive, but she did not have the courage to express this to her.

As Grandma and Carmelene became more intertwined in their own world, Harley felt ignored and pushed out of his nest. The two most important women in his life now had other absorbing interests. He was not only taking second place to the first child of his mother's affections, but came in second in receiving attention of his wife because of the second child.

With his new car, Harley had more mobility and felt free to spend more time at the store. He took in more revivals than ever before.

Alienation between the two women increased by the day. The gnawing feeling of rejection from her mother-in-law ground deeply into Effie's "craw." Even more painful was the fact that her oldest child preferred her grandmother. Effie saw no way of escape. Her husband's life was so intermeshed with his parents. They, this young couple, did not have the means to go it alone: no farm, no furniture, no anything except two small children.

Effie's sense of helplessness turned into fear, then into anger, comparable to that of an animal when cornered. The internalized anger became resentment and bitterness. The image of an aggressive mother-in-law grew in her mind. She brooded over her lot in life. She had never had any emotional support or affirmation from her own family. In fact, since her marriage they had more or less "ditched" her to the throes of her new chosen family.

After the August revivals were over, an interest in singing continued. The singing master presided over a singing school one night a week at the church. The shaped notes in some of the hymnbooks had always fascinated Harley. He was learning that each shape had a corresponding tone such as do, re, mi, fa, sol, la, ti and do. He heard of a family that played the banjo and would help anyone interested to learn. It had always been a secret ambition of Harley's to play an instrument, especially the banjo. He did feel that he must learn to play well before obtaining one. About once a week, he would drop in on his banjo friends for instruction. This challenge was invigorating to him. His interest in the sight-reading of musical notes gave him a sense of accomplishment. He needed this to fill the emotional vacuum in his life.

In the meantime Effie resented her husband's freedom to come and go while she had no choice but to remain at home with her children. She smarted at his indifference to her plight. She was never brave enough to put her misgivings into words. Her knees buckled at the very thought of demanding consideration. What was her alternative? She had no skills to become independent of her husband. She knew her family did not want her back. She had known so much rejection and put down as a child. She never felt her father cared for her, and she knew for a certainty that her mother favored her younger sister. Now she was the mother of two small children—again feeling unloved and trapped.

Summer cooled into fall, giving relief from the oppressive summer. The weather had improved, but not the climate around the two vying women. Effie was weary with caring for a fretful child and doing her part in gathering the crops. She carried an apple box lined with an old quilt to the field to hold the baby. Hallie did not take well to this ground-level bedding. After much crying after her mother, she found her thumb and with a few snivels and one snuffle, dropped off to sleep.

The toddler followed her grandmother up one row and down the other. The veteran cotton picker grabbed the locks from the sharp bolls and stuffed them into her seven-foot sack. She had given Carmelene a flour sack with a shoulder strap sewn on the top of the opening. The child was clad in rompers of tough blue denim with long legs to protect her tender legs from the stinging needles and other poisonous weeds. The youngster bounded from middle to gap in the row of cotton stalks. After a while she grew tired and snuggled down on Grandmother's sack. She was soon fast asleep. Ma carefully pulled the sack to the end of the row and took time for a drink from the nearby Mason jar and some rest.

The two women, along with their charges, kept the cotton-picking under control. When the wagon was filled with its fluffy load, the menfolk headed for the gin. After the cargo was unloaded, its contents weighed, and credit given for the amount, they hitched the team to a nearby post. The next important step was to walk across the highway to the store and pay on their account for the past year. The merchant carried their credit from one cotton season to another, as was the custom. Seeds, plow handles, bolts, screws, plus feed for the work animals, and mash for the hogs and chickens were paid for in this manner. Even large sacks of flour and cornmeal for the table sometimes had to be purchased this way.

Usually the farmers looked forward to this time of relaxation and talk, sometimes whittling as they sat around the store. The newspaper was always nearby to invoke a discussion, a heated one if it was about politics.

This particular Friday there was hushed uncertainty. The bold black headlines of the newspaper screamed about **BLACK THURSDAY** and the **STOCKMARKET CRASH** of the day before. These farmers had never had enough money to delve into high finance, but they knew something was terribly wrong. This financial crises had caused panic everywhere. One report said that eleven speculators had committed suicide.

The men returned home troubled about the future. Whatever the crash meant, however, they felt secure because they had the land to raise most of their food. Furthermore, they had voted for Hoover, and he would know how to keep the country's business on an even keel.

Soon all the crops were gathered into the barn and the family settled in for a long winter's nap—the two little ones snug in their long winter underwear. But the close confinement intensified the two women's resentment toward each other. To MaBett, Effie seemed ungrateful. After all they were sharing their home with the young couple and their two small children. They had worked hard to have a decent house and farm. She was doing the cooking and milking and helping to raise the children, especially the oldest one. Why was Effie always cowering on the edge of everything? Why did she mumble when she talked, and why did her chin tremble for no earthly reason?

Although the country was in the grip of "hard times," this farm family was quite secure. There was wood for warmth and cooking. The cellar was full of canned goods such as pear preserves, beans and kraut. The smokehouse was full of cured ham and side meat. There were sacks of dried peas to be shelled. The crib was filled with corn for livestock. The loft was crammed with hay for the two cows that provided milk, cream, and butter for drinking and cooking. Even the "dominecker" hens, encouraged by the big red rooster, were laying eggs about every other day.

Without benefit of radio or newspaper, the family was unaware of the near panic over the country's economic structure. But there was an incident in the heavens that brought interest and concern. On April 29, 1930 a giant shadow passed over the sun; they later learned that it was a total eclipse of the sun in California. Winter had come and gone. Spring had prepared the earth for planting. The calendar page was turned to May, one of the most momentous times of the year.

May was also a time for looking back, remembering and honoring the dead. Decoration Day, May 30th, was originally set aside to honor the men who had died in the Civil War. On that day, flowers and flags were placed on the graves of servicemen. The observance had evolved to include remembering all who had died. It had become a special time to tend and decorate the graves of departed family members. Each cemetery had an appointed day when family and friends came together to rake and tidy up its hallowed grounds. It became an annual pilgrimage during which the living came from miles around to visit the burying grounds of family members and friends. The renewing of acquaintances and the noting of changes or deaths strengthened the bonds of the family.

For MaBett, Decoration Day was second to Christmas in importance. Early in the week, before that special Saturday, she had made sure that their best summer apparel had been washed, starched, and ironed with the flat iron. Her very best damask tablecloth, white with embossed pattern and bordered with a side pink stripe surrounded by two smaller green stripes, was carefully laundered and starched with a week flour solution that she had boiled on the stove. After drying in the bright sunlight, the cloth was sprinkled down for a couple of hours; then each wrinkle was painstakingly stroked and smoothed out on a sheet-covered folded quilt-placed on one end of the kitchen table. She had to be careful not to scorch the sacred spread.

The day before Decoration Day at Providence, MaBett graveled the new potatoes and found enough to boil for potato salad. Early the next morning she boiled them whole, scraped off the tender skins, and mashed them in a large bowl. While they were still hot, she added vinegar, hardboiled eggs, chopped cucumber pickles, and green onions. Then she garnished the top of the dish with an extra boiled egg made into a rosette arrangement. She had soaked cured country ham overnight. After mixing flour, lard, and buttermilk into biscuits, she fried the pieces of ham until they were tender crisp. A luscious banana pudding had been made the day before; it was piled high with white egg meringue which had been browned to a delicate toast color. A jar of perfectly round pickled beets had been set aside since last canning season just for this day.

The food was prepared and put into a basket with the folded tablecloth on top. Before putting on her best clothes, MaBett gathered the choicest roses. She had been watching them for days, hoping they would be at their best this particular week, and so they were. Her favorites were the pink ones growing down by the fence that separated the yard from the barn lot. There was another bush of white roses in the yard that gave solemnity to the romantic, fragrant pink ones.

After filling Mason jars with water, MaBett trimmed the stems and snipped the thorns from the roses. Then she crushed the lower portion of each stem with the handle of the butcher knife to enable the stem to absorb more water, in order to preserve freshness Carefully she placed the bouquets into the green glass vases and then into a cardboard box to be transported to the cemetery. She dressed in her pretty floral frock and dressy black straw hat, and gathered up her basket of potato salad, ham and biscuits, canned green beans, pickled beets, and banana pudding for the solemn journey to the cemetery.

Upon arrival, MaBett placed the Mason jars of pink and white roses on the graves of her loved ones. One daughter had died only two years ago, leaving four small children. In silence she communed with her, telling how much she missed her and that the children were doing well. She strolled past the other graves, noting headstones and dates indicating the time of life. She remembered the pain of losing her father, mother, and precious daughter. Time has a way of healing heartache, but sad memories linger. The cemetery took on a pretty peaceful look. The bouquets of freshly cut flowers gave testimony to the devotion of the remaining ones. The hush gave way to happy greetings of aunts, uncles, and cousins.

Womenfolk lifted their food baskets from cars and buggies parked under the shade of towering oaks. The women spread out their tablecloths on the ground, one after the other, forming what looked like a long banquet table. Each section was laden with the best kitchen creations made from the freshest butter, milk and eggs.

The spread reached so far that if the serving women needed to get from one side to the other, they had to lift their long skirts a few inches above their ankles and step over the waiting meal. One or two of the matrons fanned the table with a kitchen towel or a limb broken from a nearby bush to discourage flies and yellow jackets.

Usually after the sumptuous meal, a local pastor would speak to the captive audience. Then as the womenfolk gathered up the remaining food, the menfolk drifted to the edge of the grounds near their carriages to smoke their pipes and share far-fetched stories.

As the mid-afternoon sun began its descent into the west, all the living started to their earthly abodes. They had sensed anew the loss of loved ones, but the day's ritual had strengthened them. Deep inside some could not help but reflect that by next year's gathering, some of these living would also be sleeping here.

Six

The third child was expected by the latter part of March 1931. I, the oldest child, was not past three years old, and my little sister was around a year and a half. Each day, each room of the farmhouse seemed to become smaller and more crowded. The coldness of the winter winds blowing against the glass panes of the puttied windows intensified the chill of emotions inside the house. Even the innocent chatter and play of the children failed to moderate the resentments and misgivings. To Effie, her mother-in-law seemed to slam each door with increasing fervor. It also seemed that each stick of wood for the firebox of the cook stove, as well as the iron eyes of the stove, were picked up and put down with a heavy hand.

The obvious avoidance by MaBett of the youngest child was painful to the young mother. The necessities of added laundry and care for the children during the winter months added stress to the already strained household. On very cold days when the wash could not be dried outside, diapers and underwear were hung on the backs of straight-back cane-bottomed chairs and placed near the fireplace and cook stove. These obstructions clogged movement through the house and aggravated the grandparents. Each inconvenience was magnified in Effie's thinking. She felt that her little family was in the way of the old folks, but what could they do? Being in their declining years, the old folks needed them.

On a milder day, when Grandma had found an excuse to leave the house for a trip to the store and Grandpa was at the barn, Harley bristled when Effie gave a short answer to an impatient comment. She erupted into hysterical rage, saying that she could no longer take the mistreatment in this house. She was leaving, but she did not know where she was going. She could not take the children with her; he would be responsible for them. Harley, too, was in a state of exasperation with the silent wars of these women, and, in desperation, he burst into a tantrum of defense, proclaiming his innocence. When the yelling subsided, and they could talk in more controlled tones, they agreed that they must find a place for themselves and their growing family. When and where? They remembered that the birth of another child was only a few weeks away. They had no choice but to remain here until after the baby came. They would need help for the delivery and care of the two small children during Effie's confinement.

After a time, the couple thought of the little house in the woods. They began talking about what it would take to make it livable. This small three-room house with a back porch had been built by one of the older sons a few years back. He had brought his bride to his parents' home, as was the custom, but the situation was two crowded for a young couple beginning their married life. Thus, he had built the simple house below the main house in the woods near the spring. After one year, they had realized that the farm was not large enough to support another family, so he bought his own farm over in the next county. This small house had been standing empty. Only the dirt daubers, spiders, and wasps had enjoyed its shelter under the towering oaks and sweet gums. It had served as storage for some small farm equipment and the Irish potatoes after digging. It could be cleaned up and papered with fresh wall covering from the store, putting it on account until this year's cotton crop was brought in, in the fall. Harley knew his mother would make available two bedsteads, feather beds, and pillows. Effie had brought several of her own handmade quilts into the marriage. Harley could make an eating table from planks lying around the place

So from this emotional explosion came a clearing of the air and a healing of wounded feelings for the young couple.

Yes, they could go it alone. They would set up housekeeping and have their own individual corn crop and cotton patch. In following days, as the weather became milder, they got their new home in order. Although Effie was in advanced pregnancy, they worked together for the first time toward their own goals. When Grandmother was not looking, the couple looked at each other and the two little ones with a special twinkle in their eyes. But I was puzzled. They seemed so happy, but I was not sharing this excitement. I liked living with my grandmother. What did all this commotion and hidden talk mean?

Early spring came and went. The flurry of activity hastened the passing of days. On the last balmy Saturday of March, Effie easily delivered her third little girl. This one had neither my fiery-red hair and green eyes, nor the black hair and dark eyes of my sister Hallie. Her hair was a warm brown color, and she had soft blue eyes that would soon turn a color that would compliment her chestnut hair and loveable disposition. Bonnie Bell seemed perfect name for her.

When the new baby was two weeks old, the transition was made from the comfortable family home to the little house in the woods. I accepted the move reluctantly, but I did have a new little sister to help care for, and that absorbed most of my attention. The baby thrived on the warm milk from my mother's more-than-adequate breasts. As she feasted on the flow, Hallie and I swung from Mother's elbows, patting and stroking the baby's soft, silky hair. Over and over, our cautious mother instructed us about the soft spot on the top of Bonnie's head where the bones had not yet joined. She emphasized that any hard blow to this soft area could seriously hurt the baby or even kill it. We quickly learned how fragile and helpless a new baby was. At night, Bonnie shared the bed with Mother and Daddy. During the day, she was placed on a pallet on the floor. With the constant attention and eager pulling we supplied, it was safer for the baby to be on this level.

April came and the garden was planted. The now separate families agreed to share the costs of the seeds and the produce. But they would go their separate ways in the planting of the cotton. In early May, father and son swapped the team of mules and equipment, but Harley did more than his share of the work because his father was becoming frail and stiff with rheumatism and lumbago. When the cotton reached hoeing stage, MaBett and Effie were on their own. Since the young family had vacated the homeplace, Grandmother had been very lonely. She missed our childish jabbering, and she especially missed my tagging on her long gathered skirt. She missed preparing my favorite breakfast of cooked rice and milk. She missed my being with her when she gathered the eggs and fed the pigs. One day while on one of her jaunts to the store, an acquaintance mentioned having a litter of nice black-brown feist pups and asked if she would like to have one. She gladly accepted and brought home a cute, loveable puppy that she named "Trixie."

Harley and Effie had chosen the areas below the little house near the bottomland for their cotton patches. Since I was showing maturity and reliability, Mother decided to leave the little ones at the house with me while she went to the fields to do the hoeing. There were no screen doors; the front door was kept open for fresh air and a cool breeze. Harley nailed strips of wood across the open space waist high to keep us children inside. The back door was kept closed and latched from the outside. The baby was kept on a pallet on the floor. As yet, I could not carry the baby. Mother went to the field to do her work but returned midmorning to check on us and to nurse the baby. I took the role of second "Mommie" very seriously. When the baby became fretful, I pulled the pallet across the floor from one room to another. Bonnie enjoyed the motion and the change of scenery. I even knew how to place a spoon of cool water on the baby's lips to pacify her.

But the "little bad wolf" shattered the placidity of the little house in the woods. Since MaBett had brought home the little feist dog, she had teased me that if I were not careful, Trixie would take the baby away. By this time I had bonded to my new baby sister and would protect her at all cost. Also I had been present when the dog had pitched a fit. As yet I was not sure about the dog.

Trixie, like most dogs, loved to be with children. So on this particular day, she slipped away from her mistress and followed the scent of the children to the little house. He anticipated a playful romp. Seizing a small rock from the yard in his mouth, he leaped up the front step and right through the opening between the strips across the door. The dog's sudden appearance frightened us children, as we remembered Grandmother's innocent jest about his taking the baby away.

Trixie dropped the stone on the floor . . . Hallie saw the rock and took it over to the pallet with the baby. I was monitoring the situation very carefully, not trusting the dog around the baby. I began to scold the unwelcome guest, who found refuge under the bed. I crawled under the bed and pulled the dog out by all four feet and flung him over the railings to the outside. Then I grabbed the broom and dared him to come back inside. Suddenly, I realized that the baby had something in her mouth. Where was the rock the dog had brought inside and Hallie had been playing with on the pallet? I guessed that the baby had the stone in her mouth. I ran my finger into her mouth, and sure enough, there was the pebble on the baby's tongue. I realized the eminent danger of the baby swallowing the hard object. With a crook of my forefinger, I soon had the rock in my grasp and out of the baby's mouth. Like the puppy, I flung the rock over the strips to the outside.

The adrenalin flushed through my veins. When I heard Mother unlatching the back door, I burst into tears. Everything seemed to be as she had left it two and one-half hours ago. Why the tears?" I explained through jerking sobs, the danger of the dog to the baby. Mother was proud of her mature, responsible child, who was not yet four years old.

There had been two days of sporadic showers that prompted the tender cotton plants to shoot up. The rains also encouraged the grass not only to grow up and out, but also down, the roots firmly attaching to the soil of clay, silt and sand. It would take a sturdy scrape of the sharp blade of a heavy hoe to extricate these stringy tentacles from around the cotton plants.

This afternoon Mama would take my sisters and me to the field with her. It would take some hard hoeing to get all of the lower patch worked out by night. Daddy would be plowing in a nearby field, so Mama suggested that he take her hoe and an apple box for the baby to the edge of the cotton patch. She filled a green Mason quart jar with cool water from the spring and screwed the zinc lid on tightly. She also filled a sugar sack with some tea cakes which were left from their noon meal. Gathering up an old quilt, some extra Birdseye diapers, and a file, she had all she needed for the afternoon job. After grabbing her bonnet to protect her head from the burning sun and sock gloves to protect her hands, she was ready. The gloves were made by cutting holes in the feet on the socks and sticking the fingers through the holes. The foot area protected the palms of the hands. Gripping the handle of a hoe with sweaty palms for hours would raise painful blisters on the spongy bases of the fingers inside the hands.

With the baby astraddle her right hip and the resct of the load under the crook of he left elbow, Mother headed for the field. Hallie and I wanted to share the load, so I carried the jar of water, and Hallie Sue tugged on the sugar sack of cookies. Down the rutted farm road trudged the mother and three small children. She found the wooden box and the hoe at the end of the rows near a tall shade tree. The old quilt was used to line and pad the box for Bonnie Bell. The box was then placed in the shade of the sycamore tree at the end of the field. Then Mother instructed Hallie Sue and me that we were to stay right near the baby in the box. I was responsible for the baby, and I accepted my job with all the sincerity I could muster.

After getting the baby settled in the box, Hallie Sue and I playing in the immediate area, Mother reached for her hoe and began her afternoon work. She worked her way up and down the row, glancing frequently to check on the three of us in the shade. After going up and down three short rows, she felt confident that we were doing fine and that Bonnie Bell was sleeping.

Then she ventured down the entire length of the long

rows. She looked up and saw me coming toward her. She scolded me for leaving the baby, but I kept coming down the row to her. Mother stepped to the edge of the field and broke a switch from a small bush growing there. I said nothing, but fearing the switching, turned back toward the box with the baby. Mama, aggravated at the interruption and my disobedience, followed me back, intending to teach me a lesson by switching my naked legs. When she got nearer the box, she gasped in horror. The box was upside down. Under the overturned box the baby was lying on her face. Her arms were flailing, but she was unable to turn over. Her nose and mouth were buried in the corner of the quilt against the hard ground. Already she had turned blue from lack of air. Hallie Sue had pulled on the side of the box, flipping it over.

Mama screamed in panic, grasped the infant, blue in her face, and worked her arms up and down to initiate breathing. With one hand she grabbed the water jar and doused the baby's face with cool water. The little one's lungs grabbed the available oxygen, and all was well with her. Mama began scolding Hallie and me as we looked on in fear. She threatened to switch us for allowing this to happen. Our stunned silence turned to yelps and cries as we anticipated the pain that was to be inflicted upon us. We did not fully understand what had just happened. But in a minute or two, sanity prevailed. Mother, her fright subsiding, realized that we were only children and were doing what children do. Once again, I, not yet four years old, had been a "smart little girl."

One morning Daddy had gone to the barn to feed the stock and had found an abandoned baby squirrel at the base of a tree. He cupped it in his hands and brought the starving creature back for us girls to see. Then he remembered that there was a medicine dropper on the shelf in the kitchen. Placing the frightened animal in a cardboard box, he filled the dropper with milk, then lifted the squirming baby out and dribbled drops of the nourishing fluid into its toothless mouth. It soon got the idea and pulled at the milk from the hard teat. We girls were fascinated with this new pet, and soon we were doing the required feeding. We kept the squirrel in the box for a few days, and before long it did not want to leave its new home. We added cornbread to its diet and it learned to eat from a bowl.

The animal was thriving on human food and care; its tummy was pouching out as it ate more and more. After some time its eagerness for food and exploration became a problem. It insisted on drinking from the water bucket. One day when we sat down for the evening meal, there was no cornbread. Mother had baked enough for two meals at noontime and put the remaining in the cabinet. Somehow the cabinet had not been closed tightly, and the squirrel had crawled up into the cabinet and discovered the bread As much as were enjoying our newly-found pet, it was still a wild animal and needed to be in the woods with its own kind. One morning, before we girls were out of bed, Father threw his straw hat over the little wild one and scooped it up into a coffee sack. It was becoming a nuisance. He took it deep into the woods down by the creek and let it go. Then, at dinnertime, he explained to us what he had done. We did not fully understand, but we accepted his word as final.

Noisy neighbors surrounded the little house in the woods. The blue jays seem to be fussing all the time. The cawing of the crows could be heard from the lower cornfields. Mrs. Bob White was constantly calling her husband from the edge of the meadow. There was a mysterious, soft, sad cooing of a bird that never came into view. It was the male call of the mourning dove. Mother called it the rain crow and said that when it made the coo-cooing sounds, it was a sign that it was going to rain.

On the inside of the house a mud dauber could be heard drumming, daubing, and sawing as its strong jaws worked up mud with saliva and built its nest in the form of tube-shaped cells.

These solitary wasps plaster their nests on the undersides of eaves and porch roofs. When the nests are finished, the female flies out to catch a spider, sting and paralyze it and drag it into the nest. Then she lays her eggs on the body of the spider and seals up the nest. When the larva hatches in a few days, she will have an ample supply of fresh food.

After a few days of listening to a mud dauber high up on an inside window frame, Mother grew tired of the noise, and with a claw hammer dislodged the mud nest. She took the dried wad of mud outside on the doorstep and broke it open with the hammer. To her surprise and disgust, it was filled with large white worms (larva) and dry spiders.

There were also crawling neighbors that scampered and skittered in and around the outside walls of the house, especially on bright sunny days. They were long, slender lizards with gray and yellow stripes, and a beautiful bright blue tail that gleamed in the sun. They played hide and seek from the outside walls to underneath the house. Their favorite resting place seemed to be the sandstone rock foundations of the house. Sometimes they ventured right into the house through the open screenless windows. They would zigzag across the inside up to the ceiling. When my mother saw one, she would let out a screech, grab a broom, and beat it out of the house. A few yards behind the house stood a section of old rail fence. Bits and pieces of old fences were all over the place. The main enclosure now was a barbed wire fence, but I found the old fence a favorite place to climb and teeter back and forth on the bottom rung. This was also a favorite place for a striped racerunner lizard to sun. When I approached the fence, it darted in and out, as if teasing, and then disappeared into the grass.

One day while we were eating our noon meal, Mama went out on the back porch to get a glass of water. On the wall right over the water bucket clung a very long lizard with scaly back and twitching tail. She screamed for Daddy to come quickly and get that creature off the porch. By the time Daddy got through the door, the frightened reptile had gone up the wall and stuck in the very top corner. Daddy reached up to grab it by the tail. When he pulled his hand back, only the tail was between his fingers. The tail had broken off, the lizard's method of defense, and it had escaped to the outside. Daddy flung the pointed thing to the porch floor where it wriggled for several minutes. We girls stared and squealed in excitement; then we realized that the lizard was

72

somewhere without a tail. "Don't worry, " Daddy explained, "it will grow another tail."

Another crawling creature that lived nearby was the mud puppy. The spring for the family water supply was several yards east of the house down an uneven slope of a hill. I liked to follow my father to fetch water, which he did not do very often. Usually that was s woman's job. When he did go to the spring, he felt it was his duty to clean it out. After filling the buckets with clear water, he would take a forked stick and rake out all fallen leaves and weeds and then dig deep in the accumulated sand, allowing any dirt to run off in the stirred water. Usually a mud puppy or two would be brought up from the wet sand. These slimy dark-colored animals with spots, four little feet, a flat tail and short head, would dart about very quickly and slither away. To me everything was alive and full of surprises.

Nosey neighbors came by now and then. Because the house was built in the pasture, the cows went by there on their way from the barn lot to the lower pasture. Sometimes in late afternoon, when the cows, with full udders, were sauntering back to the barn after grazing and chewing their cuds all day, they would venture near the house and curiously stare at us children as we peered from the front door. When we saw the cows nearing the house, we would run inside. To a child, a cow looks big and monstrous.

When the sun set behind the trees and darkness settled in around the house, it seemed to us children that the eyes of night were staring at us from the bushy fringe of the yard. The owl's hoo-hooing was frightening to our listening ears. At night we stayed in close proximity to our mother and the light from kerosene lamp. After all, she was afraid of the dark, too. She never ventured beyond the doors at night. When we children were naughty or tried her patience, she would tell us that the "booger man" would get us, and of course, he lived out there somewhere in the darkness. Often she spoke of "BOOGERS" in the dark. (Bugbear, an imaginary hobgoblin was used to frighten children into good conduct.)

One night I dreamed of the "booger man" coming for me.

For some reason I had been scolded severely and told that the "booger man" was going to get me. After I dropped into a fitful sleep, the boogey man came after me in the form of a giant red toad frog. The monster flung me over its wide back and hopped across the barnyard and into the deep woods.

There was constant threat made to children that this boogey man or bugbear, would get them for misbehaving. Very soon I realized that this was make believe, but Mother never told me that she knew better. She knew that this was the way adults had of coercing children to carry out the will of parents.

There were carefree times in the little house in the woods. The crops were laid by and the haying done. While Mother was in he field gathering peas or beans for the next day's meals, Father was left in charge of the children. Rarely did he find the time to mind the children. But one special day, he felt free from pressing obligations to the farm and his parents; Bonnie Bell, on the pallet, was cooing and blowing bubbles from her mouth and pummeling the air with her chubby legs and pink fists. Hallie Sue and I were prancing and dancing all around her. The happy infant watched our every move with great delight. Daddy got his French harp from the shelf over the bed and began playing a snappy tune. We held hands and romped and skipped across the room to the rhythm of "Old Dan Tucker." We finally became dizzy and flopped down on the pallet beside the baby. Next to us, Daddy found space on the folded quilt. With the harmonica on our level, I insisted that I wanted to play it also. But Daddy refused; first, because it had been in his mouth and was wet with saliva, and second, because anything he put in his mouth had to be absolutely clean.

Daddy put the harp back on the shelf, and still in a playful mood, took his straw sailor hat from a nearby nail and set it on his head. He had gotten it on his last trip to town. Somehow it seemed to go with his new car. After all, he previously had nothing but a work straw hat and a winter felt hat to wear. So on a whim, he saw and bought the sailor hat. It was classy with its Bon Ton Ivy adjustable cushioned sweatband, straight crown, and extended brim.

We girls were beside ourselves with joy. We were having so much fun, and so was Dad. With hat square on head, he got down right in our midst, rolling and romping on the floor. The game was to get the hat from his head. Sure enough, Hallie Sue swung at the topper, knocking it to the floor. At that instant, I did a turn-about and lost my balance, falling squarely on the hat, one knee crushing into the crown of this straw chapeau. Daddy looked at the flattened hat in disbelief. His first reaction was to scold and paddle me for such a reckless act. I was devastated that I had done so much damage to my father's cherished possession. My startled look and expression of pain and regret made Daddy feel sorry for me. He tried to push the crown back in shape but the sennit braid was forever bent. He put the hat out of sight, not wanting Effie to see the damaged thing. He did not want to explain what happened. In those days, men just did not admit to having fun with their children. Somehow it was not man-like.

Seven

Late summer found my parents still struggling to prove their independence. Even though we lived in separate houses, we still had to share some vital things. Since my parents did not have a cow for milk, they had to depend on the cows owned by their parents. Grandma suggested that she feed, milk and turn the cows to pasture in the mornings. Also she would churn from her part of the milk and share the butter with us. Mama and Daddy would be responsible for feeding, milking and securing the cows at night, taking their share of the milk then.

Then there was the matter of eggs from Grandmother's flock of chickens. She would share as many eggs as she thought we would need each week. Mama felt that her mother-in-law begrudged giving up that amount of butter and eggs, as these were the two things she used for trading at the store. But necessity forced her to swallow her pride and accept a minimum amount of these basic commodities for her family.

It seemed that everywhere Mama looked she was made to realize her dependence on the mother of her husband. Even at night when she laid down on the feather bed, she remembered that it was her mother-in-law's bed of feathers and ticking. Her head was resting on a pillow stuffed with the down of geese raised and plucked by her mother-in-law.

Going to the spring two or three times each day carrying a large bucket in each hand was a chore that no one wanted, but it had to be done. Leaving the three of us children in the house while she hurried to the spring, quite a distance from the house, was a concern to my mother. Bonnie Bell was crawling everywhere, and Hallie Sue was climbing up on the chairs and the table. Mama trusted me to watch them for the short time it took her to get a half-day's supply of water for drinking and cooking.

Doing the weekly wash was a job. She not only had to carry the water by the buckets-full from the spring to the house, but she had to rig up an old tub to set on a stack of rocks, and build a fire underneath it to heat water and boil the white things. There was only one wash pot on the place, and she could not move that heavy iron cauldron back and forth on washday. The sooty side of the tub made lifting the clothes in and out a tedious task.

By this time of the year, there was canning and preserving the food from the field to do. With three small children underfoot, Mama had to do the picking, gathering, shelling and shucking. Here again, she had to take from her mother-in-law's supply of canning jars. She was continuously being forced to admit that they could not go it alone, at least, not for the time being. Another thing she had been forced to deal with was the distance from her house to the storm cellar at the main house. When small storms and threatening clouds began to gather, she worried about what they would do if there came a bad storm. Would she dare start out with three children, walking up the road under the tall trees, to the big house? One very hot day, her fears were realized. She heard the rumbling of thunder and saw the skies darkening in the south. Harley was somewhere on the place with the team of mules hitched to the wagon. The air became thick and tight. She just knew this was going to be a bad one. She, Hallie Sue, Bonnie Bell and I would have to stay where we were in the small house. How she wished Harley would come in from the fields.

Mother re-lived the time Harley was almost hit by lightning. As usual he was taking his time leaving the bottomland as a cloud was gathering. With the mules and the wagon, he came up through the floor of the broad valley, as yet a long way from the barn. A huge bolt of forked lightning burst open the low-hanging clouds right over him, the animals pulling the wagon, the bed and spoke wheels rimmed with steel. The leather harnesses were connected with metal rings, and the long trace chains were made entirely of metal. Momentarily, he was numb—his eyes blinded with the flash; his eyelids and brows seemed to be singed. He thought the Almighty had called him in a very loud voice. The clash of noise and the flash startled the animals, and they began to lurch forward in fright. It took all the strength Harley could bring forth to restrain the frightened animals until they were safe in the barn. He had told this incident many times, but still, he did not get unduly alarmed when storm clouds were brewing.

On this particular day, Mother closed the doors and windows and gathered my sisters and me around her on the side of the bed. The lightning became sharper, the dark clouds were almost touching the tops of the trees, and the thunder reverberated with fervor. Then everything became quiet. Was it passing over? A strong gust of wind hit against the south side of the little house, causing it to tremble, then shutter and shake. The small structure was sitting only on stacked flat sandstone rocks.

From the back porch came a crashing sound. The wind had picked up the wash tubs and the scrub board and slammed them into the wall. The tubs could be seen rolling across the front yard. Mother was terrified; she held us children so tightly that she almost squeezed the breath from us. More lightning cracked and giant fingers of fire seemed to reach from one window to the other. Mother kept saying "Where is Harley? Where is Harley? He is going to be killed." We children were so frightened that our hearts were almost bursting out of our chests. For long minutes we sat paralyzed, expecting the next clap of thunder to bring down the roof, and the next crack of lightning to strike us dead.

There came a suspended moment of silence, a gasp of relief. From the angry skies, the bottom of the clouds let go with tons of ice balls that pelted and pounded the corrugated tin roof. The clattering noise brought my siblings' and my hands up over our heads for protection. Our eyes were squenched in terror. In a long short time, the banging and beating on the roof ceased. Slowly, Mother released our tightened bodies. She looked relieved; so did we. She got up and went to the window to peer outside. All danger seemed to have passed, so she cautiously opened the front door. Clinging to her skirt were Hallie and me, wanting to see outside also. The yard was covered with round pellets of ice, like buckets and buckets of mothballs. Our fear turned to curious excitement. Ice on a hot summer day!!

I wanted to touch these strange ice marbles. Mother gave in to my pleading, and allowed me to go outside and pick up some of the hail. Quickly I filled a wash pan of the melting balls for the others to see and touch. The little gray-weathered house had stood the test of a terrible storm; so had mother and we children.

One mid-afternoon that same summer, the ears of my dozing sisters and I heard the rumble of a car coming down the red-clay rutted road to the house. After we alerted our mother that someone was coming, we stood peering out the front door at the approaching car. Cars had not ventured down this road. Our father kept his car in a quick-built, shed-garage at the main house. First, there were two gates to open and close, since the road led through the barn lot into the pasture that kept the work animals. Secondly, we had no company since moving into the little house. None of Mama's family had paid her a visit in a long time.

As the two people scrambled from the car, Mama recognized her brother Samuel and his wife, Lolita. Instinctively, she feared that something was wrong. Were they bringing bad news of her mother or father? She was relieved, but saddened, to hear that her older half-sister's youngest son, age two, had died of sleeping sickness. She remembered again the death of her half-brother's young child, of diphtheria, some years back. Because Mother had no adult to talk with, she often talked to me as if I were much older. She had told me that diphtheria was a terrible, contagious disease that caused the throat to close up completely. As for sleeping sickness, she did not know the cause — maybe a bite of a mosquito. She knew it was a deadly disease that caused inflammation of the brain. I spent many pensive moments wondering how sleeping could make anyone so sick. Suppose I went to sleep never to wake up again. My sisters could get it . . .

A pervasive sadness settled down around the two separate families. The countenances of my grandfather and grandmother were constantly downcast. They seemed to be homesick even though they were home. This had been the first time in their many years of marriage that there was no one but the two of them in their house. They were so lonely.

My father, their youngest son and chief caregiver, was caught between their need for him and his wife's aversion to his mother. The first few months in the little house had been a good experience, and he had enjoyed the time spent only with his wife and young children. But his aging parents seemed to need him more and more. His mother had lost weight, which she could ill afford. His father had become frail and confused. The once patient patriarch was becoming more gruff and hostile toward his wife of forty-five years. My grandmother was afraid of him, especially during the nighttime when he would ramble around looking for some unknown thing. He was now seventy-seven years old.

As fall came and the cotton ripened, it was obvious that my grandparents did not have the strength to finish the crops. In desperation, MaBett voiced her concern to those of their children who came by for a visit. They all agreed that she must have some help with their father. One of the older sons was ready to bring his wife and younger children back to the homeplace to care for his parents and the farm. But this son and his wife were not Grandmother's choice. She wanted my father, with whom she had always had a special closeness, to move back into the house.

With dread and some delay, my father shared with my mother his parents' need for them and the dilemma that the choice was posing. Mother had been aware of the increasing frailty of his parents, especially his father. With reluctance, she consented to move back into the house with them.

So by mid-fall, while the weather was still mild, the transition was made; the families were again under the same roof. There was a time of adjustment for my two young sisters, but I was so glad to be back in my grandmother's house, share her bed, and be a sidekick to all her exciting activities.

Eight

I was now coming up on four years of age. It seemed that the eight months or so in the little house had matured me beyond my years. My sense of being trusted to help with my younger sisters heightened my sense of responsibility. My grandmother, seeing my physical growth and realizing my emotional stability, seemed to draw from my strength. She was going through some of the hardest days of her life. Her aging husband was very difficult to humor and care for. She found herself looking for more reasons to get out of the house and go to the store. Now I could walk with her. Since others were in the house, she would not be leaving Pa alone. It was a great source of comfort to have our family in the house with them as the winter days set in and rolled slowly by.

Early spring brought hope that Grandpa's health would improve with the warming days. But those hopes were dashed one Friday morning when Pa had not awakened and began stirring around at his usual time. The stillness alerted his concerned wife that something was wrong. She tried to awaken him and found that he could neither talk nor walk. She concluded that he had had a stroke. Dr. Thomas was sent for and soon confirmed her fears. The children were notified of his condition. By Saturday the house was filled with members of the family. They stood around the stick bed, faces gripped with concern.

Mother had to assume responsibility for cooking and performing outside chores. She was concerned that we children would get in the way. I, sensing her concern, stood at the edge of the crowd, listening to every utterance. After words and remarks were made regarding Grandfather's condition, the conversation turned to the kidnapping of Lindbergh's baby. It seemed some were more informed than others, especially those who lived in town and had access to a newspaper.

With hushed tones, they talked of how the 20-month old baby boy was snatched from his bed in his own home in New Jersey. A ladder was used to carry the child from his room, and muddy footprints were left on the floor. The kidnapper was demanding $50,000 for the child's safe return. Lindbergh was willing to pay the ransom, but no instructions had been given as to where or how to pay the money. This apprehension deepened the solemnity of the occasion. Kate, the daughter who lived in town, brought out cheese and crackers. She sliced the cheese thinly to ensure there would be enough. Although the children were in the side room, they were not overlooked. This was the first time they had tasted yellow, nutty-like hard stuff, but it was very good. The crunchy crackers were great. I never forgot my first encounter with this Cheddar delight.

By the next morning, Grandfather was showing improvement, and Sunday all the adults were gone except the immediate family. But MaBett knew that her husband would never be well again.

All across the country there was deepening despair. The nation was in the midst of a deep depression. Hoover had tried to stabilize the economy, but there were major financial crises everywhere. According to the newspapers, the U.S. deficit had passed $2 billion. One million was hard for most people to comprehend — especially small time farmers.

Out of desperation, eleven thousand veterans marched on Washington in the latter part of May, demanding a bonus for serving in the Great War. This bonus army, as they were called, had camped along the banks of the nearby river, some settling in abandoned buildings near the White House. Each day the men gathered at the Capitol for a quiet vigil.

Reading of the incident, my dad thought of one of his older brothers who had served for a short time during the war.

He could not imagine this brother being so brash, assuming so much in the country's bad times. Some of the men had taken their families with them and were living in tents or makeshift shanties. Pictures in the newspapers showed pathetic children looking puzzled and forlorn. One large printed sign in front of a tattered tent read **HOOVER'S POOR FARM,** and below that another read **HARD TIMES ARE STILL HOOVERING OVER US.** By the later part of July, criminals and other malcontents had infiltrated the group. President Hoover sent in federal troops to evict the seekers and squatters.

There was a glimmer of hope on the horizon: Franklin Delano Roosevelt, Governor of New York, was running for president on the Democratic ticket, and he was pledging a "new deal" for the American people.

By August the unemployment rate was soaring, with at least eleven million out of work. The government was making loans that it could ill afford to help banks and other organizations survive.

By midsummer, Grandpa's health had stabilized. He sat on the front porch most of the time, oblivious to most of the things around him. Even the jabbering and the scuffing feet of a three-year-old, plus the business of a year-and-a-half-old, did not faze him.

Harley, with constant concern for the welfare of his parents, was now responsible for all the farm work. Effie was assuming more and more of the cooking and the outside work. It had been a compact year. The pressure of the last six months was pushing MaBett to get outside and resume more of her activities, the favorite of which was to walk to the store with a basket of eggs and butter. After all, her supply of snuff had to be replenished. I was eager to go with her. With excitement, right after dinner, we were on our way. MaBett trudged the worn path in measured steps, marching as it were to the cadence of the cicadas and katydids sawing in the nearby bush-wilderness. I ran along beside her, sometimes ahead, sometimes behind, skipping and tripping to the trill of a lustful lark from a tall tree. It meant so much to my grandmother to have a road-buddy.

In her long white apron pocket, Grandmother carried her round, tin box of Scotch snuff. When she took her frequent dips, I was fascinated with the brown powder, which had such a pungent aroma. Not wanting me to be left out, she took an empty tin box and filed it with cocoa powder for play-snuff. As apprentice snuff-dipper, I had to have a black-gum toothbrush. When we came near the bottom of the ravine, Grandmother pointed out a black gum sapling with dark gray bark and oval pointed leaves. Breaking a twig from some long-hanging branches, she peeled back about one inch of bark with her teeth and chewed one end until it became soft and pliable. Then, still with her teeth, she pushed one half of the coarse fibers into soft bristles. Giving me four inches of the remaining twig, she instructed me to make my own snuff brush. After peeling the bark and chewing the green stick until just right, I jabbed my brush into the box of cocoa, while Grandmother punched her dipstick into 100 percent fermented and pulverized tobacco. Then she swabbed the loaded brush on the gums of her salivating mouth. I did likewise. Grandmother was proud of her young soul mate. I was learning fast—no harm done. Besides, it was kind of a graceful gesture to offer a friend a "pinch of snuff."

I, not quite five, had been initiated into the sorority of the Sisters of Snuff Dippers and Bibbers. Together the two cleared the woods and emerged from the hollow by the Jones' place, grinning and giggling, daubing and spitting. Soon they neared the spring at the foot of Smith Hill. Grandmother also carried in her apron pocket a collapsible drinking cup. Having four rings, it telescoped into a flat round box with a tight-fitting lid. By this time our mouths were dry, having expectorated much this day. Opening the collapsed tin cup, we caught some of the fresh, ever-flowing water from the spring, which had been flowing from this hill longer than anyone could remember. We rinsed our mouths of the amber and drank lustily of the cool, clear, refreshing water,

After our thirst was quenched, we climbed the last hill onto a level plain, where the road led to the store and Highway 70. The joy of the journey was as delightful as reaching the destination. Seldom were there womenfolk shopping at the country store. Usually the menfolk picked up the few necessary items such as coffee and kerosene. After trading and browsing through the newspaper, MaBett went next door to see her sister, the wife of the merchant. They shared their families' joys and concerns, concerns mostly for her. Her sister was well aware that it would be downhill all the way with her partially paralyzed husband.

The calendar was not the only way that the family knew August was well under way. The hot, sticky "dog days" had sapped their energy and stifled any enthusiasm for outside activities. The level of water in the water bucket always seemed near the bottom. Four adults and three children gulped water from the long handle dipper, then plunged the bowl of the dipper to the bottom of the white porcelain bucket. Near sunset, an extra bucket of water was brought up from the deep well and poured into the foot tub for the "family foot washing" before going to bed. Hands were perfunctorily washed before and after each meal. My dad could not and would not tolerate "nastiness."

The area of the body between the fingers and toes was pretty much neglected. Consequently, the places that were covered and usually moist, due to bodily functions, did not receive attention. First, the privy was literally an open-air area behind the smokehouse with only an old Sears Roebuck catalog to use as toilet tissue. If members of the family were not near the backyard when nature called, they sought cover behind a spreading bush, pulling wide leaves from it to finish up the job. There was nothing to sit on but the imagination supported by the haunches. We children, impatient with nature's protocol, many times failed to apply anything that would absorb drippings and stripping of waste materials.

Interestingly, I noticed that many times MaBett stood upright in a wide-leg position, holding her long skirt afar. The amber fluid was slightly acid and became an irritant to the tender parts of the groin area. We children were uncomfortable and fretful because our inner thighs and bottoms were galled and sometimes raw. When we finally settled down for sleep, and pulled our underclothes from the painful areas, Mother could not help but see our plight. She had only flour from the flour barrel to sprinkle on the affected areas. Unfortunately, the flour powder caked on the moist areas, creating another uncomfortable situation. By Saturday Mother would realize that we children must have a bath. In mid-afternoon, she would draw water for the foot tub and set it in the sun for a while to take the chill off. We children shared bath water and wash cloth. We danced and pranced with glee. We felt so clean.

MaBett and Effie were taking turns milking the cows, depending upon their other duties. On one particular late afternoon MaBett gathered up two milk buckets and a small portion of water to wash the udders of the cows. As usual I tagged along. I liked to help pull the hay down for the cows. There were a couple of cats that stayed at the barn. They were slick from eating mouse meat, but they liked milk as well. They had learned that when Grandmother did the milking, she would squirt some warm milk in a nearby lid for them. I took great delight in watching them lap up their milk food. I was not allowed to touch them though. After the cats had consumed their liquid supper, they stretched their bodies and spread their paws as if to say "thank you." Afterward, they skulked to the back of the barn; I followed them to a pile of discarded farm tools and debris. One of the cats jumped up on a dilapidated cultivator. I followed the animal, stepping across some broken and jagged wooden pieces lying on the ground. As I put my full weight down on my right foot, I stepped right on top of a rusty nail sticking up from a wooden scrap. I let out a gasp of pain, pulling my foot from the imbedded point of the nail. Holding my foot in horror, I began to cry, hobbling back to MaBett who was just coming out of the stable with a pail of milk. Setting down the milk, she dropped to her knees and brought me to her bosom, soothing me and assuring me that she would doctor it to make it better. Quickly, helping me to the house with one hand and carrying the milk pail in the other, we hobbled to the front of the porch, where I fell to the floor, tightly holding my throbbing foot.

Grandmother ran to the side room and pulling an old wool sweater from a box, crammed it into a tin bucket. She poured kerosene over the old sweater and struck a match to it. It began to smolder and then to smoke. She helped me into a chair and sat the smoking bucket under my punctured foot. For a few minutes, she turned the bucket, blowing on the reluctant flame and smoking the aching foot. She grabbed the kerosene can, saturated a piece of rag with coal oil, and dabbed it on the hole in the flesh.

She helped me into the house and threw an old quilt on the floor as a pallet for the night. By this time Mama had become aware of the commotion. She hurried from the kitchen to see why I was crying. She then went to prepare a remedy she relied upon for treating injuries involving nails, a frequent occurrence on a farm where children went barefoot most of the time. She took a thin slice of fat back and laid it on the puncture. Using torn strips of rag, she bandaged it tightly to the foot for the night. I tried to suppress my wails; I had never known such pain. I remained on the pallet, pummeling the air with my throbbing foot. I whimpered and writhed in pain until long into the night. She watched me from her bed, feeling the pain with me. Finally in the late hours of the night, sleep overtook my exhausted body and snuffed out the pain. The soreness remained for days.

Nine

Fall lingered. The sassafras shrubs spread their gold and scarlet leaves—from the lowly sprout all the way to the taller ones in the distance. The tall, stately sweet gum trees were frocked in brilliant red, with hard thorny balls hanging from long slender stems. An abundance of beautiful scarlet-yellow leaves clung to the black gum.

Finally a killing frost nipped the proud trees, stripping them of their colorful array. The detached leaves started slowly drifting to the ground. Sometimes a playful breeze would flirt with a flighty one in its descent.

The days were becoming shorter and cooler. Each day could be the last mild one for a while. On one particularly mild Wednesday, there was excitement afoot. This was my fifth birthday. Grandmother woke up the plans for the day. She helped with the household work, cooking dinner, with enough for supper. Since the weather was still pleasant, she saw that her frail husband was fed and then led him to the front porch to his favorite rocker. She placed a quilt on his knees and tucked it around his feet.

Anticipating this week's trading day, she had gathered and kept back two-dozen eggs and two pounds of fresh butter. She stuffed a fresh box of snuff into her apron pocket and scooped a box of coffee grounds, for play-snuff for me. Along with the snuff and the drinking cup, she grabbed her bonnet, and with basket of eggs on her right arm and butter in a sack on the other, she and I headed for the store.

We broke twigs from the black gum bush along the path,

to be used for fresh snuff brushes. After prepping the sticks, we were in business. With brisk steps we crossed the hollow and trudged up and down the next hills to the bridge that crosses the creek. We looked in wonder at the tall sycamore tree along the stream; with most of its broad leaves gone, it had a mottled and ragged look. The bark of the lower part of the trunk was a vivid reddish-brown, and higher up the branches were a shiny olive green. Much of the bark was broken and hanging in tatters. Where the bark of the upper branches was broken, an inner bark of light cream color was exposed. Small balls were hanging from drooping stems. We stepped from the main road a few yards to rest under the funny frocked tree. Grandmother reached up and pulled a few of the balls from the stems and gave them to me to touch and explore. The balls, the fruit of the sycamore tree, were wads of many tiny fruit tightly packed together. I tried to disgorge the dried segments, thinking once they were pried open, they would be fluffy. They were difficult to open and I soon lost interest. We crossed the plank bridge and went around the curve to the spring just ahead where we stopped for a drink of water. We rinsed out our mouths. The snuff was gone, but the taste and residue were still there.

When we arrived at the store, MaBett was more than glad to put her load of eggs and butter on the counter. She looked around the shelves, boxes and gunnysacks, searching for a special treat for my birthday. From the glass-enclosed case she saw a big candy bar, Baby Ruth, five cents. She asked for two of the bars and then took two bottles of Coca Cola from the drink box. She would finish her trading later. She and I stepped outside under the big porch and sat down on the wooden bench. This was my first big candy bar. Filled with crunchy roasted, peanuts and coated with caramel, it was indeed "the best bite of all." I sat happily beside my beloved grandmother, my feet dangling with gleeful sweeps and swings. A few cars chugged by on the highway. They waved at us from behind the tall, round gasoline pumps.

Mr. John, the merchant, added twenty cents to the list of items, and soon we were on our way home, our basket full of sugar, salt, and baking soda. On the far side of the creek we passed the tall chestnut tree that had been there forever and ever. The long yellow catkins of the summer had turned into prickly burrs. Under the spreading branches the ground was covered with at least a bushel of the bristle balls. Some of the husks had broken open, showing two or three leathery nuts nestled in a velvet lining. Transferring the few items from the basket to a paper poke, MaBett squatted down and very carefully filled the basket with the sticky burs. What a treat it would be to roast them in the fireplace when cold weather set in; furthermore, she would add some to the next batch of dressing.

Grandmother had been aiming to kill that old red rooster anyway! After his tough hide had been simmered for hours, the broth would make good dressing, and now she would have these chestnuts to give added flavor and crunch. It would be simple; she would just boil the chestnuts for about thirty minutes, shell, chop, and add them to the other ingredients — biscuits, cornbread, eggs and sage.

Grandmother and I, with our prickly load, reached the yard of the farmhouse as the sun was setting in the west behind the barn. Grandpa appeared tired. His sympathetic wife helped him inside to his bed. His sun was also slowly, but surely, going down.

The uncertainty of the country's crisis gave the now head of two families impetus to make preparations for the coming winter. Harley cut and gathered as much firewood as possible. One of his older brothers, concerned about their parents, and especially their father's failing health, had come for the day. While there, the brothers spent half of the day cutting firewood. It took two men to pull the crosscut saw back and forth in precise motion, cutting down trees and then cutting the trunks into sections which would fit into the fireplaces. Their cutting tool was a large, straight blade of about seven feet, with sharp jagged teeth, and a handle on each end.

The thick sections of wood were split into thinner pieces using a wedge, a piece of heavy iron tapered to a thin edge. A split was started with an ax, and then the wedge was inserted and pounded with a large maul. It took both muscle power and stamina to wield this sledgehammer with both hands. One man would split while the other piled the splintering pieces of wood. Then they would switch roles. Later Harley would bring the farm wagon and team of mules to the woods to haul the wood to the house. He would unload it stick by heavy stick onto the dwindling woodpile.

In late November when the weather had turned cold to stay, Harley's older sister and her husband, who lived nearby, helped Harley kill hogs. This entailed shooting the animal, scalding the carcass in a vat of very hot water, scraping most of the hair from its skin, and then stringing it up on a stout pole by placing a gambrel stick behind the hamstrings or tendons in the hind legs. Harley's brother-in-law then made a long cut down the middle of the animal's underside from crotch to chin. Then carefully, he made a second cut, letting the intestines drop into a tub. The leaf lard, fat that held the intestines together, would be removed later. Now the veteran butcher made one cut all the way down the middle of the backbone. Then the carcass was taken down from the pole and put on a wide sled. With an axe he chopped out the backbone. After more chops, whacks, and cuts, the pig was cut into the appropriate portions: hams, shoulders, ribs, tenderloin, and side meat. The tenderloin would be cooked for supper. Portion's of the backbones, ribs, and liver were shared with the helpers. After removing the fat from the entrails, Harley's sister and her husband left them to finish the smaller jobs the next day.

Early the next morning, while their hands were still numb from the cold, Harley and Effie tackled another day's work—working up the fresh meat. They set aside a dishpan to catch the trimmings of the lean meat that would be used in the sausage. Another pan caught the trimmings for the fat that would be rendered into lard. Besides the fat from the intestines, trimmings from the hams, shoulders and middling meat would be used to make lard. Lard was an important part of cooking. It was used for frying all the cuts of meat and chicken. It was shortening for biscuits, breads and piecrusts.

It was Effie's job to trim and cut all the fat into pieces

about the size of hen eggs and put them into the big iron wash pot, with just enough water to keep the raw meat globs from sticking as they cooked. The fat was cooked slowly all day over an open fire, and stirred often.

After several hours of cooking, the water had evaporated from the grease leaving the residue called cracklings. The hot grease was dipped out of the kettle and poured into large tin cans and allowed to harden. The cracklings were saved for use in cornbread.

It was during this frying process that Effie could no longer hide from her mother-in-law that she was with child again. The hours of trimming the fat from a freshly slaughtered hog, watching and smelling it sizzle in the hot pot, was more than her delicate, unbalanced stomach could handle. She ran behind the house several times, heaving, gagging, and disgorging contents from her stomach, a process called "pukin." Fresh meat did not seem appetizing to her at this time.

Grandmother took much pride in her sausage mixings. The lean scraps and trimmings were ready for the seasonings. To a big dishpan of meat, she added about a quarter cup of salt, a half-cup of brown sugar, two tablespoons of sage, some black pepper, and two teaspoons of red pepper. The sausage grinder was fastened to a plank about five feet long. Each end of the plank rested on the seat of a cane- bottom chair. Under the meat grinder was placed a clean zinc washtub with which to catch the ground meat after the pieces of lean meat had been crushed, chewed and forced from the steel-grinding tool.

I, as Grandma's little helper, got to sit on one end of the plank while Grandmother sat on the other and turned the crank. When all the meat was ground, some was kept for the next breakfast or two; the remainder was packed into canning jars. First the ground mixture was fried lightly until browned, and then while still hot, it was put into the jars. The hot grease was poured over the top, the lid put on tightly, and the jars turned upside down to seal and cool. Then they were stored in the cool fruit cellar for future breakfasts.

To Effie, the pervading smell of frying sausage lingered for days. She had a queasy stomach for many mornings.

As the weather became colder, so did Grandpa. The wood was kept piled high in the fireplace to make him comfortable. He was constantly complaining, usually about imagined discomforts, but no one will ever know for sure. Often he became incoherent. His talk was very plain, sometimes unacceptable for the ears of children. He kept his "slop jar" under his bed and availed himself of it — often at the most inopportune times. Grandmother had no choice but to put me back in the room with Harley, Effie, and the other two children.

This meant that three children had to share one bed. Bonnie Bell was now about one year and ten months old and had already been moved from our parent's bed. Effie was uncomfortable most of the time, and certainly sleeping with a child this large (one who was a fretful sleeper) would be an impossible situation.

The added bedmate created a lot of quarreling and complaining; Hallie Sue and I whined and tattled about each other. One of us was constantly kicking the other. This bickering at night aggravated Mother, but she would only threaten us with what our father would do to us for misbehaving. When he came into the room to go to bed, we at last pulled in our feet and curled up in our own space.

By morning the bed would be wet. Although Mother pinned a double "hippen" on Bonnie Bell at night, still there was leakage. Hallie was having difficulty controlling her bladder at night. The bed-clothing would be hung out on the line during the day to dry. If the weather was inclement, the sheets and under-quilt would be hung on the backs of chairs in front of the fireplace until they were dry. The drying urine left copper circles on the bedclothes until they were washed; the ammonia fumes made our nostrils smart.

Although the front rooms were kept very warm, our colds and coughs grew more persistent. The nights were racked with hacking coughs. During the day there were constant runny noses to be wiped. We children were prone to wipe the mucous on our sleeves, but we were scolded for our "nastiness." Instead we were encouraged, by word and example, to raise the skirts of our dresses and wipe our noses on the underside. The men would use their shirttails—all except Harley that is. Since he was a boy, he had insisted on having white handkerchiefs, which were made by the womenfolk from plain flour sacks.

Upon rising in the morning, there was a chorus of hawking as each member of the family, attempted to clear his or her throat and lungs of the congealed residue of colds—the phlegm. Near at hand were the hearth and ashes of the fireplace, which served as family cuspidors.

The lingering effects of the colds led to infections of the throat and ears. Mama tried different remedies which had been used by her mother and others. MaBett insisted on the tried and true cure of putting two or three drops of kerosene on a lump of sugar and feeding it to us. At night a poultice of kerosene, turpentine, and lard was tied around the throat. The lard was to prevent the stringent oils from blistering the skin. An additional lump of sugar with kerosene was taken to complete the treatment.

Sweet oil was kept on hand. The soothing oil was warmed, and a few drops dropped into an aching ear. If the pain persisted, a small sack of salt was warmed by the hearth and placed on the pillow underneath the hurting ear. Usually the applied heat eased the pain and calmed us.

The same poultices were used on deep chest congestions. A piece of flannel cloth smeared with the healing ingredients was kept on our chests at night by pinning the cloth to our underwear.

Croup was the dreaded malady of the night. We children were constantly warned about playing in cold water during the day. Getting our clothes wet would surely bring on an attack. A death knell or croup knell hung over our playful moments which involved water. Effie had known of children turning blue and nearing death because their windpipes literally closed up. So at night she listened for the croup cough. If one of us began to develop a hollow, barking sound with wheezing from the throat, she knew this could be a life threatening situation. Quickly she would put a gob of Vick's salve in a pan of boiling water and force the one of us who coughed to breathe in the vaporizing fumes.

The hot rooms up front were in direct contrast to the cold kitchen at the back. The fires did die down in the early morning hours, but before the warm air had escaped, one of the adults stoked and fed the live coals with new wood.

In the kitchen, separated from the front part of the house by a side room, there was no source of heat except for the cook stove. By early morning that room was very cold! During very cold weather, some mornings there would be a skim of ice in the water bucket. Even with a hot fire in the firebox, the kitchen remained cold. The biscuits would come out of the oven hot and perfect, and the milk gravy would be steaming, but by the time the food was placed on cold plates, surrounded by cold air, the gravy had set up and everyone ate cold food.

The year of 1932 ended on a solemn note. Only Christmas had been celebrated, and that in a quiet way. All thoughts and activities for the family revolved around the grandfather's confinement. Cold weather kept us children inside bursting with energy. Mother was beside herself trying to keep us quiet. We wanted to run from one room to the other, making noise and letting in cold air from adjacent unheated room. One of my favorite quiet pastimes was musing over the Sears Roebuck catalog. The almanac, that always hung on a certain nail, also fascinated me. The adults were frequently referring to it for future weather and the rising and setting of the sun. From time to time the clock was forgotten and allowed to run down. The timepiece was rewound and set according to the almanac.

I watched the adults' activities, especially when they pertained to books with pages. I began to ask questions about the numbers on the calendar and the words that were the names of the months and days of the week. Grandmother realized that I was ready for learning my numbers and ABC's. She took brown paper bags and cut the sides into large writing sheets.

A pencil was found in the top dresser drawer and trimmed with the butcher knife. Thus at the knee of my grandmother, I began my education.

Eagerly I wrote the letters over and over, and then put them together to make my name. Seeing how the letters became words, the proud teacher helped me find words like boys, girls, you, hats, caps, men, coats, socks, shoes, doll and buggy on the pages of the Sears Roebuck catalog. Then I saw the use of numbers and how the pages of a book were counted from page one all the way to the back of the book. The amount of money for each item was shown from fifty cents for a pair of boy's overalls to one dollar and twenty cents for a pen. Grandmother was able to get enough money together to teach me the value of coins and dollar bills, and what a certain amount of money could buy from the catalog. Before long, I could count all the way to one hundred. Now the numbers on the calendars made sense, as did the numbers on the bottom of book pages. I soon learned the weather signals of the calendar — the white flag for fair weather, the blue flag for rain or snow, the checkered flag for a storm, and the black triangle for a change in the temperature. I became aware of the seasons of the year — that we were now in the winter season and that spring, summer, fall and again winter would come.

I was fascinated with the moon phases shown on the calendar and in the almanac. With Grandmother on a clear night, I looked for a new moon or the first or last quarter or for a full moon. I also looked for the man in the moon, but all I ever saw was a bear.

Ten

The family (old, young, and very young) were absorbed in their own battle for survival. Care for aging parents with failing health, a fourth child on the way, and uncertainty about the future were staggering concerns for this young couple, not yet tried by the fires of life. It was just as well that they did not fully understand the turmoil going on out there in the world during the early days of 1933. There were fifteen million Americans without jobs; one out of every four households had no paycheck. In many cities, entire families were living in tarpaper shacks, scavenging for food in the city dumps. On March 4, amidst deep despair, Franklin Delano Roosevelt was sworn in as the new President. He tried to assure the troubled nation that they had "nothing to fear but fear itself." But so many were gripped with fear and uncertainty, they could not fathom his challenging remarks. The people had to believe him, however, and trust his program of recovery and restoration for the country.

One of the first Cabinet members chosen by the new President was Cordell Hull as Secretary of State. The people of Tennessee were proud of their native son from Overton County. He had already proven himself in the state legislature and as a circuit court judge. In 1907, he was elected to the United States House of Representatives. During this time he wrote the income tax law, and later on, the inheritance tax law. He also became Chairman of the Democratic National Committee. In 1930, he was elected to the United States Senate. Hull was instrumental in getting Roosevelt nominated to the Democratic Presidential ticket. So Cordell Hull had already made himself an effective and influential person in the Halls of Congress. Hopefully, he would remember the humble folks of his home state, especially those in West Tennessee, so far away from his Eastern Cumberland roots.

On the 5th of March, the new President ordered a four-day holiday for all banks to halt massive withdrawals, but more time was needed for passage of emergency legislation in the Congress. By March 13th, banks found to be sound were allowed to re-open. At this time, the President began an intimate radio program that he called the "fireside chat" to comfort and encourage the American people. But many of the people of the nation, including many struggling farmers in Tennessee, did not have radio sets. This transition period in Washington seemed worlds away. Grandfather had another stroke and remained in a coma for a short time. All his children and their families gathered for the deathwatch.

It had been a cold winter, and everyone was racked with colds and flu. Grandfather's weakened body and spirit had succumbed to pneumonia. An agreement had been made between the aging parents and their youngest son that he was to give them a suitable burial after their respective deaths.

Effie, seven months pregnant, remained in the kitchen most of the time cooking meals, drawing water and washing dishes. The farm chores of feeding chickens, gathering eggs, slopping hogs, and milking fell to her. She kept us children in the kitchen with her. Harley's older brothers and sisters, most with large families of their own, looked askance at their youngest brother and wife for having "one youngin after another." Effie was especially sensitive to the insinuating remarks and stares at the little ones. She vacated their bedroom for company and bedded down on an uncomfortable narrow bed in the side room. We children slept on pallets on the floor. It was as if the adults had formed a barrier around the departing patriarch, and he was soon gone.

The wake and the funeral closed the book on Mr. John Stephen Kirk's life. It was a mystery to us children since we were not made a part of the closing scene. In making the necessary arrangements for the funeral with Smith Funeral Home, there would be a charge of seventy-five dollars cash that would include using a truck to take the casket from the home to the cemetery. If this amount was not paid within one week, the charge would be one hundred twenty-five dollars. Son and mother could only come up with fifty-five to sixty dollars. One close family member turned down their request for help. In desperation, Harley turned to the husband of an older niece, a reputable businessman who gladly made the loan without signature for security.

The house was strangely quiet for a few days. Grandmother mutely emptied the closets of her husband's coats and heavy winter clothes. Only the stoneware jug stamped "A.T. Akin Co., Wholesalers, Liquor Dealers, Jackson, Tennessee," remained in its place. From the dresser drawers Grandmother pulled two pairs of union suits (mostly threadbare) and some tufted knitted socks, stretched and shapeless. Grandpa had been a much larger man than was Harley, so a pair of black rubber knee boots standing in the corner was too large for him. A pair of work shoes was pulled from under Grandpa's bed. Two pairs of overalls and a jumper were hanging from a large nail on the wall in the side room. All the clothes and belongings of the departed were gathered up and taken to an old quilt box in the corncrib at the barn.

April ushered in an early spring. Even though Effie was heavy with child, she and MaBett managed to get the garden out. My dad had done as much preparing of the ground as he could with a plow and mule.

Grandmother seemed to have a new lease on life. The last year's responsibility and concern over a sick one had drained her energy. She looked pale and drawn. But she had accepted her husband's passing, knowing that the aging man had been fed good meals and made as comfortable as possible. Now with another child due shortly, she could be of more help to the young family. One of the first things she wanted to do was make some light bread for the children and adults. It had been quite a while since she was able to get that involved. On her last trip to the store, she had ordered some cakes of compressed yeast.

To one-half cake of yeast, she added one teaspoon of sugar and worked them together until they were liquid. Three-fourths cup of lukewarm water and a teaspoon of flour were added to the yeast and set aside in a warm place on the top of the stove. Six cups of flour and a teaspoon of lard was rubbed into the flour. Grandmother's nimble fist made a hollow in the center of the flour. Then she poured in the yeast and nearly all the remainder of the lukewarm liquid. She began to knead the mixture into a soft, elastic dough, using the rest of the liquid. Kneading steadily for about twenty minutes, she worked in all the dry flour, adding more if the dough began to stick to the bowl or her fingers.

She covered the dough with a cloth and placed it on the backside of the stove where it would be free from drafts, until it doubled in bulk. It usually took about four hours for this process. The dough was then punched down and turned onto a lightly floured dough-board, divided into portions, slightly kneaded, and put into greased bread pans.

Again the pans of dough were covered and allowed to double in bulk. The oven was ready, but not too hot; after the bread was put in, it would rise to its fullest extent. The fire was stoked for higher heat to allow the bread to form a good crust, and then lowered to let the loaves cook thoroughly. Altogether, it took about three-quarters of an hour to bake the bread. The loaves were removed immediately from the pans and put out where the air could circulate freely around them until they cooled.

The smell of yeast in the hot baked bread permeated the kitchen and beyond. We children could hardly wait until the loaves were out of the oven and cool enough to eat. Using a knife MaBett smeared the fresh slices of bread with newly-churned butter and pear preserves and handed them to us. This, and a glass of sweet milk would be our supper for the night.

When this took place early in the day, the kitchen was quite warm. When Grandmother made light bread late in the day, the fire in the cook stove was allowed to die down. The dough was put down to rise so as to be ready to work up the next morning. There were times when the dough was ready before Grandmother was ready for the pummeling process. If this happened, the dough was "cut down" from the sides of the bowl and allowed to rise again. This prevented over-rising and consequent souring.

One day Grandmother noticed that the whole family seemed listless and in need of a good spring tonic. Earlier in March, she had sent Harley to the far field behind the barn to bring back a clump of sassafras that was growing there. By the hairy leaves and twigs, she knew this was "red sassafras" which is better for tonic and tea than the white sassafras that grows rampant over cutover lands. In fact, the white kind was a scourge to early planting because sprouts would spring up over the fields, and they had to be cut and piled for burning; an acrid smell always came from the slow burning, spitting pile. The red sassafras was harder to find and was protected for their roots.

My dad had taken an axe and a basket and dug by the base of the trees, cutting off sections of the roots. He remembered his mother always saying, "Drink sassafras during the month of March, and you won't have to see a doctor all year." He hoped she was right. She believed that it was a blood purifier that toned up your whole system, and that it was good for colds. She also believed it was good for sore eyes and bad diarrhea. Harley gathered a whole basket of roots for her.

MaBett slipped off the outer bark and washed and scrubbed the inner bark of the sassafras until it was pink and clean. After cutting the roots into five-to six-inch sections, she dried them and put them into a flour sack. She placed the sack on a high shelf where it was dry. When the time was right, she would use the sassafras to make an appetizing tea. We children needed to drink some of the tea, too; it would give us a good appetite and sweeten our breaths.

Into two quarts of water Grandma put two pieces of the roots after she had pounded them with a hammer. She boiled them for about twelve minutes then strained the amber tea and sweetened it with sugar. The adults drank with gusto, but we children had to be coaxed and threatened with worse things such as Black Draught.

To his amusement, Daddy had recently seen the words to a song praising sassafras. It went like this:

> In the spring of the year
> When the blood is too thick
> There is nothing so fine
> As a sassafras stick.
> It tones up the liver
> And strengthens the heart.
> And to the whole system
> New life doth impart.

He wished he knew the tune.

We children, especially the younger ones, still seemed sluggish and restless at night. Our continual itching in the groin area was a sign of pinworms. Mama knew that pinworms crawl out of the stomach through the bottom to lay their eggs on the surrounding skin, causing itching. Eggs lodge under the fingernails after scratching; some also lodge on bedclothes and towels. When ingested, the cycle starts again.

There was fear that a child would become infested with parasites, such as hookworm, that live in the intestine, sucking up blood and tissue fluids. Often when a child was weak and pale, adults would say that they looked "wormy." They had known of children who were dull and listless, with swollen stomachs and legs.

Unfortunately, adults did not know that hookworm disease was picked up by walking on ground that contained the young worms, which burrowed into the bare skin. Once in the body, the hookworms entered the bloodstream and were carried to the lungs. They burrowed into air channels and passed into the throat where they were swallowed into the intestines. In the intestines, the hookworms became adults.

Later their eggs passed out of the body with the waste and hatched in moist, warm soil.

Outdoor toilets, many merely the bare ground behind some outbuilding, were perfect hatching places for the larvae, and bare feet that stroke the private ground were perfect magnets for perpetuating their serious health problems.

No government agency provided information or enforced regulations to improve sanitary conditions.

One prevalent cure for worms was putting three or four drops of turpentine on a lump of sugar and eating it. Children were made to do this quite often. Grandmother had her favorite remedy, which was to make a sugar syrup with horehound (a weed that grew around the barn lot). This she faithfully gave to any child in her charge. Effie remembered that her father and mother had given her and her sister calomel when they were children.

May came, which meant that the cotton must be planted. Grandma helped my dad all she could by measuring out the cottonseed into the hopper. She held the reins of the team as he made switches from the middle buster to drag to planter. In the midst of the planting season, Effie gave birth to their fourth child, another girl. The two older girls of Harley's sister came and took the three of us children for the day. The new baby was fair-skinned with blue eyes. Now there were four girls with distinctly different features: one with red hair and green eyes; one with black hair and dark eyes; one with chestnut hair and brown eyes, and the new little one with blond hair and blue eyes.

This was a difficult time for the young family, with so many things to do in the field. Daddy had no one to help him with the farm work. His widowed mother was willing, but her strength was limited, and now Effie was confined with the baby. Harley's oldest brother and his family came by on the first Sunday afternoon to see how the family was faring. He was surprised to see that the little one looked so much like his children. To everyone's surprise, he blurted out, "Why don't you name this one JoBethe?" He was an avid reader of Zane Grey's books, and this could have been a name or combination of names in a recent story. Besides, the name came from the Bible. So Martha JoBethe became her name.

This had been a very good season for strawberries. On Grandmother's weekly trip to the store, she learned that her sister, the wife of the merchant, had a large patch of berries, more than she knew what to do with. The next morning Grandma gathered up two large baskets and a shoe box, and with a bonnet on her head, headed for the store and the strawberry patch. I wanted to go with her, but Grandmother remembered that when I went into the fields where the plants and weeds were, my legs began to itch and welt up and, in a few days, would be covered with sores. Besides, I was needed to help with my two sisters. By dinnertime, Grandmother returned, tired but gripping the handles of well-laden baskets of berries. After the noon meal, she began to hull and wash the berries. First she sugared some down for supper. She would make some short cakes to go with the berries. She mixed together one quart of flour, one-fourth pound of butter, two teaspoons of baking power, and some salt. To this mixture she added two eggs and one cup of sugar that had been slightly beaten together. A small amount of water was added to make soft dough, which was patted into large biscuits and baked in a moderate oven. The biscuits were split and spread with butter while still hot. At eating time, the sweetened berries were ladled onto the short cakes and covered with cold cream.

Before Grandmother could do more with the berries, she had to go to the smokehouse and dig out enough quart and pint jars to can and preserve the rest of them.

After washing supper dishes, Grandma used the same dishwater to wash the canning jars. She put a batch of the berries in a large porcelain pot and added sugar to taste. She stoked up the fire and brought the berries to a boiling point. Then she pushed the container to the back of the stove, where she would let it stand overnight. The last batch of berries would be made into preserves. In a smaller kettle, she placed equal amounts of sugar and berries, then boiled them hard for five minutes without stirring; she packed the cooked whole berries into very hot pint jars and sealed them immediately; she set them upside down and left them overnight.

The next morning, when breakfast and chores were completed, Grandmother tackled the remaining canning. The quart jars were placed in a kettle and boiled for a few minutes. In another small pan, she put the zinc lids and rubber rings to boil. Then she brought the berries, prepared from the night before, to the boiling point, stirring them carefully. Then she put the hot berries into the hot jars, placed the rubber rings around the top of the jars, and screwed on the zinc lids.

Canning was done by the open kettle method, wherein food was cooked completely and packed, boiling hot, into sterilized jars and sealed immediately. When the jars were completely cooled, Grandma wiped the sides until they were whistle clean. She carefully carried them to the shelves in the cellar that were used both for storage and as a refuge from "bad clouds." (Bad clouds or tornadoes were called cyclones.) Each filled jar gave her a sense of fulfillment as mother and grandmother. She was so glad that she had a family who still needed her, and whom she needed.

I was assuming my role as big sister with responsibility. In fact, my two younger sisters, who were now two and almost four years old, began to call me "Sister," encouraged by my mother and grandmother. I was able to help both my mother and grandmother with some chores around the house. I was ready to bring Mama a dry diaper when the baby needed changing and to see that the chamber pot was handy for my sisters. I could get the smaller ones a drink of water from the water bucket with the dipper and return it to the bucket. Since the wood for the kitchen stove had been cut into small sticks, I could bring in arm loads for Grandmother when she was cooking.

My eagerness for learning was obvious as I kept the family aware of the days of the week and the numbers on the calendar. I was also attempting to read words from the oatmeal boxes and flour sacks. My father took note of my readiness for school. One day while he was at the store, the first grade teacher of Hickory Flat School came into the store (she board-

106

ed next door at Mr. John's house.) Daddy became aware of who she was by comments directed to her by others in the store. He began talking to her of his oldest girl, who would be starting to school at the next term. He could not hold back his pride, but told her how I already knew my ABC's and could count to high numbers. The teacher glowed with interest and went to her room next door and brought my father the primer that would be my first school book.

Daddy could hardly wait until he got home to show me the reading book. I was standing out in the backyard beside the well. Grandmother had just drawn a bucket of fresh water and gone back into the kitchen. I, with no reason to follow her inside, was standing alone, lost in a world of fantasy. When my father gave me the book, my eager hands grasped the small hardback and my face broke into a happy smile. I sat down on the back step and began turning the crisp pages with the exciting pictures, letters and words. With my father's help, I read all the stories before bedtime.

The first story was a funny one about Goose-Goose the tidy, hardworking neighbor and Pig-Pig the big fat pig who made a "pig of himself." I read and reread the book. Soon words like "dinner," "hunger," and "garden" became my own. There were many exciting stories like "The Little Tin Train" and "Singing to the King." In this story there were songs of the Hen who sang, "Cut, Cut, Cut-tar, Cut," and the Ducks who said "Quack, Quack, Quack." The Goose could only sing "S,s,s,s,s!" The king said, "You shall go into a pot. And the fire shall be hot, Away with you." My favorite story was "Bunny in the Garden" that told about the animals nearby, such as Mother Rabbit, a squirrel, a fox, a bumblebee and a little ant. I laughed with glee as I read about the ant biting the rabbit's ear: "As Little Ant bit harder, Bunny ran faster around the garden and then hid under the cabbage leaves. The squirrel, the fox, and the bumblebee laughed and laughed at the Bunny and sang, 'See Bunny run! Little Ant is having a fast ride! Bunny is Little Ant's horse.'"

The story my father liked best was about Big Dog Rover who was going to catch a fat little woodchuck for a fine dinner. Woody Woodchuck ran as fast as he could down into a hole where he lived. The dog caught him by the tail and pulled and pulled. The wee end of Woody Woodchuck's tail came off and some fur was all that Big Dog Rover had for his supper. My father and I reviewed all 424 words in the Word List in the back of the book. We did the exercises to double check my comprehension. Riddles on one of the last pages were fun.

The reading lessons made everyone happy. The younger children, except the baby, stood on tiptoes to get a peek into the book with pictures of pigs, geese, rabbits, mice and bumblebees. I protected the pages from the eager hands of my two sisters. Mother intervened, and soon their curiosity was satisfied and their attention turned to other forms of play. After a few days, Grandmother brought out two yellowed school notebooks from the high shelf in the closet. She had kept Daddy's last school papers and tests from the eighth grade. There they were — tests on reading, arithmetic, geography, and spelling, with A's on most of them. Grandmother felt that with my maturity and early learning, I would be proud of my father for doing well in school. This being Sunday, Harley was in the house and heard his name repeated by us children. Yes, he had known that the papers were there for the last fifteen years or so. Their presence and the memory of his good grades and good behavior in school was an affirmation to him that he was a good person with a good mind.

Daddy was so pleased that his mother was showing the school papers to me. He felt confident that I was going to do well in school also. With pride he thumbed through the notebooks and then put them back in their nook on the shelf. I knew that my mother, father, and grandmother, had high aspirations for me. I would try to make them proud.

Eleven

By the middle of May, the cotton was coming up; very little had to be replanted. With good weather and hard work, Daddy and Grandmother had managed to plant more than last year. Mother was getting her strength back after child-birth. JoBethe was a good baby, thriving on Mother's milk and the stroking and patting of three noisy sisters.

From our little corner of the world, our family felt quite secure about the future. Things had been calm in Washington. The country was waiting for the "New Deal" to begin. The New Deal was the sum of the new president's policies and programs to be passed by Congress. The term was new; its meaning, as yet, vague. It had been explained as a new deal of old cards—no longer stacked against the common man. Certainly the farmer had become the forgotten man, the one in need of much help and understanding to bolster his sagging spirit and empty pocket book.

Early in April a farm relief bill was passed by the Senate to aid the struggling farmers. They were anxiously waiting to see what help was forthcoming provided the House passed the bill. With strong faith and hope for the future, the farmers planted every available acre with seeds, purchased from the local storeowner. They especially needed more markets for their products and improvement over the current low prices. On May 12, the Agricultural Adjustment Act was adopted un-der the direction of the new secretary of agriculture, Henry A. Wallace (editor of a farm journal and the world's greatest authority on hybrid corn). A bold program was adopted. It was a plan, administered through the county agents of each state, to reduce the planting of commodities such as corn, cotton and tobacco that had already been planted. There would be a small monetary compensation. The breeding of pigs and meat cattle was to be curtailed. A directive was given to slaughter six million piglets within the year.

Destroying food and crops and paying farmers not to produce certainly went against the grain, but other efforts the past thirty years had failed to help the farmers. Soon letters with the AAA government symbol of the county agent were being put into mail boxes almost every day. Concern and lack of understanding were expressed often at the general store. Farmers seemed to be waiting to see how fellow-farmers were going to handle the disturbing situation. They had waited for a new leader to show them the way out of depression and farm crisis. They had no choice but to accept the new president's mandates. They were relieved to hear that slaughter of meat would be frozen and over one million pounds of pork would be distributed to families on relief.

The farmers tried hard to understand the continuing communiqués from the county agents, with such words and phrases as "parity," "acreage allotment" and "price supports," They soon learned that this new government measure was an attempt to raise farm prices. The government would buy crops from farmers at a support price. But farmers would have to meet certain conditions, such as planting only the acreage of each year's crop allotment. Parity seemed to be the heart of the matter. This was from the agriculture Adjustment Act which was intended to measure agriculture equality. Parity was the level of farm prices that would give farmers the same buying power that they enjoyed during the period from 1910-1914. This time was chosen because it was the period when farmers had been the most prosperous. So if a farmer could buy a pair of overalls in 1910 for the same price that he sold two bushels of corn, he should be able to do so today. Farmers would have to subscribe to the steps outlined to achieve the desired end.

The new school year began the middle of July. The

school year was broken into two parts, the first part being July and August. Farm families needed their children to help pick cotton during September and October. I would be starting to school, having turned six years old in the fall. I was so excited, but my younger sisters could not understand why. Grandmother was also excited about her star pupil going to school, knowing I could already read the primer. With a twinkle in her eye, she imagined the surprise of the teacher and the other pupils as I read every word in the first book of the first grade.

On a recent trip to the store, Grandmother had chosen a piece of cotton cloth with a pretty print for my first day of school. She had prevailed on her older daughter, a good seamstress, to make a dress. A small lard bucket was washed, dried and set aside for my lunch bucket. MaBett boiled some eggs and made some fried chocolate pies for my lunch. Sometimes, biscuits left from breakfast and a piece of fried fatback were my mainstay. Other times, early tender boiled field corn made up my lunch. One time for a special surprise, I found a fried chicken leg tucked in behind some cold biscuits.

First through fourth grades were on one side of the two-room schoolhouse and the higher grades on the other. The school day went fast. I not only enjoyed my reading group and work, but I listened intently to the other grades reciting and doing their spelling and arithmetic lessons. I heard so many new stories: "Goldilocks and the Three Bears," "Peter Cottontail," "The Three Billy Goats Gruff," and on and on.

The schoolhouse was over a mile away. I walked through the hollow and up a hill to my neighbors' house; from there I walked to school with the two older Jones girls, Irene and Portia. Portia, the older girl, usually walked ahead a few paces. Irene, two grades ahead of me, became my companion and school mate. The road from the Jones' house descended downhill and was surrounded on one side by large craggy rocks, half buried in the side of the hill, overshadowed by trees.

Portia, being older and wiser, convinced me that the rocks were a den for panthers. Each time we passed the rocks, she pretended great fear, as she looked for the animals in their hiding place. I could almost see the red eyes of the wild beasts staring out from the cave. I had no reason not to believe my older friend. I hid my fear, not wanting to appear like a child, even to Mother and Grandmother. Perhaps I wasn't quite sure that they were there, but I wasn't quite sure that they were not there either. I trembled as I passed the hillside, but being with Portia made me brave. I grew fearful that the same wild animals, hungry for human blood, might be in the hollow, which I had to cross alone. My fears grew more than I could bear, and I started putting off going to school alone. Mother, knowing that I loved school, was puzzled. She started having Hallie walk with me to the neighbors' house in the mornings and meeting me on my return from school. My uncertainty regarding the panthers kept me from confiding in the adults about my fear. I might appear foolish.

This little country girl was fascinated with the antics of the three Billy goats. The story lingered in my mind. I didn't exactly know what "gruff" meant, but I thought that it suited the goats, as did "rough" and "tough," though spelled differently. There was the youngest little goat with its tiny voice and little hooves, squalling and bleating as he clip-clopped across the bridge. (I realized that the bleat was the cry of a goat.) Then the middle Billy goat, chomping on a clump of grass, in his middle sort of voice, also dared to cross over the bridge, making a clip-clop with his medium-size hooves. I could see and hear that old troll with his big quivering nose, eyes shining like burning coals and a bloated belly, bellowing from under the bridge. Finally. the biggest Billy goat with his big hooves and fine manners started across the bridge to find some fresh grass for breakfast.

By this time the old troll's mouth was slobbering, thinking that now he had his breakfast and lunch. But the brave big-big Billy goat growled, lowered his head, pawed the ground, and charged the trembling troll. He butted the wicked creature with his strong head and sharp horn—up in the air, over the bridge, and down into the water. The troll sank like a big rock and was never seen again.

I mulled the story over and over in my quiet moments, entertaining myself with the spunky animals. Then at an opportune time, I asked Grandmother why they did not have some goats as well as the cow, mules, and pigs. Grandmother explained that only the poorest of people kept goats for milk. They did not need much food since they ate mostly grass, berry and honeysuckle vines, and sometimes tin cans (she supposed that it was only the paper labels they ate from the discarded tins). It was true that they were a small, scrawny type of cow that gave a white, sweet nourishing milk that only some people could drink. They chewed the cud and had split hooves like cows. Grandmother had known of people who had goats that would go through or over fences and even climb on top of barns. Besides, male goats had a nasty beard and stank. She explained that the nanny goat was the "momma goat" that gave milk and had babies. The little goats were called kids until they were a year old.

Nevertheless, I remained fascinated with the mischievous animals and thought that one day I would have my own goats.

By the first of August, I was knee-deep in school, enjoying every class every day of every week. Grandmother missed my presence around the house, especially when she went to pick peas as they became ready — black-eyed, crowder, or speckled. The green beans had come and gone, and many jars had been canned for the coming winter. Now peas were the heart of most meals. In the past, I would tag along with Grandmother, sometimes skipping on the path; I would stand at the edge of the field watching her gather whichever food crop was ready. The family had become aware that weeds poisoned my legs, so she avoided weeds and other plants as much as possible.

Now that I was in school, the paths and patches seemed lonely to MaBett, but she had Trixie, the little black and brown feist dog, following closely on her heels. The two, tiny woman and tiny dog, made many tracks in the dusty trails around the farm, checking on animals, chickens, and food crops in their different stages of growth.

After picking many pecks of peas and toting them to the house, Mama grabbed two dishpans—one to hold bundles of pods on her lap and the other to catch the green seeds that her stubby fingers dug from the tight slender hulls. Around Mother's knees and the pans, my sisters pulled and poked the green peelings. Nearby, the baby cooed and kicked from a pallet on the floor.

Mama enjoyed these domestic time-outs as she stripped the legume pearls from the dimpled pods. When she looked closely, she could see that there were large fly-like specks on many of the seeds. Somehow insects had managed to sting the tender hulls and impregnate many of the embryos with eggs that would in time turn into larva. After the peas were shelled, they were rolled handful by handful over the open palm to cull out the big bug-bitten green seeds. Bug-infested peas were obvious from signs such as stunted growth and ill-shapen bulging sides. Often there would be a white squirming worm right in the midst of the peas. Fortunately its presence would be spotted before it was put in the pot. Seasoning consisted of small strips of fatback. One dishpan was soon emptied and the other one filled. There was a growing pile of the stripped hulls on the floor; these would become forage for the milk cow's supper.

From day to day and from patch to field, MaBett garnered the summer's yield of peas, okra, and hickory cane corn. With tow sack in hand, she waded through the corn middles of straggly weeds and cockleburs. She checked out the ears with black silks that indicated the corn was ready for plucking and shucking. Dent corn, commonly called field corn was food for the family at its milky stage and food for the animals after it had hardened and dried. Then a dent appeared on the top of each kernel. Corn was one of the main foods for the family. Cornbread was eaten for both dinner and supper.

We children were constantly chided to eat bread with our other foods or suffer a stomach ache. During growing season, corn was eaten for breakfast with hot biscuits as well as for the other meals. Although corn was sometimes boiled on the cob, the family's favorite way to eat corn was the fried-in-the skillet method: about ten ears of freshly picked corn were shucked and cut off the cob. The corn was then fried in about two tablespoons of lard in the large iron skilled. The milky kernels were carefully turned and scraped until lightly browned. Salt, black pepper and about one-half cup of light cream or top milk was added and the mixture headed thoroughly. Strips of selected fatback, fried and crunchy and golden brown, completed the meal.

Sometimes after the school day, as the sun swung low in the west, I would go with MaBett to the garden to get food for the next day's table. All gardens were enclosed with paling fences to protect the growing vegetables from marauding livestock. It was quite common for someone's cow or cows to escape from the barn lot or go through a pasture fence during the night. I stood in the open garden gate, guarding my tender legs from the weedy culprits.

The main vegetable during these late summer days was okra. The pods needed to be picked almost every day while they were immature and about four to six inches long. If left to grow, the pods could reach ten to twelve inches, become hard and inedible.

MaBett always carried a small pocketknife in her apron pocket for picking okra. The prickly, sticky pods grew on very tough stems from stalks to grow about four feet or higher. She cut off the pods, handling them as little as possible. The pods were covered with infinitesimal bristles that inflected a stinging sensation that could linger for hours. (When she got back to the kitchen MaBett would use a baking powder wash to relieve the smarting.) Since I could only look at the sticky operation, I began to observe carefully the dark green rank okra plants. The leaves resembled my hand with the fingers spread out; the blossoms were large and pretty. Of course, from the big blooms came the elongated pods that enclosed the baby seeds.

I thought of the cotton plant that had similar leaves, blossoms, and also a pod. The cotton pod was called a boll, but both had sections inside with the same arrangement of seeds. My mind ran to a third similar plant, the hollyhock growing at the corner of the house. It had the same-shaped leaves and big showy blooms white to pink. The three similar plants found on the farm fascinated me. Later on in life, I would discover they were all of the mallow family. With the okra gathered for the next day's dinner, along with a kettle of speckled peas and a pone of cornbread, the family could enjoy the victuals provided by nature.

The pods of okra were cut into coin-size disks and coated with a cornmeal and flour mixture, seasoned with salt and black pepper. The sliced spiked pods were fried in hot grease in an iron skillet, covered part of the time for light steaming. The menfolk would eat only the sautéed version. Sometimes the womenfolk, especially Effie, would cook the whole tender pods in a small amount of boiling water for about fifteen minutes and season them with butter, salt and a smidgen of vinegar. She enjoyed the sticky, substance inside the ribbed, tapered pods. Another favorite way of preparing okra was to drop the whole pod on top of a pot of green beans for about ten minutes while the beans were still cooking.

The last food crop to come in late August and September was the Kentucky Wonder pole beans that were planted in the corn so that the stalks became the support for the climbing vines. The plump, thick-hulled pods were filled with white-pinkish, almost developed beans. Young tender snaps were mixed with shellie beans and cooked slowly with a piece of fatback. This provided substantial, satisfying meal for the entire family. Of all the foods on the farm, I liked the summer ones best. I was especially fond of peas, okra, corn, and cornbread, always served with a glass of cold, sweet milk. During the day, milk was kept in the milk box in the cool flowing water of the spring. Not all peas were gathered while green; some were left in the fields to dry before being picked, then stored in tow sacks in the barn. On the first frosty days, when confined inside by the fireplace, we shelled and bagged the peas for winter meals.

Pease porridge hot,
Pease porridge cold,
Pease porridge in the pot,
Nine days old.
Some like it hot,
Some like it cold,
Some like it in the pot,
Nine days old.

Twelve

Being the mother of four small children and a young farmer's wife, Effie was mentally and physically occupied with the chores at hand. But she did think often of her father, mother, and younger sister. Only in family emergencies did she hear from them. Little effort had been expended to make visits back home, as she knew her family, especially her father, had never accepted Harley, considering him a "ne'er do well" from across the county line.

Effie had learned from her sister that her father had succumbed to the world of whiskey; to what degree she did not know. Sadly, she remembered as a young girl how faithful he had been to the Methodist Church, serving as a steward and proudly carrying the *Methodist Book of Discipline*. Also, he had been active in local and state politics. Fondly, she carried a memory of a visitor who ate at their table, later becoming Governor of Tennessee. She wondered what had happened to her "Pappy," a well-known and well-liked country gentleman.

This she did know: he had turned from tilling a large farm to running a small country store on a mostly inaccessible road. The location puzzled her because there was a well-established store and post office on the main highway, a short distance away.

This was the time of the Great Depression and of Prohibition. That was really of no concern for Effie's family because they were upright law-abiding citizens and maintained a self-sustaining lifestyle. She did not know, nor did she need to know that Prohibition forbade the manufacture, sale, or transportation of alcoholic beverages. This law caused widespread changes in American behavior down to the ordinary man. There was extreme violence. Making moonshine became a lucrative business. Even though it was illegal, few bootleggers were considered criminals by their neighbors. Many agents failed to enforce the law, choosing to look the other way; some accepted bribes rather than arresting lawbreakers.

Although Effie was not aware of the many facets of illegal whiskey making, she grieved that her father was now tainted with such an unholy reputation. She resented the fact that he, once a member of the upper crust, had belittled her husband, who was upright and honest in every way. Her concern for her father was soon brought to an abrupt end. Her sister's husband sent word that her father had died suddenly. The mystery and regret of his last years would remain with her the rest of her life.

A new law had been passed in June to help bring the nation out of depression. The newspapers called this law the most important bill ever passed by Congress. The new law, giving the government control over industry was called the National Recovery Act. Objectives were to regulate working conditions, fix minimum wages, and provide federal funds for a public works program. Some of the public works would be constructing state roads and building Navy ships. The President expressed hope that the thousands who were jobless would "be back on the payroll by snowfall."

The blue eagle, with wings and legs outspread, became the emblem of the National Recovery Act. It was seen on everything from envelopes to business establishments. The newly-organized movement guaranteed jobs with decent pay. There was to be a shortened workweek, only eight hours a day. Unfair competition and overproduction of crops and commodities were to be curtailed. A new dance craze swept New York; it was called the Nira, in honor of the NRA. But the growing plight of the needy permeated the country. By the later part of September, President Roosevelt had organized the distribution of seventy-five million dollars to clothe and feed the jobless. At that time, an estimated three and one-half million people were on the nation's relief rolls.

The coming winter meant that more assistance would be needed. President Roosevelt brought forth a new program at the estimated cost of seven hundred million dollars, to meet the continuing crises. Figures with bony faces stood in line for free bread and soup. Much of the food would come from surpluses held in storage by the U.S. Department of Agriculture.

By the end of September, half of the cotton had been picked and taken to the gin to sell in order to pay the year's debts at the store. There was now some loose change in the pockets of the farmers.

Thirteen

The autumn days were mild, and the nights bathed by a glow from a mellow golden moon. The sweltering heat of the summer was a vague memory, and the dread of the coming winter's cold, with its accompanying influenza and pneumonia, was in the future. On one of the trips to the gin and the store, my daddy caught sight of the top of a tent pitched in the field behind Dr. Thomas's place. Guarded glances and indirect questions were exchanged between the ginning-farmers. They didn't want to appear too curious. Their remarks might reveal their ignorance. But the word got around about the moving picture show to be shown afternoons and evenings inside the tent.

Perhaps the good doctor saw an opportunity to bring a little levity into the lives of these hard-working people during this discouraging era. The weather was still mild, and the tickets to the show were less than a dime. This would be a new experience, great entertainment for everyone from far off Hollywood, California. School closed in September and October so the children could help pick cotton.

MaBett had never been to a moving picture show. She and I would certainly go one afternoon. She still had some of her cotton patch money in her coin purse. My fare was free.

We made our way down the path, across the hollow, up one hill and down another, across the creek, around a curve and up another hill, on to the highway and to the tent. There was semi-darkness in the canvas top supported by poles, which was the theatre. Portable chairs were lined up on the dirt floor. We made our way down the dirt aisle, almost to the edge of the makeshift stage, and chose our seats.

The sign outside had announced "Max Sennett's Keystone Cops." We had never seen such antics. We were enthralled by the outlandish pratfalls and slapstick comedy. The crazy cops were up and down and all around trying to enforce the law. All these antics were set to a ring-a-ling, thumping, snapping, tapping music. The picture show ended with a cavorting, crazy chase of the cops, their stunt cars, and some trains. We were so excited; we made plans to come back in two days to see another show, featuring a tramp called "Charlie Chaplin."

Sure enough, there on the screen was that funny little man with a moustache and sailor hat. The name of the moving picture was *Tillie's Punctured Romance*. It went all the way back to 1913. To me, a child of almost six years, that seemed so long ago. Words were flashed on the screen to explain the story. Many of the words were now incomprehensible to me. But the action and the pictures gave meaning to expressions such as "dapper stranger" and "shady characters." Some phrases, such as "two timing" and "the plot thickens" were also new to MaBett. Tillie (the farmer's daughter), after being tricked by Charlie Chaplin (the city slicker), inherits three million dollars from her uncle. I had never heard of such shenanigans as slapping, bopping, and cuffing each other around. Even kicking and poling in the rump were shown. They couldn't even dance without slipping and sliding all over the floor.

Finally Tillie went berserk and shot up the place when she found her new husband fooling around with Mabel, the cutesy former girlfriend. Tillie wound up being tossed off the pier and rescued by the Keystone Cops in their water-patrol skiff.

MaBett and I were exhausted from watching the fast-paced antics. As we left the tent, Grandmother mumbled something about "all that horseplay." I could not see what horses had to do with it, but I didn't ask questions. I was delighted when Grandmother said that we would come back one more time before the show closed the next week.

The weather continued to be mild and accommodating for the cotton gathers. The family was working on another bale. MaBett hoped that it would be picked and ready for the gin by Friday, the last day of the picture show. She had said that when the cotton patch north of the house was finished, we could go back to the store to see the last show in the tent. So we hurried and filled one sack after the other. I pulled my shortened sack, snatching locks of the dried cotton bolls on the other side of the rows covered by Grandmother. MaBett realized that her strength was diminishing by the day. The muscles in her slender back strained with each tug of the cotton sack, and lifting up of the cotton to the scales was especially painful. Her strong shoulders had begun to slump. Her once limber fingers were beginning to stiffen. Grasping each boll took special effort. She had not told anyone, but the field work of this year's crops had taxed her strength, and she had found herself tired most of the time. But she had to help her youngest son and his growing family. There was so much to be done gathering the crops and picking and preserving food for the coming winter. Each day she started by getting up and getting breakfast for the family, milking the two cows, and preparing food for their dinner—the main meal. She enjoyed cooking, but she enjoyed the outside work more.

By mid-morning, MaBett and I would go to the field to work. Mama would do the rest of the housework and join us in the fields in the afternoon. There were three little ones, one only about six months old, to take to the cotton patch and care for in the edge of the field, while picking the cotton, filling up sacks, and dragging them from one end of the row to the other. Sometime Daddy would show up to help weigh the cotton and empty the sacks, but he did little picking. His masculine instincts usually urged him to tackle more demanding work.

By Friday, right after dinner, the thirteen hundred and sixty pounds of cotton was in the wagon, with the extended sides holding the voluminous load. Daddy climbed up on the buckboard, twitched the reins on the back of the team of mules, and was off to the gin.

MaBett and I hurriedly washed off some of the surface dust, changed clothes, and Grandmother changed shoes. I put my Sunday shoes and socks on my calloused bare feet. Down the path the two of us skipped, but MaBett only in her fantasy. We were rushing to see *The Gold Rush.* When we reached the flaps of the tent, we were surprised to see so many other people converging on this canvas nickelodeon in the middle of an open field.

We waved at some of the familiar farm-folks. Some had sheepish grins on their shy faces. They self consciously sauntered down the dirt aisle to their usual places. Then they turned and looked behind themselves. In the semi-darkness, they saw a host of rustic, curious, faces staring at the darkened screen. They did not fully comprehend, nor did their unsophisticated fellow spectators, the role of Charlie Chaplin. Up until this past week, they had not heard of this funny little man, with his too-small derby hat, oversized shoes, second hand jacket, bamboo cane, and odd walk.

Soon a portable generator lighted the screen. There, before the hushed voices and focused eyes, came Charlie Chaplin playing a prospector with a backpack and gold panning-pan slung on his back. The wobbling funny fellow was at Chilkoot Pass in Alaska, slipping on a snowy slope. There he encountered a black bear. (How could they tame this wild animal to play these scenes?) A storm closed in on him and his only companion, a lonely, very hungry man. In desperation, the gold seeker boiled his shoes to stave off starvation. The other man, in hallucination, saw Chaplin as a life-size chicken. (How did they get those feathers to stick on him?) The beak and the clawed chicken toes looked so real.

I did not fully comprehend the characters or the plot. But the experience of seeing these three moving picture shows became building block to a greater understanding of places, costumes, and humor.

The year came to a jubilant end for those who enjoyed strong spirits. A repeal of the 18th Amendment, a law forbidding the manufacture and sale of beer, gin, rum, and whiskey, had gone into effect in January of 1920. The Women's

Christian Temperance Union and the Anti-saloon League had spear-headed the battle.

For nearly fourteen years prohibition prevailed. But F.D.R. fulfilled his pledge to repeal the 18th Amendment. With the cooperation of Congress the resolution passed, and once again, strong drinks were legal. President Roosevelt called on the nation to practice moderation. Also, he implored states not to allow the return of saloons, but public bars sprang up everywhere. The nation's long dry spell had ended.

Fourteen

Now in late July, with the intense heat of summer, the hay had to be cut, dried, and brought to the barn, pitched up to the loft or stacked in mounds behind the barn. Daddy, though small in statue, must keep pushing himself almost beyond his strength. Now solely responsible for an aging mother and a growing family, he must meet the demands of a father and the work of a farmer.

School had begun for the summer term. Since this was an agriculture-based economy, children were needed to help in growing cotton. Older children and their mothers did most of the tending of the young cotton plants. Then in the fall, with graduated sizes of cotton sacks, they also picked the cotton. So during the middle of summer, the country schools were on full schedule. Not only were the children doing "reading, writing and arithmetic," but for one week, attending religious services. August was the usual revival time for most country churches because this was the only free time for the farmers. There was a vintage Methodist Church adjacent to the Hickory Flat School yard. They held two services each day for one week. Morning service started at eleven o'clock. The teachers, the two of them, with the children marched over to the church for the services.

This was my first time in church. I was fascinated with the singing and the preacher-man up front, pounding on a high table with such urgent words. We children were impressed and entertained by these out-of-class experiences. The following days, during recess time in our play area under

Carmelene - early Memphis days.

Harley, Effie, and eight of their children. Michael was away in college.

MaBett's butter mold.

Michael, who missed the family photo.

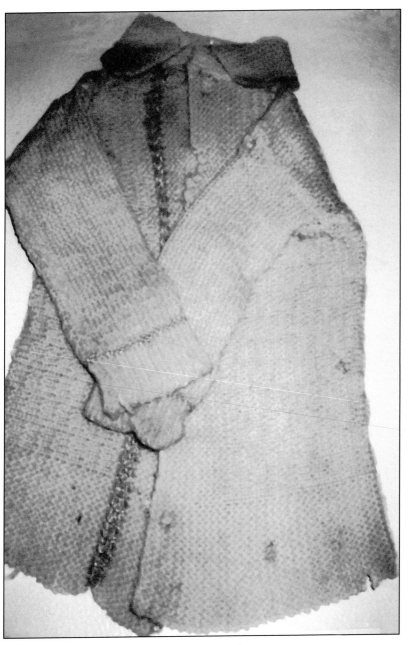

Carmelene's first dress.

Pa Kirk and MaBett.

**MaBett with Carmelene -
early spring 1928.**

Effie with Carmelene.

MaBett's button hook and shoe horn and collapsible drinking cup.

Harley, with his son and grandson, surrounded by piglets.

MaBett's bonnet.

MaBett's coin purse.

Scale on which Baby Carmelene was weighed.

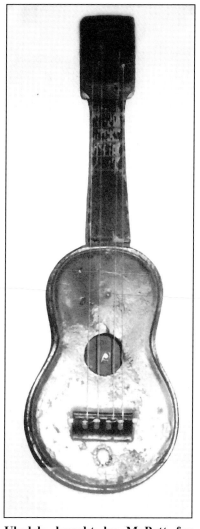

Ukulele bought by MaBett for Carmelene.

Effie in her garden.

Harley, Effie, and their first four little ones.

some nearby shade trees we play-acted being in church. We formed a block group, and different ones of us played the part of the preacher.

In early September, school was out for a few weeks. With time-out from picking cotton, my grandmother and I continued our trips to the store. (With no electricity and no refrigeration, eggs and butter could not be kept fresh for many days.) On one of the jaunts to the nearby market, Ma overheard the key-buddies and the store man express interest in the day's newspaper headline. Since almost every home had a jar of Vaseline, the petroleum jelly, this really got their attention. The inventor of Vaseline had died at the age of ninety-six. On his deathbed, he had attributed his long life to taking one teaspoon of this clear jelly every day of his life.

No doubt there would be greater demand of this salve. They all knew it had many uses. Besides healing cuts and burns, it could be used to grease hinges and doorknobs, and even keep mildew from leather. It was also sometimes used on the hair and for shaving cream.

All agreed this was a great remedy for a lot of things. Besides it was easy to swallow. Ma quietly added a jar to her list of sugar, salt, and soda. But when Mr. John compared the total cost with her dozen eggs and pound of butter, he found she was short the amount needed for the added item. The merchantman nodded that he would put in on her account until her cotton was brought to the gin and sold.

Fall was fading into winter. The crops had been fair — just enough to take care of what was owed for cottonseed, nuts and bolts, and several gallons of kerosene. Grandmother's strength was fading also. She realized she was passing from the fall of life into the winter years. The once feisty, energetic, petite woman was now a frosty, frail granny-woman. She was becoming more contemplative of what the future might hold.

Christmas was not many days away. As usual, the Sears Roebuck catalog was the in-home shopping center. There had been an increase in prices, but a decrease in her pocket cotton money. She remembered the glee of many former Christmases. The thought of those joyful times turned to gloom. So little money for the now four children in the home. What could she get them with so little? She had been amazed at how her little girl had learned to wind the (Victrola) gramophone in the front room. A record of Jimmy Rodgers, the Singing Cowboy, seemed to be her favorite. Still undecided, Grandmother turned the pages of the catalog. There before her eyes was a page of guitars; on the next page, ukuleles. Of course, these were for adults. Could there be others for children? A few pages later were some, perhaps toys. They were much smaller and less expensive.

That was it! She would find the money somehow. Now for the other little ones; a pair of socks each would be her limit. She got the order ready for the mailman the next day. A week later a small package came from Sears Roebuck. There was the guitar, or was it a ukulele? It was over a foot in length, with a metal body and a wooden neck—complete with four steel strings, frets and tuning keys. There were also the socks for the other little ones.

The long nights of winter shortened into the milder days of March. Even as spring was approaching, Grandmother's body was not responding to the warmer air and sunshine. One day in early April, she awoke puzzled and alarmed. The entire right side of her body was numb. She managed to get out of bed and call for help. Her speech was slurred and she could hardly see out of her left eye. Harley went for the family doctor who lived near the store. He diagnosed a stroke.

During the day, other members of the family were notified of Grandmother's condition. By the next day, most of the adult children surrounded her bed. Grandmother, in her failing awareness, motioned for me, her favorite grandchild, to be brought to her bedside. Bert, one of the older sons—the domineering one—refused to allow me to be brought into the room.

Mother and we children huddled in the kitchen. The gravity of the situation kept us quiet. In a few hours Grandmother slipped away. We children were puzzled by the stony silence of our aunts and uncles. We never saw our grandmother again.

It had been a somber Sunday, the twenty-second day of April, 1934. Grandmother had been gone one week. It was so quiet and lonely. Not one of the many members of the surviving family had come by for a visit. A sense of loss and helplessness gripped the soul of my father. We children sensed our father's sadness. He struggled to get out of bed and hobble to the breakfast table. Mother was frozen with concern. She could and would take care of the livestock and chickens today. No other farm work would be undertaken since this was the Sabbath.

Daddy felt guilty returning to bed but had no strength to do otherwise. We children were uncharacteristically quiet, sensing an unusual situation. I crept into Grandmother's room and up to her bed. The plump pillow and counterpane were still there, but Grandmother's slight body was not. Alone, I realized that Grandmother was really gone. My body trembled as tears sprang from a broken heart. Now I understood more fully my father's sadness. I wanted to share with him my pain but could not find the words. I wished that he would talk to me, but all I heard was a groan and a sigh.

Daddy pulled the quilt over his head, appearing to be asleep—but sleep would not come. Although emotionally and physically exhausted from the recent stresses, his mother's sudden illness and death, the funeral, the family decision, his mind kept replaying events from the past: He knew he had been privileged to be the youngest of nine children. His mother loved him, taking delight in her handsome baby boy. His older sisters coddled and adored him. But he shuddered as he remembered the taller, older brother, who constantly intimidated him. He felt again the fear and need to be ever on his guard. Moreover, he thought of his father, who had seemed old to him even when he was a little boy—perhaps rightfully so, since his father was fifty-one years old when he was born.

Grandfather had always been uncommunicative, sullen, and glum. But he had been a hard worker, who took the care and upkeep of his family seriously. As he aged, he became more gruff and grouchy; but due to his age and failing strength, this seemed acceptable.

Grandmother had tried to make up for her husband's indifference to the boy. Daddy realized he had been pampered. Perhaps his older siblings resented the special attention he received from his doting mother.

Being the pet of the family, Daddy had determined at age twenty, to show them that he could become a person in his own right. He was not an avid lover of the soil and so was open to other possibilities. An older cousin invited him to go with him to St. Louis to seek work. The cousin's older sister lived there, so they had a place for lodging. After a few days of job-hunting, he decided the big city was not for him; he caught the next train back to the family farm, leaving the cousin there. After some time, the cousin also took the train back home.

After winning the heart and hand of a good country girl, Daddy settled down on the farm, in the bosom of his father and mother. In their later years, they needed him. Now with four young children, he assumed full responsibility for his growing family and the homeplace. How he missed their help.

As the hours of the day dragged by, Daddy's strength waned. He had no desire for food. The dread of tomorrow almost suffocated him. It was now the last week of April. The Irish potatoes and English peas had been planted. The first week of May was coming up and the ground had not been turned and readied for the planting of cotton. Finally, after Mama's insistence, he downed a glass of sweet milk and cornbread. Slowly, sleep came to his weakened body and troubled mind.

On Monday morning, the sunrise awakened Daddy, but his body did not respond to the demands of the day. As he got to his feet to put on his clothes, his head swam and his eyes would not focus—even with the aid of his glasses. His heart was fluttering, and he was gasping for breath. His knees buckled as he fell back on the bed. Fear overwhelmed him. What was happening?? In desperation he sank into the featherbed and pulled the covers over him.

If Sunday had been a somber day, Monday was a frantic one. Mama had managed to get up and build a fire in the kitchen stove. Hurriedly she had mixed up and patted out biscuits for the oven. Then she sliced strips of fatback and fried them in the iron skillet. Knowing her husband had eaten little the day before, she scrambled a hefty portion of eggs. The baby, with a wet diaper, was crying to be nursed. The other two little ones were up, whimpering and whining. They sensed the concern of their mother. I was banging my lunch pail, wanting it filled for school. Also my hair needed to be combed. By this time Daddy should have been ready to eat; he always enjoyed a hearty breakfast. But this morning, there was no sign of him. Mama scurried to his bed and pulled the covers back, finding him face down and breathing heavily. She shook his shoulders and called out his name. He slowly turned over and clasped his chest. She could see and feel the rapid heartbeat. Panic stricken, she constrained herself because of the children. She surmised that his weakness was due to lack of food the day before. Helping him to his feet and into the kitchen she pushed him up to the table. With her help and a smattering of Karo syrup on his biscuit, he was able to chew slowly and swallow a portion of his breakfast. By now, I was out the door and on my way across the hollow to join the Jones girls on their way to school.

The dizziness and weakness continued as Daddy struggled to get to the barn to tend the stock. He knew he was not up to the fieldwork today. Back in the house, he slumped into a chair, wincing with pain. Later in the day, his older sister Maudie and her husband dropped by for a short visit. This was the first company he had had since the funeral of his mother. Their presence encouraged him, but the pallor and pain was obvious to all of them. They sensed the seriousness of his condition and urged him to see Dr. Thomas. But he felt it was a matter of time, and he would be feeling better. It was just the weariness of the last few days that had worn him out.

The following day he felt more helpless, realizing the fieldwork must be done. By then both Mama and Daddy agreed that he must have the doctor come and help him get back on his feet. The doctor came, not knowing what to expect. He knew Daddy had always been little, but lively. The doctor's perfunctory diagnosis gave no clinical evidence of serious hearth problems. But Daddy was convinced that he had heart trouble. The doctor suggested another cause could be the food he was eating. Just recently in a medical journal, there was a caution against consumption of white bread and other starchy foods. Perhaps whole wheat bread would be best.

Word had gotten around that Daddy was having health problems—specifically his heart. This meant he was unable to get his crops out. Sure enough, in a short time, a neighbor farmer and his three sons came with a team and equipment to plant the cotton. I came home from school to find the man and boys helping my father. The youngest son, perhaps two years older than I, was so cute and attentive to my presence. After they were gone, I fancied the boy was my boyfriend. The next day I was still thinking of the young fellow. I printed our initials, in bold letters with the plus love sign, on the back of the house.

By now, the realization that Daddy was unable to carry on the farm work made him more anxious and desperate. He was becoming more agitated, and the children were getting on his nerves. Finding the markings on the back kitchen wall ignited a mini-storm. With scolding and threats, Daddy demanded that I wash the wall, and he said that he was going to send me to reform school. Somehow I knew it was a jail for disobedient children. Momentarily I was terrified, but soon I understood that my father was sick and not himself. It was only a threat.

Fifteen

Things were not getting any better. The cottonseed was in the ground, but the corn had to be planted and the hayseed sown for the livestock's winter food supply. Daddy's strength was diminishing, and he became picky about his food, especially white bread and dry beans. No longer would he drink coffee but found Postum good and better for him.

Stark reality was staring him in the face. The crops had to be planted and tended. They were the livelihood of any farm family. The neighbors had been helpful, but they had their own crops to till. Daddy must have full-time help. As he weighed the situation, he thought of the little house his family had lived in for a while. If only he could find a reputable person to move in and do the hard work. He did not fancy the idea of a sharecropper, but there was no other way.

Through his older sister Maudie, two brothers heard about the idea and were interested in working out a deal. They were both single and lived with their father on a small farm. The older brother would move into the little house, and the two would work the land under sharecropper terms. Besides providing the house, Daddy must provide the work animals, farm equipment, feed, seed and supplies; they would share part of the net worth of the crops.

Although the two brothers had lived nearby, they had not been close friends with my father. Soon suspicion superseded trust. After three or four days of wrangling over working conditions, a heated argument almost led to a physical altercation. The two brothers dared Daddy to remove his

133

glasses. Needless to say, the plowboys left the premises with only their footprints in the dust of the barnyard.

As Daddy shared the incident with Mama, we children overheard the pitiful account of our father's plight and sensed the heavy heart of our mother. In our innocence and bewilderment, we began to turn on each other. Hallie Sue and I got into a spat and exchanged pinches and punches, which led to our crying to our mother. This was more than our nervous father could take, and in a fit of fury, he tied my left hand to the right hand of my sister and sent us to the spring for a bucket of water. Of course we were blaming each other for our predicament and pulled away from each other. We brought the pail of water back. I tattled that my sister had resisted all the way. Father justified the awkward punishment saying he was teaching us the benefit of co-operating with each other.

The setback of the attempted sharecropper arrangement intensified Daddy's condition. Heavy pressing pain in his chest almost took his breath away. His shoulders throbbed, and a sense of despair spread over his whole body. He became more listless and withdrawn from the family, spending most of the daylight hours in the floor on a pallet.

Mama was now carrying all the chores of the house and barn. With a baby at her breast, two toddlers at her feet, and me in school, she was pulled in all directions—trying to be a good mother, nurse, cook, and farmer's wife. Moreover, she was trying to be a peacemaker to a troubled family. With my red-headed rambunctious ways, it was not always easy.

After one family squabble, Mama complained to Daddy that she could not take anymore. He rebounded by snatching me by the dress tail and marching me down to the barn. A surge of anger enabled him to totter down the worn path. He shoved me into the corncrib and locked the door. Since this was Saturday morning, he shuffled back inside the house and changed into clean overalls. He remembered he needed a new bottle of tonic, Peruna, a box of Black Draught, and his favorite drink, a bottle of Dr. Pepper. With crib key in pocket and ignition key in hand, he drove off to the store.

In the meantime Mama's sister had heard — and was concerned — about Daddy's heart trouble. Her husband dropped her off for a short visit. The two sisters were glad to see each other and to get updates on family happenings. Since I was not there with the other children, my aunt asked about my absence. Mama was hesitant but had to admit I was being locked up in the corncrib as punishment. My aunt furiously insisted that she see me. The two sisters hurried to the barn and there I sat, slumped on a crate of corncobs behind the crib door. With anger for such an uncalled-for act, my aunt huffed, "If that was my youngin, I'd take an ax and chop the door down."

More and more, I seemed to be bearing the brunt of all my parents' frustrations. Another time at the dinner table, the taste of kerosene was in a pot of black-eyed peas. Again I was blamed and punished for the unexplainable, distasteful ingredient. If only Grandmother was here, these things would not be happening to me.

Being busy over the cooking stove, bringing water from the spring, and milking two cows two times a day, Effie had little time to help with picking the cotton,. With three small children to take to and from the field, she was encumbered about with each day's duties.

By mid-May the spring sun was encouraging the crops and garden to full growth. Aunt Maudie was very concerned about her young brother's situation with health and field-work. She knew an older man in her church, Mr. Frank Landers, who was able-bodied and available for farm work. He was be reputable and responsible, as he had been a deacon in a Baptist Church for some time. She sent Mr. Landers and his wife down to her brother's place for talk and inquiry. They were interested and could live in the little house in the pasture. Mrs. Landers did state that she would not be able to work in the fields, doing the normal woman's work. It was urgent that The Landers move in and take over the field work immediately. Mrs. Callie Ann, the sharecropper's wife, was of no help, as she remained secluded behind the modest walls

135

of the tenant house.

After the Landers had moved in, the first order of business was that Mr. Landers hitch up the team of mules and take the wagon to the cotton patch. The wagon was positioned at the end of the rows, and a pair of scales was suspended from the back of the wagon bed. As the cotton was picked, it was weighed and the pounds tallied for a bale.

Daddy was relieved, but remained on the pallet on the floor for the summer. He was absorbed with his health and sought help in eating the right foods. From some source, he heard of a drink made of beaten raw eggs, milk, sugar and vanilla flavoring; this he consumed daily. With the others out in the fields working, he was not lonely, as he had a pallet-pal. The baby JoBethe, now a year old, shared his summer mat, crawling and scooting all around him. He taught her her first jabbering words and coaxed her first steps.

During the baby's long naps at his side Daddy pondered his role as father and mentor for his children. There was emptiness in his life that an occasional presence at church had not filled. He needed help for his soul's longing—help that only prayer could bring. There was a preacher of another denomination who lived near the store. He had always liked the man and had confidence in his calling. He sent for the preacher to come and pray with him. Right away, Brother Goodman came with his Bible, knelt beside him, and read a portion of the Scriptures. They talked about his health and spiritual needs. After a prayer, the preacher went on his way, and Daddy sighed a prayer of deep relief in his soul.

The summer slowly cooled into early fall. By the middle of September, the buds of cotton with their white creamy blossoms had matured into golf ball-size bolls. Now the bolls were cracking open, releasing four or five locks of white fluffy fibers. The hull of the dried bolls with prickly tips was not the bur.

The first phase of the harvesting was ripe for picking. For the first time, I—not six years old—was big enough to pull a cotton sack with wide straps over my shoulders. Brimming with energy and ready for the task, I became the sidekick for

Mr. Landers, the sole manager of the farm at this time. My father, the head of the farm, was still reclining on the pallet on the floor, engrossed with his heart trouble. Effie's whole concern was for his care and comfort. She spent much time in the kitchen cooking and preparing food for his special diet. He would not eat boiled vegetables, such as potatoes, but wanted them fried. Cornbread was acceptable, but now he would not eat biscuits and white bread. He loved and devoured sweet things such as pies and cakes. The cows could hardly give enough milk, as he drank sweet milk by the quarts.

Mr. Landers was a tall, strapping man, always hustling in his work. Consequently, he required lots of water to quench his thirst. Carmelene became the water girl—going back and forth to bring his fruit jars of the cool, refreshing liquid. He was always kind and appreciative, speaking in gentle tones and giving her a pat on the back. She thrived on this attention, since she had never known affection from her grandfather, and now her father had become so harsh and punitive toward her.

Mr. Landers was becoming chummy and taking more time to rest on his stuffed cotton sack. After drinking the water, he would pull the young girl down beside him. Some rows of the cotton had stalks four to six feet high. This became a perfect cover from the eyes of others. Later on, he coaxed her into the corncrib, whispering to her that they had a secret no one should know. And the secret she kept in her heart and mind for many years.

During this time, she overheard her mother in exasperation tell her father that while walking through the hall of the barn after milking the cows, that Mr. Landers pushed her up against the wall and rubbed his body against hers. This puzzled the child, and she pondered the honor and uprightness of this man. As soon as the crops were gathered in, the sharecropper received his share of the crop's worth and he and his wife vacated the little house, but left questionable memories in the mind of the young girl.

Daddy's mother was gone; so was the year. More depressing, his health was also gone. He was relieved that the sharecropper was gone. But Daddy was blessed, for he had a good wife and mother for his children. He must find strength and courage to carry on. There was still one unfulfilled commitment—that of putting monuments at the graves of his deceased father and mother. He had sent for two catalogs that sold grave markers. After careful consideration, he chose and ordered two rocks that he could scarcely afford. After a short time, they were delivered—small, but with the correct names and dates for their births and deaths.

Daddy was aware that his living rights to the farm were coming to an end. One of his older brothers, the brash and domineering one, wanted to buy the farm. Grandmother had made known that she wanted Daddy to have the household items and farm machinery for taking care of Grandfather and her in their declining years. So on an agreed-upon day, the brothers and sisters came back to the homeplace to finalize the disposal of the farm and assets. Rightly so, each one wanted something of their mother's. Some of the choice items were her quilts, feather beds, and pillows, filled with the feathers and down plucked from her own geese.

It just happened that days before, Mama, knowing this day was coming, had tried to arrange things as Grandmother had left them. While making her bed and plumping up the pillows, she felt a round object inside one of them. She had noticed that the aging woman had been overly protective of this particular pillow. Mama took the scissors and snipped the seam of one end of the pillow. Carefully, her fingers felt until she found a round clump of feathers. To her amazement, she pulled out a perfectly-formed crown of feathers. She felt she owed it to her mother-in-law's memory to keep and cherish this memento of her life. So she put the cluster of feathers in her own trunk—safe from the children and the curious eyes of others.

Sure enough, the pillows were the most sought after items, leading to some cross words. There was little family felicity remaining, so the visiting relatives soon departed, taking with them hard feelings that lingered for years.

With his part from the sale of the family farm, Daddy

was able to obtain a small farm a few miles from the home-place. Since he got the basic pieces of furniture and most of the farm machinery, he could manage a new beginning for the family. His health was better; the new venture invigorated his slight body and boosted his confidence in the future. Along with the furniture came the utilitarian things such as the iron kettle, wash pot, cast iron utensils, boiling pot, teakettle and skillets.

Sixteen

As Daddy loaded the wagon for moving, he put one of the most precious things under the buckboard. This was the dome top trunk of his mother's, containing her black cape and Sunday straw hat, three dresses, and some small personal items. He felt he was going with her blessing and wanted to make her proud.

On that early spring day in 1935, the wagon bed was lined with pallets from my grandmother's handmade quilts. Even her smell seemed to linger as our eyes fastened on her prized possessions. At least we were taking a part of her with us. The wagon was hitched to the team of mules once owned by my grandfather—now deceased. My father slowly mounted the wagon and took the worn reins in his hands. "Gid-up-gid-up"! There was pain in his command. The obedient animals heeded the call. They headed up the familiar road, often used for farming tasks and family errands. When they got to the main road, instead of turning to the left as usual, my father yanked the reins to direct them straight ahead. Soon their hoofs were trudging the loose gravel of an untraveled way.

On the buckboard sat my father and mother, gripped with fear for the future, but somewhat relieved of the tension brought on by the contentious acts and words of my family members since the death of my grandmother. We children sensed my father's sadness in leaving the only home he had ever known. I, feeling the need to break the silence, reached for Trixie, Grandmother's feist dog. Even Trixie seemed puzzled by this bumpy ride. My puppy talk brought a grin to Bonnie Bell, now four, as she sucked harder on her thumb. "Get away, get away" yelled Hallie Sue, age six. "I don't want that dog to touch me." My mother's arms were wrapped tightly around JoBethe, as the two-year-old squirmed for breathing room. When we realized we were on our way, we relaxed a little bit.

As my father switched the reins, he scanned the planting fields along the road. He knew all the farmers along the way, the first farm belonging to Uncle Fenner, his mother's brother. The next was a tenant house owned by a large landowner further up the road. Soon another country road led to the right, ungraveled but well-worn. With a jerk, the mules would turn with their cargo of anxious hearts. After going uphill and down a gentle grade, we saw a humble house. From the right side, leaning over the rim of the wagon on my knees, I yelled, "Look Daddy, our new house has a big, pretty cedar tree." The other children crawled to the edge to look over also. My mother, always protective, turned around and yelled "You all sit down and stay still 'til we get stopped. Do you want to fall out and get run over by the wagon wheels?"

We were coming near a mailbox and the entrance to the yard. A culvert of splintered planks covered a scant ditch. Within a few yards, we were in the yard of our new home. Daddy sprang down from his high seat and hitched the team to a nearby telephone pole. I would discover later that there was no telephone in the house. One by one, he lifted the little ones from the wagon to the ground—all except me. I had scampered down with Trixie and dashed up the two steps onto the porch. The front door was closed, but unlocked. I yanked the door open and peered inside. Then I slipped inside, finding two front rooms, both smaller than the rooms at our other place. There was a kitchen and a back porch.

In the backyard, a few feet away, was a well with a windlass and a long bucket. Down below the well was an old hen house, with dangling roosts and a dirt floor covered with gray chicken droppings. On the other side of the house stood a weather-beaten smokehouse; I would explore later. A few feet away was the garden, enclosed by the usual fence to keep animals and chickens out. Last year's growth of vines and weeds still clung to the wire webs. The gate was hanging on one hinge. Even so, my mother would be pleased to have a garden so near by. The garden was her main area of work and the source of food for her family.

Next, I spied another shed hanging over a small cliff like gully. Yes, it was a toilet, something we never had at the other place. There was a door and two holes, but no closure down below. Crinkled leaves from a Sears Roebuck catalog and dried sassafras leaves gave evidence of its use.

Further down, I could see another fence of posts and sagging barbed wire. As I came closer, I could see a small barn in need of repair. There were holes in the roof, and the hayloft had fallen into one of the stables. The crib had no door; "Where would we milk the cow?" Behind the broken-down barn was a pond of water that collected rain, but it was covered with a skim of gray matter. This was the home of baby frogs, called tadpoles, and baby mosquitoes, which we called wiggle tails.

The pond would be the main source of water for the livestock, including the mules and the cow. This had been a day of departure, but also a day of discovery. The empty house would soon be filled with familiar furnishings, including a cook stove. Aunt Maudie and Uncle Henry were following close behind — their wagon loaded with Ma's furniture, now ours. Their older son, Robert, was leading the milk cow. A coop of hens and a rooster would be brought later, along with plows, the disk harrow and small pieces, axes, shovel, and hoes (especially the grubbing hoe).

It had been a long, tiring day; the little ones were hungry and sleepy. Mama, knowing the uncertainty of the day, had filled two Mason jars with water — one for my father who would not drink from the same jar as the kids. The other was soon emptied by sips and gulps from thirsty mouths.

Since the house was empty, there was no need to go inside to sleep. Mama gathered the pallets from the wagon and spread them on the porch. The little ones crawled onto the comfy mats and were soon fast asleep. Even Trixie soon joined them on the edge of the pallet, but not near Hallie Sue. Mama and Daddy sat on the edge of the porch, with their tired feet dangling to the ground, and their eyes fastened on the road for the sight of the wagon bringing their belongings. Soon they heard the jangling of chains and the lumbering of the loaded wagon as it came into view. They did appreciate the help and encouragement Maudie's family had been through these trying times. It was difficult to express their thoughts, but they knew the feelings of their hearts.

They had hardly gathered at the porch steps when down the road came Gloria and Esther, Maudie's two older girls, bringing two baskets of food she had prepared for their supper. In the cool of the evening, as they ate the potato salad, string beans, cornbread, cold biscuits, and chess pie, the chatter and laughter seemed to warm the walls of the house. Needless to say, the food nourished their tired bodies and weary spirits. The last gleam of the setting sun shined through the kitchen window — a blessing for the day and event.

The first items to be taken from the wagon were the lamps and globes. Night was coming, and light was needed inside the house to prepare makeshift beds. Fortunately, a half-filled can of coal oil had been tucked in the loaded wagon at the last minute. A lantern was placed alongside the oil can. With its light, water could be drawn from the well. Daddy remembered that the water bucket and dipper had been tied to the buckboard. Everyone was thirsty after a full meal. Surprisingly, the water from the well was clear with a fresh taste. The heavy pieces of furniture were unloaded and placed on the front porch so that Aunt Maudie and Uncle Henry and their children could leave for home and rest. It would take some time to put the furniture and necessary items in place. After a night of rest, the task would begin.

Many things needed repair or replacement. First, the stove pipe in the kitchen had rusty holes — a fire hazard when using the cook stove. The rope of the windlass at the well was unraveling. The propped-up clothesline was rusted. Even the nest box in the henhouse was without straw.

Inside the house, there were no closets. At the other house, there had been a large one by the fireplace. Here nails had to be driven along the walls to hang bonnets, caps, and coats. Pasteboard covered some windows. There were no screen doors for the front or back, and no screens for the windows. We settled in to the present realities, with hopes for the coming tomorrow. My young ears and eyes were open to my parents' despair, yet determined to make a go of this new beginning—one day at a time.

Right away, a neighbor from down the road came by to see us. My dad had known of him and was glad to see him. "Howdy, I'm Dave Mills. See you have moved in. So glad to have you; this place was empty for a while. I know you will be a good neighbor. But I see that you need some help, especially fixin' that barn. I've been thinkin', what are neighbors for? So I'm going to gather up some others around here and do something with that barn. You've got to have a decent place for your livestock. The weather is good now. Since it is not quite time to plant cotton, we will take a day or two and give you a hand."

My dad was speechless, but so appreciative. "You don't have to do that, but I will be so much obliged." His lips quivered, and there were tears in his eyes.

Sure enough, the next morning right after breakfast, Mr. Mills and four other men showed up in their wagons with lumber for the side walls and timber for rafters. For two days, we heard the buzzing of saws and the banging of hammers. Soon there were stables for the mules, a stall for the cow, a crib for the corn, and a hayloft overhead. It was nearing cotton-planting time—always the first of May. The most pressing job was to choose the land for the cotton patches. The most suitable spots had not been worked last year and were covered with sedge grass and sassafras sprouts. I was not yet big enough to wield an axe, but I would gather the sprouts by the armfuls after my father had chopped the roots out of the ground. Then the turning plow, pulled by the team of work animals, he would turn the hard ground and break it up into soft, crumbly workable soil.

About half of the farm of ninety-some acres was covered with trees and bushes. There were oaks, hickories, sweet gums, sycamores and, of course, the pesky sassafrasses. We were glad to have the hickory trees, knowing there would be nuts to crack in the fall. The kernels would be baked in cakes by my mother and enjoyed by my dad who loved all sweet things.

My first chewing gum had come from the sweet gum tree. There was a gummy goo that oozed from cracks in the bark of this tree. The gum was hard to chew and made my mouth sour, but I champed it anyway. I was fascinated by the long limbs of the sycamore tree, with its white mottled bark and fluffy balls hanging from drooping stems. There were only a few of these trees, which did not grow on the upland but hovered along the edges of the streams, which we called branches.

Only one chestnut tree grew on the edge of the field behind the barn. Somehow, it had escaped the blight that had killed most of these trees. I knew about the prickly bur with nuts inside. The nuts were good to eat, but getting them out of the sticky, stinging hull was difficult.

There were thickets everywhere—bushes and thick weeds galore. On the edge of these clumps were huckleberry bushes that would be bursting with dark blue berries later on. They were nature's treats for the farm hands, big and little, as they hustled by, doing their chores.

As I ventured beyond the barn, I came upon an orchard of big apple trees in full bloom with their rosy pink petals. What a beautiful sight! There would soon be green apples to eat, and later on, apple pies. The trees were buzzing with honey bees, gathering nectar for their combs in the nearby hollow tree, which we later found. My dad loved honey and began to plan to place some bee hives nearby.

Our neighbor, Mr. Mills, came by on his way to the store. He saw our delight in the big fruit trees. "You know these are Horse Apple trees. The apples are big and yellow when ripe. The trouble is, being this far from your house, they do get picked by roadside thieves. Just thought I would warn you." We had not thought about this. We had other fruit trees around the house. There was a pear tree behind the well, two peach trees beside the smokehouse, and some plum bushes beyond the garden. All were now in bloom. Below the far side of the barn lot was a long, deep hollow — almost like a gully — but thick with trees and dark shadows.

I heard my father speak of a spring at the foot of the hill being a second source of water for the farm animals. Being curious, I ventured off to see for myself. As I made my way down into the ravine, the dead leaves became deeper. Fallen limbs and rotten logs lay enmeshed as I picked my way around them. At the very bottom of the gorge, I found the spring of water coming from an opening in the side of the hill. Its self-made basin was filled with soggy leaves and sand. With a piece of broken limb, I dug out the muck and scooped out the sand with my hands. The mucky mud began to move; I was disturbing a mud puppy's home. It slithered into the running stream below. The water was so cool and fresh, and no one was enjoying it. Next time, I would bring a mason jar to carry some back to the house. It was rather spooky being down there alone; I wondered if there were wild animals watching me. I could handle beavers or possums, but wolves or bears. No, please.

My father readied the garden with a plow and the mule team. After that, no more plow or animals, with their four big feet, would flatten any growing plant as they turned from one row to another. My mother laid off the garden rows with hoe and rake, and would further till with the same garden tools. She planted her garden by the signs of the Zodiac, so the green beans, lettuce, and onions were already in the ground, as dictated by the Farmer's Almanac. The Irish potatoes were planted in the nearby fields; cucumbers would be planted on the first day of May. The peas, Crowder and speckle, would be planted later.

It was now time to plant cotton. Three spots had been chosen since the patches were not very big, being limited by fence rows and towering trees. The land was made ready, with the middle buster plow making the row. The tops were scooped over, and the cotton planter, pulled by a mule, would drop the cotton seeds into the loose soil. Corn would be planted next, in the bottom land. Hayseed would be sown on remaining spots and patches. By the first of June, the tender cotton plants would be up and ready for thinning by the gentle strokes of the hoe. The second time around, the grass would be scraped out with a sharp hoe. This work would be done by the women and older children. By the first of July, the cotton would be "laid by" by the male of the family. With mule and plow, he would scoop up soil from the middles of the rows and heap it around the plants for support. Also, the corn had to be thinned out and grass and weeds chopped away from the tender shoots. It was the goal of most farmers to have all the crops "laid by" by the Fourth of July. They could then take a break from planting and plowing, but hay had to be cut, raked and dried, then hauled to the barn by wagon and mules, and stored in the hayloft or piled into haystacks.

It was time for school to begin for the summer. School was in session during July and August and out for September and October. School-age children of farmers were needed for harvesting crops, especially picking cotton. During the hottest months of summer, we walked to school. There were no busses. We sat at our desks in hot rooms with no fans. There was no electricity; open windows brought some relief by way of an occasional cool breeze. The school was only about one-fourth mile from our house. By taking a shortcut across an open field, we made the distance even less. Ours was a two-room schoolhouse, connected inside by two large window-like openings which were open for group meetings and closed for classes. Grades one through four were in the front part of the room, and grades five through eight were in the back area, which included a small stage for performances.

There was a large playground area, but only one basketball post and net. An outside pump provided drinking water, which was contained in a bucket with a dipper. Each student haD his or her own drinking glass.

Toilets for the boys and girls were placed a distance apart

on the edge of the school grounds.

I was in the second grade and eager for school to start, but uneasy about being accepted by different classmates. I was aware that my dresses and underwear were made of floral flour sacks, but so were those of the other children. During the summer, many of us went to school barefooted. Walking up the dusty dirt road, I could look back and see my footprints following me.

Our school supplies were brown wooden pencils, that cost one cent, and a Big Giant tablet that cost five cents. These were obtained at the country store. Second-hand school books were available. Our lunch boxes were small lard buckets with bails. Lunches were mostly cold biscuits with a piece of meat. We had loaf bread only on rare occasions. Sometimes an ear of boiled corn on the cob was our lunch. A special treat was a fried chocolate pie. At times I would walk home for lunch, since we lived nearby. School was my joy. I loved to read and study. I looked forward to any assigned homework, studying at night by the light of a coal oil lamp. It was not easy, with the little ones pulling and jabbering.

For some reason, my parents never took notice or checked my school work. Even worse, if I misbehaved or failed to carry out on order, the punishment was that I could not go to school the next day. English, reading, and spelling came easy for me, but I did struggle with arithmetic. Later on, in upper classes, I found geography and history very interesting. Unfortunately, there were no classes in music or art. Also I would have loved spelling bees, but there were none.

As I passed from one grade to the next, books became my best friends. There were a few lending books at the school, which I took home for reading. From the early grades, I took great delight in *Aesop's Fables*, especially "The Tortoise and the Hare," "The Fox and the Grapes," and others.

Later, my favorites were *The Five Little Peppers* books, *Heidi*, and *Rebeccah of Sunnybrook Farm*. In the upper grades from my school textbooks, I was exposed to the challenging and rewarding stories and poems of Henry Wadsworth Longfellow. I will never forget the excitement of "Paul Revere's

Ride" and "The Village Blacksmith." Others I fondly remember are "The Courtship of Miles Standish" and "The Song of Hiawatha."

I do not remember Many seasonal programs, but one patriotic one was very special. One of the teachers, Mrs. Cora Mae Gately, planned and directed a presentation, "Columbia, the Gem of the Ocean." We students waved flags and marched in cadence up on the stage to this rousing tune and stirring words:

> Columbia, the Gem of the Ocean
> The home of the brave and the free
> When borne by the red, white, and blue
> When borne by the red, white, and blue
> Thy banners make tyranny tremble
> When borne by the red, white and blue.

We probably did not know what tyranny meant, but were sure that Columbia was America.

There was no emphasis upon recreation. Recess was allowed, but there were no structured activities. Some of the students took advantage of the basketball goal, especially after school hours. I was not one of the few who donated a few cents to purchase a basketball, and we were compelled to come straight home after the dismissal bell. There was much to do: drawing water from the well, feeding chickens, gathering eggs, bringing in stove wood for the cook stove in the kitchen, and helping with little ones.

As I grew into adolescence, my hair seemed to get redder and thicker, and my arms and face more splattered with freckles. I felt unattractive, and some of the boys re-enforced my poor self image by calling me "Peckerwood" and "Rusty," asking if I had been out in the rain too long.

I had no one to share my inward pain. My parents were weighed down with basic survival needs—food and clothing for a growing family. Education and social training were low on their priority list.

Seventeen

Days passed into months, and eventually, the year came to its end. The cotton had grown, produced, been picked, and hauled to the gin. The gin master paid money for each pound. The proceeds were used to settle the account at the country store, where we had charged the basic necessities such as flour, meal, sugar, and coal oil. The corn had been gathered and stored in the crib, along with the hay. The larder for the livestock was full.

We warmed by wood cut from our trees. That same wood stoked the firebox in the stove that cooked our food. Also the wood warmed the water with which we washed our hands and faces and the clothes we wore, in summer and winter. The water that we drank and that supplied our household needs came from the well. Our hens gave us eggs for breakfast and the cakes for my dad. The hogs were the source of our meat and lard. Milk for our drinking and cooking, and butter for our bread came from our cow. The garden, tended by my mother, provided vegetables and pickles, canned in Mason jars. The fruit trees gave us jams and jellies, preserved by my mother.

There must have been a sense of accomplishment by my parents. They proved to themselves and others that they could make it on their own, without being propped up by aging parents. They could enter the coming year with hope and confidence that things would be even better, with good health and abundant crops.

During the winter months, our house was heated by a

wood-burning stove, with a pipe, that extended up through the ceiling. The demand for wood was ongoing. My father, with axe, would comb the timbered fields to find the right tree for wood. It took two men to pull the cross-cut saw across the grain of the wood. A stripling of a boy would come in handy, but there were only girls. He would ask a neighbor man or one of Aunt Maudie's menfolk to give him a hand. After the tree was cut into block sizes, it took splitting and chopping to reduce it into firewood pieces. Then the sticks of wood were thrown into the wagon, pulled by the team of mules, and hauled to the yard near the well. Since there was a continuous need to fuel the fires, they did not bother to stack the wood in an orderly fashion. It was pitched into a pile.

Fire was kept burning in the heater during the day and banked at night. My dad's early morning job was to jump out of bed, in his long-johns, and stir up the fire before the rest of the family's feet hit the cold floor. During the day, fire in the kitchen stove warmed that area, but at night it became very cold. Sometimes there would be ice in the water bucket in the morning.

After a breakfast of biscuits, fatback, and gravy, and sometime scrambled eggs, we were on our way to school, slinging our dinner buckets — packed with leftover breakfast biscuits and a piece of meat. If the weather was very cold or wet, we wore galoshes over our shoes to keep our feet warm and dry. Each room of the school had a wood-burning heater, with the older boys assigned as firemen.

Even with constant effort to keep warm, colds — the contagious infection of the nose and throat were common. At home and at school, there were coughs, sneezes and runny noses. Those were the days before Kleenex or any kind of paper tissues. Most children wiped their dripping noses on their sleeves. Some resorted to using their shirt tails. Some girls used the bottom of their slips.

Around the home, when the mother was nearby, her apron became the handkerchief. The usual remedy for colds was Vicks salve, so that aroma pervaded the home and the school. The dreaded outcome of a cold for children was the croup at night. The nose and throat became acutely inflamed, causing labored breathing, hoarse coughing, and spasms in the throat. Breathing the vapor of Vicks steam was about the only known relief.

Winter thawed into spring. My mother had gained weight and found it more difficult to make the beds. Milking the cow twice a day was even more of a struggle. She was depending on me to do more around the house. I was drawing all the water and helping on washday. Then one day, unexpectedly, right before dark, my dad rounded up us kids and took us to Aunt Maudie's house for the night. He had never done this before; we were puzzled. Aunt Maudie seemed to be expecting us and bedded us down for the night. In the morning, after a quick breakfast, the older cousins walked us back home. What a surprise! Our mother was still in bed. My cousins seemed to know something already. My mother had a baby boy—her first boy, and our baby brother. Now I knew the reason for the night visit at Aunt Maudie'. For the next four or five days, my mother remained in bed while my dad struggled to milk the cow and do the many other jobs of my mother. I was now old enough to do more of the housework—washing dishes, and feeding the animals and chickens.

In about a week, my mother was back on her feet, diapering and nursing the new baby. As yet, the baby had not been named. Mother knew I liked to read; this gave her an idea that I could suggest a name from a story. I was proud of our new baby and pleased when Mother asked me to think of a name for him. I came up with the name Adrain Arzell. I coined the name Adrain and had known of someone named Arzell. I put them together, and my mother and father liked the name.

Since my mother had not delivered until the ninth of May, even in her condition, she had planted her garden. Most of the seeds were now peeking through; all except the cucumbers, which she always planted on the first day of May. Now the baby was a few days old, and Mother and her hoe were stroking the soil and scraping out the grass, almost as if she was caressing the tender plants. We were eating radishes, lettuce, and green onions, which my dad never touched.

I was the baby watcher; baby cribs were rare with farm families. New babies slept with their mother. During the day they slept on the parents' bed. The baby was placed in the middle of the bed, surrounded by pillows to keep him from rolling off the bed. The small siblings, curious about the little one, were apt to climb up and pull him onto the floor. As the baby grew, he was put on a pallet on the floor for nap time.

By the time the cotton was ready for the second hoeing, my mother was out in the field, doing the woman's work, and I was watching the baby and changing his diapers. One of my favorite baby-tending jobs was holding my little brother as I churned the milk into butter. I sat in a cane-bottom chair beside the churn, grasping the dasher with one hand, going up and down, bouncing him on my knees to the rhythm of the splish, splash, splosh of the butter being beaten out of the milk.

My brother was a cute little fellow with blond hair and blue eyes, always smiling and doting on the attention of his four adoring sisters. My mother and dad were so proud of their baby boy, taking care to protect him from harm such as falls, bumps or illnesses.

My mother and dad managed to get the crops up, hoed, plowed, and cultivated by "laying-by" time. It was the middle of July, and we two older girls were back in school. A heat wave was sweeping the country. There we were—many squirming bodies boxed in a classroom with no electric fans or ice for drinks—sweating, whining and learning very little. Our teacher gathered up some funeral home fans that gave us some relief.

We endured the summer, and shortly after Labor Day we were back in the cotton patch. I could now almost pull my weight in cotton. I went up and down the rows, snatching the locks from the dried bolls (called bur) and cramming the fluffy tufts into a seven-foot canvas sack.

It had been a sweltering summer and a warm fall. The hot, dry weather had powdered the earth into tiny bits sus-

153

pended in the air. Dust clung to every flat surface. Since our house had open windows, any movement of the air brought in the dust, which settled on the furniture, walls, curtains, bedding and floors. Our feet, most of the time bare, tracked in the clinging particles from the yard and barn lot and dried droppings of animals and chickens. Since there was no electricity, there was no vacuum cleaner. The only tool for removal of the dust was a broom made by my mother. She always grew broomcorn, a sorghum-like plant for making brooms and brushes. A bundle of stems was bound with twine and wrapped on one end of a wooden handle. This crude sweeper was not used every day, and consequently, there was a backlog of debris underneath beds and tables.

Fall brought cool weather and the need to take the chill off with a fire in the heater, especially at night. The wood, brought in from the woodpile, was covered with dust. The burning wood made ashes that were poked, stirred, and caught up in the air. There was dust everywhere, and we were breathing it. We were not aware that dust could be a carrier of bacteria and could cause serious illnesses.

It was November; little Adrain was six months old and spending most of his time on a pallet on the floor, propped up by pillows. He was growing and learning to sit alone, but was getting the sniffles and a runny nose. There was not much concern. My parents thought the change of weather was bringing on a cold. After a few days, his nose was stopped up, and he was coughing. Vick's salve was not helping. He became warm and fretful, meaning he was running a fever and having trouble breathing. It was time to call the doctor. Dr. Thomas came right up to diagnose the baby's condition. He laid his cigar on the window ledge and took his stethoscope from his black bag to listen to Adrain's heart and lungs. The doctor shook his head in concern. "This baby is real sick. In fact, he has pneumonia, in his left lung. Make a poultice soaked in camphorated oil, and wrap it around his chest and keep it there for twenty-four hours. I will give you some medicine to keep his temperature as normal as possible." (Those were the days before penicillin was available for medical use.) "I will

154

be back tomorrow to check on his condition."

When my mother and dad heard the doctor's evaluation, they turned pale; their hearts almost stopped. They knew that pneumonia, inflammation of the lungs, was life-threatening. They remembered that it had been fatal to some adults they knew. How would it affect a baby?

Camphorated oil was a solution of camphor, mixed with oil and used as a liniment. It was put on a poultice for chest colds. My dad hurried to the store to get a bottle of the oil, a large one of at least twelve ounces. His throat was tightening, maybe from a coming cold—or could it be his nerves? With the bottle of camphorated oil, he got two boxes of Luden's cough drops, his mainstay for coughs and colds over the years.

My mother found a piece of flannel, called outing. As soon as my dad returned with the oil, she saturated the cloth with it, and with safety pins, pinned it to the baby's undershirt. Since the baby was very sick, he was held constantly. When my mother went to the barn to milk the cow, and when she made the meals, I held him on my lap—my arms wrapped tightly around him.

All night my mother walked the floor or sat on the side of the bed with the sick baby in her arms. He was burning up with fever and struggling to breathe. His constant whimpering made us feel helpless. By noon the next day, the doctor returned, and the diagnosis was even more critical. The baby now had pneumonia in both lungs—double pneumonia. The treatment was to continue as prescribed, with hope and prayers that the absorption of the liniment into the lungs would break the congestion and free the lungs of mucus and phlegm.

For the next few days, the baby's condition remained the same—no better, no worse. But the doctor knew the child's body was under an attack of the worst kind of infection to a critical part of his body. So with his suggestion, another doctor was called in, Dr. Kyle from Milan. After examining the child, the two doctors walked out on the front porch to consult. They agreed it was mycoplasma pneumonia, prevalent among children. In those days hospitalization was rare. Whatever the two doctors decided, the treatment remained the same. Several bottles of the camphorated oil had already been used.

By Christmas, our little brother was showing improvement, breathing better and taking in more nourishment. The baby's sickness had been a concern for Aunt Maudie and her family. She was a devout Christian and prayed earnestly for the baby's recovery. To show her concern, she brought a token of her faith and a present for our home, a Bible. I had never had one in my hands. I began to scan the pages and read with interest some of the Old Testament stories, but found them hard to understand.

School was back in session, and I was in the fourth grade. Although our little brother was better, there was concern of a setback. To insure his warmth and well-being, he continued to be held during the day, either by my mother or me. For the winter months, I was needed at home to help take care of the baby. One day a week I was kept from school, while my mother washed our clothes and bedding.

Reading and spelling came easy for me, but missing arithmetic lessons would be a problem for the remainder of my school years.

My father and mother had been under an emotional strain for weeks, due to my baby brother's critical condition. He continued to wheeze and struggle to breathe — an asthmatic condition that would linger through his growing years. My father became more stern with his growing family, especially me, the oldest. I was not allowed to play with or visit anyone my age, except for a cousin or two. When they would drop by, they could sense my father's gruff attitude and would soon be on their way.

Eighteen

When I was not caring for one of my younger siblings, I found fun playing with animals. Some of the most frequent ones were frogs hopping around, waiting to snatch a lunch of flies that were feeding on the castaways of the chickens that roamed the yard. I would scoop up the squatty, cool creatures in my sweaty hands and stroke their dimpled backs. My mother constantly chided me, saying that I was going to get warts on my hands from the defensive drips of the frog. Sometimes my quest for fun went from the gentle to the goofy. There were always hens nearby, peeking and scratching for grit and tidbits. It was easy to catch one by throwing down some crumbs of bread or grains of corn. With an old shoelace, I would tie a frog to the leg of a hen and watch the tussle as she yanked her foot and pecked at the frog as it hopped helplessly, trying to free itself from the lasso.

At one time, I had a medium-sized mixed dog of mellow tan named Bowser. He was my buddy; we strolled through the pasture and into the woods, gathering chestnuts and hickory nuts. One day, as it was nearing Halloween, I put on an old ragged coat of my dad's and made a mask out of a brown paper bag. Sauntering on the front porch, I called Bowser gruffly. When he heard the disguised voice, saw the scary face, and smelled the musky old coat, he charged at me, growling—his teeth bared and his hackles standing on end. I snatched the paper bag off my head and spoke to him in a calming tone. I'm sure he was embarrassed for being so easily fooled, and I felt like a fool for tricking my faithful friend.

I did enjoy my pets, but there were unhappy endings. Our most beloved pet was Trixie, a black and brown feist that had belonged to my grandmother. Now the dog was up in years, slow in movement, and seldom barked. She had never had a litter of pups, due to my father's alertness to nature's promptings. When there was a ripple of restless, he would lock her up in the crib for the necessary time, while male dogs clawed at the door.

It was assumed that she was past the period of bearing pups. She slept every night on the front porch, on a mat of tow sacks. One night, she was missing from her usual place. We thought she was taking a late-night stroll and would soon return. The next morning, she was still missing, and we were concerned, calling her with a piece of bread in hand, but to no avail. About dinner time we looked out the back kitchen door. And there she was lying under the lilac bush by the garden fence. It was a hot day, and she was panting furiously, her tongue swollen and dry, lopping from the mouth. Her back was lacerated with cuts from the claws of some animal. Supposedly, she had come into heat but was too small and weak to defend herself from the aggression of rival males.

I ran for a cup of cold water to pour over her parched tongue. It was obvious that she was suffering, and the cuts on her back were gaping open, with flies flying about. I remembered that there was a bottle of medicine in the crib at the barn that my dad and the neighbor men used when operating on male hogs. I ran to get the bottle; written on the side was the word "chloroform." I hoped that this would ease her pain and give her some rest. I held a rag soaked with the medicine to her nose. She whimpered and breathed deeply. The panting stopped, and her body went limp. She went to sleep and never woke again. I was heartbroken but realized there was no hope of her getting better.

When my dad came in from the field, he was very sad, remembering that this had been his mother's beloved pet. He put the lifeless body in the tow sack that had been her bed. My sisters and I followed him as he took a shovel and mattock and dug a grave down by the barn lot fence.

My dog Bowser also came to a tragic end. One cool fall day, when all of us kids were inside, we heard Bowser yelping as if he were being attacked. We ran to the front door to see what was the matter. Sure enough, he was being attacked by a larger dog. The mangy mongrel was growling and snapping at poor Bowser's head, as he tried to avoid the bites. The stray was slobbering and stumbling as he rambled in circles, bumping into objects in the yard and snapping at everything. Bowser ran under the house to hide from the crazed animal. Right away, we knew it was a mad dog. The term comes from the Latin word "rabies" which means rage or fury.

Luckily, my dad was in the house and heard the commotion. He pulled the shotgun from under the bed and grabbed some shells from the dresser drawer, quickly putting two into the gun. Knowing the bite of a mad dog would be fatal, he dared not confront the dog up close. He ran into the garden, which was enclosed by an open wire fence. As the dog wandered aimlessly around the yard, he hoped it would come close enough for him to get a good shot. After a few minutes, the dog headed toward the barn. Dad knew the livestock were now in danger, so he left the garden and cautiously followed it to the barn. Shortly it staggered in his direction, and with a steady hand, Dad took aim, pulled the trigger, and the dog fell to the ground.

By now Bowser had come out of his hiding place, but his head was clawed and bloody. We knew he was now infected by the bites of the mad dog, and we dared not go near him. My dad took the pitchfork and a shovel and loaded the dead dog onto a make-shift sled. He pulled the carcass a far piece from the house into a ravine-like gully. I tagged along and helped him gather some dry leaves, sticks, and dead limbs to build a fire and burn the animal. After we got the fire going, we hurried away from the fumes and smell and watched ghastly smoke twisting and swirling afar.

Back at the house, there was Bowser, who had been bitten and was destined to go mad also. Telling all of us to stay inside, my dad put a rope around his neck and led him off into the woods. There, he pulled the trigger, firing the other shell, and left the poisoned body in an undisclosed place.

There were other animals on the farm, the most necessary ones being the cows. At least two were needed to provide milk and butter. They were milked twice a day, morning and evening. They spent the day in the pasture, grazing on tufts of grass and chewing their cuds.

Periodically, from the far end of the pasture, one of the cows would begin to bawl in an urgent manner, different from the usual lowing and mooing. Then my father would tie a halter on her and lead her off. We were never told why or where, but as I got older, I surmised that there must be a bull out there somewhere. When the cow returned, she was contented, but remained "dry" for the nine months of gestation.

A cow cannot produce milk unless it has given birth to a calf. Then she is known as a "fresh" cow and continues to give milk for about ten months. For a while, a baby calf has to share its milk with our table. After a few days, it is weaned. At about six months it is sold at a market. If a new calf is born weak or deformed, it is taken to the market at six weeks and sold for veal.

It is my mother's job to do the milking, but when I turned twelve years old, it became my job to do the morning milk while she was making breakfast. I soon learned how to grip the four teats, to squeeze and pull, making sure the stream hit inside the bucket. Then I was off to school for the day.

Other animals we owned were hogs—our main source of meat. They provided us with fatback (known as country bacon), ribs, ham, sausage, and lard. The brood was made up of different ages and sizes. The adult males were called boars, and the adult females, sows. Pigs were little ones; older, weaned ones were called shoats. There was inside propagating; no need for outside excursions. The sow usually had two litters a year, giving birth to eight to twelve pigs at a time. Males marked for butchering were castrated with the help of neighbor men. It was not explained to us, but we could hear them squealing, protesting going from boar to barrow. Also in the crib in the bar, was an instrument and bottle of medicine for the operation.

Hogs were the garbage collectors of the farm. All waste from the kitchen, with the exception of meat given to the dogs was pitched into the slop bucket, the receptacle for leftovers and spoiled food. The waste and slush made up the main liquids for the hogs. They used their snouts to root for tender roots and acorns. Corn and mash were the main foods, especially during fattening time. Sometimes it was necessary to slip a metal ring through the snout, which is sensitive to the touch, to discourage them from rooting and tearing up the ground. They liked to wallow in mud holes because it helped to keep them cool, but it is believed that they are cleaner than most farm animals.

The fatted hogs were butchered in early winter. We feasted on fresh meat the first two days, with fried liver, boiled lights (lungs) and backbone—pushing out the cooked marrow as a delicacy. My mother always ate the brains. We never ate the feet, snout, sweetbreads or stomach, called chitterlings. The fat from the intestines was trimmed off and rendered into lard for frying.

Within two or three days, the shoulders, sides (middlings), hams and jowls, were salted down and packed into the smokehouse. The name smokehouse was a misnomer; smoke was never used at our place. Salt was the ingredient for curing and preserving pork meat.

These were the days before TVA brought electric power to our area to light our homes and run the radio and washing machine. Consequently, all energy was homemade. We did not have tractor power for the farm, but we did have horsepower and mule power. To maintain and operate a farm, a team of strong and agile mules was an absolute must. Preparing the soil, planting, cultivating, and harvesting the crops were all done with horse- or mule-drawn implements.

Turning plows were used for turning the soil each year. The harrow with sharp-edged disks broke the chunks of soil into smaller pieces and smoothed the surface for planting. The cultivator stirred up the soil between the rows and uprooted and covered any weeds. The wagon, also horse drawn, was the only conveyance for hauling loads of corn, cotton and hay. The four-wheeled vehicle made the weekly trip to the country store for the basic needs of the home and farm, such as flour and kerosene.

Brought from my grandfather's farm, our beasts had many years of plodding and plowing behind them. My dad, seeing the need for younger and fresher stock, bought a feisty filly, satin black with feet as big as dinner plates. We named her Polly. She was already trained for working and became the new member of the team. Her gait did not synchronize with that of her plow-partner (the mule), their feet hitting the ground at different beats and different speeds. Consequently, the team was always a bit lopsided.

The following year, Polly gave birth to a brownish-black colt, which my dad named Dan. He was a perfect specimen of a mule, with small feet, long ears, a short mane, and a tail of long hairs. We kids were fascinated with the frisky, new animal but were not allowed to go near the livestock at the barn. The kick of a mule or horse could seriously hurt anyone.

Since we were girls, we were never allowed to ride a horse or a mile. There were no saddles in the barn. As I grew into my early teens, I wanted to ride Polly to the field, but my mother said "No," explaining that I would be like a married woman. I did not understand the reason, nor did my mother know, that this restriction went back to fourteenth century Ireland.

One time I did over-ride Mother's forbidden word. We were in the bottom land on a very hot day. My dad disconnected the team from the cultivator and led the mule back to the house, leaving me to bring Polly. I stood on the wheel of the cultivator and climbed on her back, water jug in hand. I was clinging loosely to the bridle rein, when we came to a steep incline. Polly stumbled, her back legs slumping, and I slid down her back and over her hips to the ground. Luckily, I landed on thick grass and weeds and nothing was hurt except my pride. Of course I never told my mother of my short, slippery ride.

At the age of two, Dan the colt was broken. He was

trained and taught obedience to vocal commands, plus a yank of the bridle and a twitch on his rump. At first he rebelled at the weight of the leather straps and metal pieces which were fastened to a plow or wagon. The most basic piece was the bridle, the head gear with the bit that goes in the animal's mouth and is used to control it. The next most important piece was the collar, the part of the harness which fits around the base of the neck, and against which the animal exerts pressure in pulling a load. The next important pieces were the hames, the two rigid pieces placed along the sides of the collar to which the traces were attached. The traces were chains connecting the animal's harness to the implement or vehicle drawn.

Needless to say, it took force and perseverance, several days, and many attempts from my father and some neighbors to conquer the stubborn will of the young creature. But with the cooperation of an older mule with which he was hitched, he accepted his role as a work animal. Quickly he learned that "haw" meant to turn left, and "gee" to turn right. "Giddap" and "whow" he had learned from the beginning. He became an excellent addition to the farm's work force.

One day, my dad was finishing a field of corn using the cultivator. The edge of the field and the ends of the rows were overgrown with weeds. When the team reached the end of a row they had to go straight for about five or six feet, bringing the plow to the end of the row. As they turned around to the next row, they were treading where a copperhead snake lay. From its coiled position, the snake hurled its body forward, striking Dan on one of his legs. Right away, my dad realized his prized mule was in serious trouble. He quickly unhitched the team from the cultivator and tied them to a nearby post. He hurried to a nearby farm and asked the neighbor to get the local veterinarian, who arrived in about thirty minutes, along with two other neighbors. Before the Vet could administer a shot of anti-venom, the animal had to be subdued. The men tied ropes around the frightened animal's leg and threw him to the ground. After the shot was given, the mule calmed down and the swelling subsided. The men untied the ropes and pulled him back to his feet. He remained listless for the

163

rest of the day. After that day, he was never listless again. The trauma had shocked him beyond recovery. He recoiled at any touch of a harness and resisted any normal activity. Even when hitched with a calm animal, he would lurch back and forth, kicking the single tree, and breaking the tongue of the wagon. After several attempts to do normal work with plow and wagon, my dad gave up and sold him. Whether or not Dan ever recovered from the encounter with the copperhead remains a mystery.

Nineteen

I had been fascinated with the world of words since pre-school days. My eyes and mind feasted on any paper dotted with words. Aside from my school books, there was nothing of interest to a child to read at home. There were no newspapers, except *The Nashville Banner*, which would occasionally be thrown in our yard with the hope of enticing us to subscribe. I would scan the pages and pictures and delight in the funnies.

We did get the *Progressive Farmer* each month. There were articles to instruct farmers on new farming techniques, such as crop rotation and contour plowing. For the farmer's wife, there were gardening tips and recipes. Patterns for dresses and other attire could be ordered. Perhaps these suggestions were too progressive, as my dad and mother stuck to the tried-and-true ways of doing things. The routine of same crops and procedures lingered on, as did the monthly magazine. The subscription price was minimal. A salesman would come by to collect the yearly fee. I remember one time when he came to collect, my mother took one of her fatted hens that she kept for trading, and paid the man. It must not have been unusual, as he showed no reluctance to the feathered cash. So the *Progressive Farmer* kept coming, and I kept perusing its pages with growing interest. I came across a recipe for cole slaw, something we had never eaten. It called for cream, vinegar, salt, and sugar, mixed with chopped cabbage. All of the ingredients were near at hand, so I mixed up a dish for the noon meal. All liked it except my dad, who did not like cabbage or anything with vinegar in it.

The Sears Roebuck catalog that came in the fall and spring was our in-house shopping mall. The merchandise had different levels of quality and prices—especially the shoes and galoshes. My mother made our dresses, slips, and underwear out of feed sacks, but there was printed material to be ordered by the yard to make our Sunday dresses. Other items we ordered were coats, my dad's long-johns, and lisle stockings for us girls and our mother.

Since we lived on a rural route, we had an RFD mail carrier who was the direct contact between us and Sears Roebuck and Company. His name was Brown Arnold, and he always drove a coupe loaded down with mail and orders. My mother made out the order and my dad waited—cash in hand. The mail carrier would stamp the envelope and write out a money order, and our order was on the way to Memphis, the district's mail order house.

Even the Sears Roebuck catalog became a plaything for rural children. We cut out paper dolls from the used catalogs, pictures of men, women, boys, girls, and babies, making up a family and giving them names. Then we would put them in an empty shoe box in a sitting position and slide the box across the floor, pretending that they were going to church. In my imaginary world, I cut out pictures of furniture for each room, pretending it was my new home. In my world of fantasy, I was a young mother with black surly hair, a loving husband and two small children.

The most necessary and used packet of pages was the *Farmer's Almanac*. It could be called "the other Bible" of the home. The compact booklet always hung from a nail on the most accessible wall in the kitchen. My mother planted her garden in the signs of the Zodiac. Even the pulling of teeth was arranged by the phases of the moon. The Almanac was also the weather forecaster for each day of the month. It was the time-keeper, giving the time for the rising and setting of the sun for each day.

The Almanac was a pharmacy in paperback. It was filled with medical suggestions for the farmer's health and his family's well being. There were pages of advertisements of medicines for whatever the ailment. These were available at the nearby country store. There were salves and ointments for skin rashes and muscular soreness and remedies for stomach pain and gastric disorders. It praised Fletcher's Castoria, a medicine for children and Black Draught, the dependable regulator. There was also a tonic for women's health, spelled with a big C, which we pre-pubescent girls didn't understand.

Besides the medical remedies, the Almanac offered first aid helps for such things as snake bite and rules for storm safety. It was filled with important dates and historical events. Also, there were proverbs and timely tidbits. It was amazing in its varied contents, both amusing and informative. *Benjamin Franklin's Poor Richard's Almanac* was the forerunner of this practical, but informative and entertaining, literature. Thank you, Mr. Franklin.

In the late 1930s, my father acquired a small battery-powered radio. He built a shelf on the wall over the sewing machine in the front room for it. In those days, radio was the only source for family entertainment and news. From its waves through the air, came adventure shows for the children. Soap operas, sponsored by soap companies, were directed to the women. Gang Busters and The Lone Ranger got the attention of the men. Situation comedies like Amos 'n Andy, Fibber McGee and Molly, Jam-up and Honey, and Lum and Abner entertained the whole family. Gabriel Heater, Edward R. Murrow, Lowell Thomas and Walter Winchell became household names.

The highlight of the radio week was the Grand Ole Opry on Saturday night over WSM in Nashville, sponsored by the National Life and Accident Company. We did not know that the call letters WSM meant "We Shield Millions." The emcee was George D. Hay, a familiar voice to thousands of listeners. From the stage and over the radio came stars ranging from musicians and singers, to comedians. There were Cowboy Copas, Kitty Wells, Earl Scruggs, Red Foley, and Roy Acuff singing the "Wabash Cannon Ball," and many more.

I especially liked the antics of the Duke of Paducah, and I saw him in person, in his green suit, at a radio picnic. His line in closing was always, "I'm headin for the wagon, boys these shoes are killing me." I did not want to miss an act or a song and would cling by the radio, with the volume turned down, until the end of the show at midnight. Surprisingly, my parents, already in bed in the same room, endured my insistence on hearing the last song and George D. Hay's "Goodnight."

The following day out in the cotton patch, hoeing or picking — depending on the season — I would try out the songs of certain singers. I would even mimic Minnie Pearl's sketches of "How-dee! I'm from Grinder's Switch."

Since I liked country music and this was my only exposure, I listened to programs that featured local talent on the radio station during the noon meal. My favorite singer was Eddie Arnold and his lonesome "Cattle Call." As I returned to the cotton patch I would be doing the "Cattle Call." Another singer I liked was Zeke Clements on the Nashville Station. I sent and received his picture. His smile and thick chest hair became my pin-up delight. My brief encounter with the outside world made my work lighter, and me, more determined to have a life beyond the cotton fields and tall corn stalks.

Radio was my first window to the outside world. I had time during the winter months to listen to the radio. Most of the daytime programs were soap operas for adults, about how adults were involved with romance, relationships, and commitments. Even as a young teen, I could visualize Ma Perkins, the matron of the lumberyard, and her involvement with others. There was Our Gal Sunday, an orphan girl from the mining town, married to a titled Englishman. Young Widow Brown was trying to support her children by running a tea room. Others were Helen Trent, Stella Dallas, and Lorenzo Jones. These characters and plots gave me insight into the world outside my rural confines. Somehow I would make my way up from a country road to the paved streets of some city, with a joy and security for the future.

From my emotional desert, there was an oasis at the end of a rutted winding road. When the fields were too wet for working, or sometimes on Sundays, I was allowed to walk to my favorite Uncle Perce and Aunt Nina's place. Their farm was literally in the boondocks—a remote piece of land covered with towering trees, situated on the Forked Deer River. From its banks, there was a spread of bottom land, an asset to any farm. The road to the folks' place veered off the main-traveled road and wound through low scraggly bush land and then through bare, red gullies, on to a tree-shrouded rise. This is where their house stood.

Even though this was remote area, other winding roads veered to the left and right to other houses. My main acquaintance was Uncle John Barr. His wagon and team of mules were known to us, as he frequently passed our house on his way to the store and gin. Another narrow road turned to the right, to the place of a mysterious character known as Tom Sheck, the inventor. He supposedly had assembled something like a moving belt, enabling him to stand on his back porch and pull up a bucket of water from the spring several yards below. Nearer to my uncle's place lived a hermit in a moldy gray house. When he died, Uncle John Barr and his son B.D. brought the body out in a casket by wagon and team, past our house and to the graveyard.

Uncle Perce's house had two main front rooms, a kitchen and side room, and a front and back porch. There was no well, so water had to be carried from a spring below a steep hill.

Since my uncle was the eldest of my dad's family, his older children were already married. This left only a boy and girl at home. The girl, my cousin, was slightly older than I, and we were friends in a sisterly way. They were farmers like my family, but my aunt never went to the field to work or had to carry water from the spring. She kept a clean and orderly house and prepared wholesome meals. At the table before meals, she would ask us to bow our heads as she asked the blessing on our food. She kept the radio on, especially on Sundays, for the Charles E. Fuller's Old Fashioned Revival Hour. She was faithful in attending church services, which were held once a month. They did not have a car, and consequently, traveled by wagon—pulled by a team of mules—to the church several miles away.

My aunt had a keen sense of wit and a gentle laugh. I felt comfortable in her home and admired her varied interest in reading. There were always magazines around, such as *True Romance*.

Uncle Perce was stoical, but calm and steady, working hard with his son to till and grow his crops. He hunted rabbits and squirrels, which he sometimes shared with my family. Sometimes a possum was caught in his trap. I have eaten such at their table. He also trapped small animals such as raccoons and muskrats for their furs. He hung the skins on the outside walls of his barn to dry. Although farm work demanded his daylight hours, he found time to read by the lamp light at night. Limited in schooling, he liked to read, especially western novels by Zane Grey. His favorite was *Riders of the Purple Sage*. He enjoyed comic books such as "Dick Tracy," "Little Orphan Annie," and "Pop-eye the Sailor Man." These were big little books, short and cube-shaped, which cost a dime. I was aware of these books, but considered them to be for men and boys. I found Aunt Nina's magazines about love and romance more interesting. I took one home with me to finish reading an article; my dad discovered it and gave me a tongue-lashing for reading trash.

Although this was a farming family like my own, there was time at the end of the day, or on Sundays, for leisure activities—such as table games. There were dominoes and Chinese checkers, which I had never seen before. I was fascinated by the board with holes arranged in the shape of a six-pointed star. I learned quickly to move the marbles across the board to win the game.

Their son, still at home, sold *The Grit*, a weekly newspaper filled with articles of interest and household hints. Its contents were varied and entertaining, and their advertisements for soaps, tonics, and freckle cream amusing. Even though Uncle Perce was a hard-working man, my dad complained about his hunting and trapping on Sundays. His list of "Thou Shall Nots," had work or fun on Sundays at the top. Dad held

Aunt Nina equally guilty, as she cooked the game that had been caught or killed on Sunday. Even worse, Uncle Perce played pool — sometimes for hours at a time — to my dad's absolute condemnation.

Uncle Perce and Aunt Nina's home was indeed an oasis. The calm, caring atmosphere and the varied items of interest helped me face the rigors of my family. Many times I wished that I had been born into their family.

We were in the hot, dusty days of August, and in the last days of summer school. The two teachers at our two-room school were loosening the rules. They gave us older girls permission to take our lunch buckets and stroll on the back road for the rest of the day. We had been good and considerate students for the most part. The oldest, Gloria, took the lead and urged us on, as the younger children gaped in wonder, wishing they too were going. We left the main road and took the road that went by the Spain cemetery, heading for old Smith Schoolhouse. But then, another road led off to the left — one we had never been on before. Not knowing what was around the next bend made the event more exciting. Gloria, our leader, knew of a mysterious cave in the side of a hill which visitors often sought. Not knowing the exact place or distance, but energized by the excitement and freedom, we followed her.

Within three or four miles, we found a large sandstone cave that extended far inside a hill. The ceiling of the cavern was low, and we could hardly stand erect, so we walked around the entrance gawking in wonder at what might be far back in the damp, dark interior. As we continued, we could see a large two-story house, enclosed with a high metal fence down the lane. Gloria knew that it was owned by two Memphis doctors. The gate was locked, so we walked around the yard of solid stone. We were curious and captivated with this big house, and, we wanted to know what was inside that demanded such security.

As we walked around the outside of the fence, we could see windows with shades. On one corner of the house, the fence was right under a window. Our curiosity turned to boldness as we climbed up the fence and pushed open the windows. Following our leader, we bounded into the house, which had very little furniture. Right away, we assumed that since this house was owned by doctors, there must be a skeleton somewhere inside. Knowing we were doing something wrong, we went from room to room, looking into each closet. We came to a blanket box on the floor and touched the lid, thinking this was it. Hesitantly, we flung open the lid, but there was nothing there except an old musty quilt.

We found the door to the cellar, but no one dared descend into that dungeon of cobwebs. We found our way back to the open window, crawled out, over the fence and down to the ground. There were concrete steps leading down the hill to an old barn, but our sense of adventure was dwindling. We had had enough for the day.

We had done no harm to the house or its contents, but we still had a sense of wrong-doing. Certainly I did not know the seriousness of trespassing on private property. This had once been a resort developed by two physicians. They had moved their families here during the yellow fever epidemic of 1878. There were seven springs on the 200-acre site, and the mineral waters were said to have healing powers. In the 1920s the sons of one of the physicians replaced the aging building with the present day lodge, which was seldom used.

We scampered back the way we had come—hot, dry, thirsty, and hungry. We still had our lunch buckets, but nothing to drink. We did not know there were seven springs somewhere nearby.

We arrived back at the schoolhouse as the other students were leaving. Subdued and tired, we said nothing, letting them believe we had had an average day walking along a country road. Furthermore, I was not going to let my dad know about this escapade. Surely his reaction would have been, "You need to be sent to a reform school."

Twenty

I was gaining more self-confidence, blessed with good health and bursting with energy for farm tasks. I was splashed with freckles, and my hair grew ever redder, coarser and thicker—much to my mother's disdain. She would take her blunt sewing scissors and yank up locks of my hair and whack them off. I remember one time, while talking to our neighbor, Mary Patton, my mother made a remark about my hair. The neighbor replied, "I'll tell you one thing: there's something under that hair." Even in my naiveté, I knew she was talking about my brain. For my freckles, I kept my arms covered while out in the hot sun. I kept a straw hat jammed tightly on my head. I had read that water from an old stump would remove freckles, but I knew there were germs there also. We were all required to work in the fields of cotton, and I chose the outside work, such as feeding the chickens, gathering the eggs, drawing water from the well, and bringing in wood for the cook-stove for my other tasks. My sister Hallie preferred inside work, such as washing dishes and sweeping floors.

Life on the farm was humdrum but stable. There were a few irritants, such as bed-wetting and thumb-sucking from some of the younger siblings. One amusing incident remains in my memory: one sister walking in her sleep and using the apron of the heater stove for the chamber pot.

Sunday was a day of rest—more or less. There were necessary chores, such as feeding the chickens and hogs and milking the cows. Other than that, we were not allowed to "strike a lick" of work on the Sabbath day. There was no

173

Sunday School in our community and preaching service only once a month. We seldom attended. Sunday morning was special since we usually had fried chicken and gravy with our biscuits for breakfast. This entailed my mother pulling a frying size chicken from the coop and wringing its head off, then slinging it to the ground, with blood gushing out its neck. I was right there to gather up the lifeless body and douse it in hot boiling water to loosen the feathers. When the feathers were all plucked, the pin feathers were singed over a piece of burning paper or a blaze in the cook-stove. My mother washed the plucked bird, cut it into pieces, battered the pieces with flour and dropped them into an iron skillet, bubbling with melted lard. The crispy fried pieces of breasts were for my dad, the legs and thighs for us "younguns," and the back, gizzard and liver for my mother.

Kinfolk — such as uncles, aunts, and cousins — used Sundays for visiting one another. Many Sunday afternoons brought the excitement of catching up on aches, pains, and crops. One of my dad's older sisters, Aunt Kate, lived in town with all the comforts of city life — indoor bathroom and player piano. We looked forward to her and Uncle Charlie's infrequent visits to our home. Her last visit was troubling.

She sat on our front porch in one of our straight-back cane-bottomed chairs, in her fine clothes. She was restless, trembling, while tears trickled down her flushed cheeks. Uncle Charlie, concerned, helped her to his uptown car and back to their home in Jackson. We did not know that she had been confined to an asylum for nervous disorders and had just been released to return to her home and family with orders that all sharp instruments be removed from her surroundings. In a few days we got word that Aunt Kate had gone down to the basement of her home, doused her clothes with kerosene, and with a match made a torch of paper and set her clothes on fire. By the time she was discovered, her body was so badly burned that there was no hope for survival. She died (at the hospital) a few hours later. We were puzzled that our aunt, only forty-two years old, could be so disturbed without our knowing it. Her funeral was held on a sunny Sunday afternoon at a nearby church. To this day, the sight of her monument in the church cemetery brings back memories of her sitting on our front porch in the sunny Sunday afternoon in tears—our family wondering why.

From the rising of the sun until gray twilight, the food, chores, and field work never varied. I looked forward to the beginning of the school year, although it meant extra work for my mother, making dresses for us girls. The dresses were made from floral feed sacks. Plain sacks were dipped in dye to make bloomers and slips. Not having a pattern, Mama would pin the material on a completed garment with safety pins, since there were no straight pins. She would then cut the sack into pieces to fit the proper size. Thread for the stitching and elastic for the bloomers were purchased from the country store.

I was twelve years old and ready for the seventh grade. We were in for a surprise! We had a new teacher who was a handsome young man in classy clothes, shiny shoes, "brilliantine" hair, and smooth hands. Perhaps he was right out of college, assigned to this two-room schoolhouse on the far end of the county. Grades five, six, seven and eight settled down on our side of the schoolhouse with subdued wonder. The eighth grade girls sniggered, trying to hide the attraction they felt toward him.

From day to day, the teacher led us through our lessons of arithmetic, geography, history and reading from our worn school books. But his emphasis was on handwriting, which we call cursive today. Since about the third grade we had gone from printing to handwriting. He stressed that our eye, hand, and arm control must be developed by practice. And practice we did, over, and over as he stood at the blackboard directing our movements on paper. He would draw three straight lines on the blackboard and show us how to make a capital letter over and over and then on to the same letter in small case. Then we were shown how to make joining strokes between the letters to make words. We could not raise our pencils from the papers until the entire words were finished. Then we could dot the "i's" and cross the "t's." Over and over, from day to day, we were drilled to write well, so our words could be read by everyone.

Our teacher was aware that we country girls were lacking in toiletries and grooming know-how, so at Christmastime, each one of us was given a small box wrapped in pretty paper as we left the school for Christmas break. I hurried home and unwrapped the gift while my family looked on. It was a manicure set with fingernail polish, polish remover, and an emory board. My father, seeing my delight and realizing its use, snatched it from my hands and threw the red polish into the fire of the heater. Gruffly he grumbled, "No girl of mine is going to wear such stuff — or high-heeled shoes either." As I grew older, my father's rules and expectations became more strict. Perhaps I was becoming more headstrong, and the sting of the switch was no longer effective. Other punishments were tried — doses of castor oil and Epsom salts.

There were other stubborn creatures on the farm, namely the mules. Many times an uncooperative mule would be unhitched from a plow or cultivator and tied to a tree, then soundly thrashed with a whip. One time a mule evened the score with my dad. Seems like the animal had not obeyed the commands and was placed in a stable with only a two-by-four as a partition between stalls. My dad was thrashing the culprit through an opening in the side of the stable. After a lashing on the mule's hind quarters, it kicked the two-by-four out through the opening. Like a missile, it hit my dad right in the face and mouth so hard that he fell to the ground. With my mother's help, he was able to get up and on his feet, spitting out his broken dentures. Six months later, he coughed up a tooth that had been embedded in his lungs.

My dad could be tough on some of God's creatures, but soft on more fragile ones. We were never to touch a bird's nest as the human scent would keep the mother bird from returning to its nest and her babies. We were forbidden to catch a butterfly as our touch would destroy its delicate wings. Even granddaddy-longlegs were to be carefully lifted from inside the house and put outside in their natural domain.

Days became weeks and weeks months as I waited another year for my thirteenth birthday and the eighth grade.

The new teacher was much older than last year's. She was a local person whose husband was a farmer. They had a baby, which the father kept during the day. Often during lunch time, she would go home to nurse the baby. She was a no-nonsense teacher, demanding study and accountability. As we were finishing up the school year, she called me aside and told me I did not know fifth grade arithmetic. No doubt the drills in penmanship had not helped me in adding, subtracting, multiplying and dividing. Somehow I managed to get through simple fractions, numerators and denominators, with her support. Since reading was involved, English, history, and geography had never been a problem for me. I was able to finish the eighth grade along with my classmates.

In 1941, all 8th graders of the county schools were to come to the high school at Lexington, the county seat, for graduation exercises. I looked forward to this event, and my mother ordered me a new dress and new shoes. I chose a navy crepe dress with red trim from the Sears Roebuck sale book. Our teacher made arrangements for the class to go together. Since our class was few in number, we rode in one of the parent's pickup truck with bench seats in the back.

It was a miserable day for me. I felt so awkward and ill-at-ease among strangers in the big auditorium. In addition, in the last week my body had changed from that of a child into that of a mature woman.

Within my restricted world of boundaries, my father limited social interactions. But I had the blue sky over my head. My lonely spirit was soothed by the fluffy white clouds floating across the vast space above me. Alone in the dark, in the early hours of night, I would gaze up in the blackness and see stars like shining jewels sparkling in the night sky. The myriads of twinkles excited me. Sometimes I could see the Milky Way, a galaxy of stars arching across the night sky. Now and then, a shooting star appeared as a meteoroid and made its way into the earth's atmosphere. Here I, a lone figure, was witness to the mysterious works of the great God of the universe. Even though my feet were on earth's ground, my heart and spirit were reaching out to the vast expanse of the unknown.

Twenty-One

My school days were over; it was already determined that I would not go to the high school. As I got older, I became more and more my dad's sidekick with the farm work. There were now six younger brothers and sisters, the youngest a bright-eyed little brother only a few months old. When my mother was outside with my dad for any reason, I was "second mommie" and took over with authority. In later years, my siblings would tell me how bossy I was to them.

As summer came, so came the gathering of vegetables from the garden and peas and potatoes from the field. My mother did most of the picking of the peas—both Crowder and speckled. This was a daily job since we ate them almost every day. It was the girls' task to shell them for the next day's meal. After supper, as it was getting dark, we sat on the front porch, our laps full of peas (legumes), zipping them from their hulls. While swatting mosquitoes and gnats and scratching chigger bites, we sang songs we had heard on the Grand Ole Opry and the local radio station. One of the new ones was one of our favorites, "You Are My Sunshine."

We knew real sunshine with its blistering rays shining down on us as we hoed crops of corn and cotton. The road by our place was rutted, hot, and dusty. Passers by were usually familiar faces in well-used cars and trucks, waving as they went by. If a strange vehicle came down the road, we would grin and say "uh-huh, there goes a revenuer." Even though we were isolated from society, more or less, we still knew about the law and moonshines. Our family was really aware, since one of my mother's older brothers had spent some time in a federal penitentiary for making and selling illicit whiskey in the adjoining county.

One day when our work was caught up, my dog and I were strolling through the woodlands. For no reason we crossed over onto another farm. There, among scrubby brush, was an old abandoned whiskey still. If my father had known that he was neighbor to a whiskey-making operation, he would have been shocked. He detested everything about liquor. He was proud that whiskey had never passed his lips. But he would have had to bear the situation, since the owner of the farm was his cousin.

Since I was no longer in school, the battery-powered radio was my only window to the outside world. I enjoyed the antics of "Amos and Andy" and looked forward to Ted Collins presenting Kate Smith who sang "When the Moon Comes over the Mountain" and "God Bless America." By radio, we were made aware of the war in Europe. Gabriel Heater, the nightly newscaster, told of German armies, called Nazis, invading Czechoslovakia, Poland, Austria, and Yugoslvaia. These countries were unfamiliar to us, but France and Russia we knew about. We knew the war was getting closer to America when Germany torpedoed and sank the USS Reuben James. President Roosevelt had been warning America of a pending national emergency. Compulsory military service had been designed to draft and train young men to defend our country.

The war came even closer as the Germans began bombing the cities of Great Britain. Edward R. Murrow broadcast from there as the Nazis attacked London. Listeners could hear bombs exploding in the background. To hear that 60,000 buildings had been destroyed or severely damaged during a massive 500 bomber attack by the Germans was beyond our comprehension, we sensed the impending danger to America.

At home, our family experienced a tragedy of heartbreaking proportion. My father's sister, who lived about ten miles away, had a loving family of three boys and two girls.

This aunt, my Aunt Ardie, reminded me of my grandmother, who was also petite and energetic. Their family farmed also, but were a little more upscale. We would visit them once or twice a year. Their home was a cottage style with pretty pictures on the wall.

The oldest son, Leon, twenty years old, was involved in an accident. He and some friends were cruising down Highway 70 on a Saturday night. As they slowed down at a major crossroad, the car behind them failed to do so and rear-ended them, doing a lot of damage to their car. Fortunately no one was seriously hurt. But two weeks later, Leon was visiting his aunt in a nearby town. She and her husband had a nine-year-old daughter. The uncle, his daughter and Leon went out in the uncle's car for a short ride. About sundown, they came to a very familiar railroad crossing, and the uncle drove the car into the path of an oncoming train. All three were killed instantly.

The funerals were held on Sunday, December 7th, at my aunt's church. There were three hearses, three caskets and three open graves in the church cemetery. We were all saddened. Why did this happen? They were at a familiar railroad crossing and knew the usual time of the train's passing.

We arrived home from the funeral as the sun was setting. It was time for the evening news. As we listened to the radio, we were stunned to hear the happenings of the day. Some 360 Japanese Warplanes had reached the Hawaiian Islands and attacked the American military base at Pearl Harbor. The Japanese planes had sunk or severely damaged five U.S. battleships, including the USS Arizona and the USS Tennessee. Thousands died or were wounded. The news continued the next day, reporting burning battleships, painfully wounded sailors and soldiers, and describing the unrecognizable corpses. President Roosevelt was on the radio, attempting to calm the fears of everyone.

The next day the United States declared war on Japan. "We Americans will prepare for a long war," declared President Roosevelt, "of which we are going to win." He said that December 7th, 1941, would live in "infamy." We did not know the meaning of the word "infamy" but we knew it was a strong message to the Japanese. "Remember Pearl Harbor" became the rallying cry for our nation. On December 11th, the U.S. declared war on Germany and Italy, since they were the Axis pact that plunged the nations into world war.

Almost overnight our country went into war mode. The draft began calling young men into military service. Rationing of gasoline, sugar, and other products went into effect. Even scrap iron was in demand for the war effort. Only a few miles away, a large area of farms was bought by the Government and turned into an arsenal for making ammunition. This site was strategically chosen, being inland, distanced from the oceans and enemy aircraft carriers. On our peaceful plot of farmland several miles away, it was normal to hear the explosions of shells being tested at the arsenal several times a day. The skies overhead were filled with large military planes on course from one training airfield to another.

Many of the men and women from surrounding farms who had never held public jobs were now industrial workers. The drone and rumble of motors could be heard in the early morning hours as the workers hustled to punch the time clock. Even though the public pay was tempting, my father chose to keep the farm going as usual with the crops, cows, hogs, and work animals. I was now in my early teens with a strong body and an eagerness to prove myself. Soon I was plowing and running the hay mower and cultivator, which were pulled by a team of mules.

After our work was caught up, my sister and I would work for neighbors. One farmer with large patches of strawberries would hire us to pick berries for a few cents a quart. This is how I got money for my first permanent, which cost one dollar at the beauty school at Jackson. In the fall of the year, after our own cotton was picked, we would hire out to pick cotton for neighbors. This gave us enough money for a new pair of shoes and a trip to the county fair. To get to the fair, we rode on the back of a pickup truck, standing behind the cab, holding down our skirts, with our hair blowing in the wind. In those days, girls wore pants only for field work.

We were well aware that the war was still going on. Now and then, a convoy of Army trucks would go through on Highway 70, with soldiers waving and throwing out their names and addresses. Some of the girls would gather up the notes and write to them, but I was never present to be in on those toss-outs. I did write to a soldier a time or two, after his name appeared in the county newspaper. I took delight in any young man in uniform. Listening to songs from the radio, such as "Praise the Lord and Pass the Ammunition" and "Don't Sit under the Apple Tree with Anyone Else but Me," became my favorite form of amusement. But "Coming in on a Wing and a Prayer" impressed upon me the solemnity and uncertainty of many a young men's future.

The United States was now going into the second year of the war, with battles in both the Pacific and European theatres. There was sad news in our country, too. A terrible fire killed 300 people and injured 150 at a nightclub in Boston. Many of the victims were American sailors, soldiers, and Coast guardsmen, in Boston for a weekend of rest and relaxation. There was some good news also. World War I flying ace, Captain Eddie Rickenbacker, and his crew of seven had been forced down in the South Pacific after their bomber ran out of fuel. They were found after having drifted twenty-four days on rubber rafts.

It became necessary to add a side room to our house. Besides five girls, ages five to fifteen, there were two brothers two and seven, who needed their own room. One cold January night of 1943, we were taken to our aunt's house. When we returned the next morning, our mother was in bed with a new baby girl. She was beautiful, with dark hair and ivory skin. She thrived on the loving care of five doting sisters. Again, my mother let me pick a name for the newborn; the little one was called Bernita Lynne. Besides needing more sleeping area, we needed more room for eating. My dad made a wooden bench that reached the entire length of the dining table.

Now with eight children, my mother and father maintained a few acres of cotton, a field of corn, hay for forage for the livestock, and a garden of vegetables for eating and canning. Two cows provided milk and butter for the table and baking bread. A few pigs grew into hogs and provided us with bacon and ham. The scratching hens layed all the eggs we needed for breakfast and baking. Food rationing did not affect us, except for such items as cornmeal, flour, sugar, Karo syrup, and Postum for my dad's breakfast. Shoes had been rationed to three pairs a year, but we were fortunate to get two pairs.

By the end of 1944, we were numb to the war news. Would it ever end? Most of the eligible young men had been drafted into the armed forces, and the other able-bodied men and women were working at the arsenal. There was need for help at the general store—where most of the people bought gas and oil for their cars, kerosene for lighting, and canned items for their meals. The owner of the store was my dad's uncle. The manager was a local friend, who knew my dad was reliable, and asked him to give them a hand. He did so, with me as his backup with the farm chores.

When the crops were gathered in by fall, and I had turned seventeen, the manager asked if I could also help at the store. Riding with my dad each day to work, standing behind the counter, greeting the customers and filling brown paper bags with their needs, were just a few of my duties. There were piece goods to be cut by the yard, kerosene cans to be filled by the gallon, gas to be pumped into their cars, eggs to count and chickens to weigh for trade. The job was invigorating; I was meeting and helping people from all the surrounding areas. Truck drivers making deliveries from Memphis and Nashville, with their grins and sneaky glances, were the highlights of each week.

FDR had won an unprecedented fourth term as president. This gave the local men a reason to mumble and grumble as they chewed their tobacco, using the pot-bellied stove as a spittoon.

The country store served as a central location for telephone calls, since there were no telephone connections in some areas. One call came from military headquarters, requesting that a certain family be notified that their son was missing in action. As soon as the store closed, my dad and I drove a few miles beyond our place to bear the sad news to the family.

It was now April 12, 1945. The news of the war was encouraging. The Allies, including the United States, were winning many battles. The radio at the store was on all the time, supplying farm news and weather. I was on a stepladder rearranging items on a top shelf. From the radio came the news that President Roosevelt had died suddenly at Warm Springs, Georgia, where he had gone to rest from the rigors of trying to bring an end to the war. Some of the codgers, from their feed sacks circle, were stunned, other expressed unbelief, and still others said, "Good riddance." I stepped down from the ladder, glaring at them, horrified at their lack of respect for our fallen president.

We were in the last days of the war in Europe. Hitler, the "Fuhrer" committed suicide as the Soviet Army encircled Berlin. On May 7th, the Germans surrendered unconditionally to the Allied forces. The war in Europe had lasted five years, eight months, and two days, but we still had a war to win in the Pacific.

My earnings from working at the store gave me the means to buy a suitcase and still have some pocket money left. The few months at the store gave me confidence that I could make it on my own. I knew there was another world out there somewhere for me. Seeing the Greyhound bus each day, hearing the whir of the wheels, knowing it was going from Nashville to Memphis revved up my dreams.

For the last nine months I had been working at the local country store pumping gas, cutting dry goods by the yard, and doing general clerking duties. The eighteen dollars per week had earned me enough money for the suitcase, a bus ticket, and a few dollars for my developing plans. The plans came gradually as I read *The Commercial Appeal*, the daily newspaper from Memphis that came to the store. This was during the World War II years and the newspaper was full of classified ads of available jobs. The ad that for days had captured my attention was the Sears Roebuck and Company Retail Store. Following the job ads were those for Room and Board. Invariably, some of the ads would state: "In walking distance to Sears." I found a small notebook and began jotting down possible jobs and addresses for living arrangements.

Working in this little country store in this small village brought me in close contact with the families as they traded for food, farm supplies, kerosene and all the necessities of their limited lives. One of the teen-age girls, Juanita whose family frequented the store, wore a leg brace, the result of infantile paralysis called Polio. She went to Memphis regularly to a clinic for therapy. It was time for a scheduled trip and I suggested I could go with her, which met her parents' hearty approval. Her father drove the two of us to Jackson to catch the early morning bus to Memphis. When we arrived at the station, she took a taxi to the clinic, and I, with my little black notebook, caught another one for Sears Roebuck. No problem, in those days with gas rationing; city buses, streetcars, and taxis were the normal way of transportation. Very few young people could afford their own cars, anyway.

I entered the multi-storied building—retail on the first floor with mail order on the upper ones. The employment office seemed to be waiting for me. The application form was short and simple. I was only seventeen years old, but I put down eighteen. With pride and truth, I disclosed that I had some job experience, working at the general store, operating a cash register and taking care of customer credit accounts. A job was offered to me if I could be available in two days. Yes, I would be ready. Then, with my little book of addresses and in walking distance of Sears, I found a certain street and the house number and secured me a place of lodging. Then back to the bus station by another taxi, where Juanita, having returned from the clinic, was waiting for me. We boarded another bus back to Jackson; her family waiting patiently for us.

When I got back to the store where my father worked, I announced my immediate plans to go back to Memphis for a new job. The store owner was not pleased with my abrupt departure, which he expressed to my father. Up until this time, when in a rebellious mode, I would threaten to leave home; my father would verbally chastise me. But this time he saw the resolution and bearing. Since I would be catching the bus and returning to Memphis the next day I would not be going back to work at the store.

Packing my suitcase, washing my hair, pressing my clothes, and primping the best I could, I was ready for the great adventure I had dreamed of. My father sent a local boy from the store in his car to bring me down to the highway. Crossing the road in order to wave down the Greyhound bus, I stood in front of Fred Rowe's Pool Hall. Here on Route 70, the highway to Memphis via Jackson, I waited for the bus.

So on this night, an ever-waiting taxi took me to my new, temporary home. The owners were an elderly, sedate couple. I was to share a room with another Sears employee, Margrita, from Mississippi.

I arose with the sun the next morning, dressed in my best attire and walked to my new job, which was in the lingerie department, which also included swimwear. My supervisor was a tall, stern, blond matron named Miss Hahn.

The store cafeteria that served all personnel of retail and mail order employees was only a few aisles over. Since the lingerie department was between the store entrance with the elevators and the cafeteria, there was a steady stream of foot traffic, especially at meal times. The cafeteria also became the main place for my meals. One of my favorite desserts, new to me, was Boston cream pie.

On the first Sunday in the city, no job to report to since all department stores, and most other businesses, were closed on Sundays, my landlord and his lady took us two new roommates out to show us the town.

The mellowed sedan crawled over the wide quiet streets of Memphis filled with Sunday traffic. From the back seat with windows half-rolled down, I was gulping in Mississippi River air and breathing out whiffs of air from a vibrating chest. As we glided along, there were palatial mansions, well-established homes with well kept yards, and modest cottages with small gardens in the backyards, the new frontier to learn and claim for my future.

Soon our hosts arrived at their destination, the gentlemen's place of business. This was also new to me, a small casket factory. With subdued pride, they gave us a tour of the small plant from the construction of the boxes to the shimmering satin linings of the coffins. The solemnity of this place seemed as a benediction for the day.

With the beginning of the new week at work, things were going well. I felt comfortable and confident with my surroundings. I was now eligible for the employee's discount. So on my lunch hour, with money I had saved from the country store employment, I bought my first wristwatch, convinced that every working girl should have one. My new friend and co-worker was surprised that I could make such a purchase before my first paycheck from Sears.

My job was quite uneventful. Selling underwear, gowns, housecoats, and swimsuits was not too exciting, except for the men customers, and there were some, buying for wives and mothers, who always asked my size. A military officer bought a gown for his wife and asked if I would model it for him. Of course, he was only joking.

Another purchase revealed my lack of creativity and expertise in wrapping gifts. In those days, there was no customer service for such amenities. A lady customer had purchased a housecoat as a gift and requested that I gift wrap it. This had not been part of my job orientation, but I found a box, wrapping paper, and ribbon underneath the counter. Without the aid of clear tape, I wrapped, pressed down, folded and tied knots with the ribbon. The more knots I tied, the more the customer squirmed, scowled and smirked. With embarrassed relief, I handed the knotted package to her and with a very weak "thank you" she scampered out the front door of the store.

Another time I was showing some swimsuits to two ladies, which they took to the fitting room. After a few minutes, I glanced up over the counter, and they were going out the front door with swimsuits over their arms. I quickly buzzed the store detective, and he went after them. When apprehended, they convinced him they had worn them into the store, since they were damp. There was a water fountain near the fitting room where they could have been doused from the spout. I was not reprimanded for a supposedly false alarm. The store detective's subtle presence blended in with the shoppers. His tweed suit and matching tie gave a sense of security and propriety to the store. I was always aware of the imprint of his revolver under his jacket as he strolled nonchalantly through the store.

One slow day, as I was standing near the front entrance of the store, some acquaintances from my hometown in Cedar Grove came in and were surprised to see me. They inquired about different departments and layout of the store. They were much impressed with my help and went back to my home community and told that I had a very important job at Sears Roebuck.

Since I was only working five days a week meant that I had Sunday and another day off from work. About once a month I would go back home for a short visit, going of course by Greyhound. Since there was no regularly scheduled stop at Cedar Grove unless a passenger wished to disembark, the driver would jokingly ask me at which traffic light to stop. After spending two days with my father, mother, younger brothers and sisters, I returned again to Memphis. A few days after arriving back in Memphis, I received a letter from my mother saying that I must have the whooping cough, that since my recent visit all the "young-uns" were coughing their heads off. I had been coughing for some time. Many times at work, I would have to run to the stock room to blow my nose in a fit of coughing and gagging. As a child, my siblings and I were never exposed to this childhood disease. When my parents would hear of an epidemic of this dreaded contagious ailment, we were kept home to avoid the possibility of exposure. In all probability I had contracted this infectious disease at work, and consequently, exposed many other children that came into the store. By this time my coughing had subsided, and I didn't miss any work. Surprisingly, my supervisor, Miss

Hahn, had not detected my malady.

Miss Hahn ran a tight ship. One day with no customers in my department, I stepped across the aisle to the men's department to chat with a co-worker and new friend. She stomped over and literally shoved me back into my department. Since she seemed to be tightening the reins on me, I went to the personnel office and requested a transfer to the auto center and service station. Pumping gas and checking oil at the country store had given me experience that I could use here. But my request was denied, saying I was too feminine for the job.

After a while, my roommate and I became discontented with our dour environment in the modest home, and the meals we chose to eat here were bland and skimpy. She invited me to move with her to her brother's home in another section of Memphis. Transportation would not be a problem since the cross-town streetcar ran from this location across town to Sears. With suitcase in hand, I made the move with her. In less than a week, we were informed that wartime regulations forbade this many persons living at this residence. Again, I scanned the classified ads for "Room and Board." I chose a place on Lamar Avenue.

Twenty-Two

This location on Lamar Avenue was the corner where the cross-town streetcar made many runs daily across town to Sears. It was a large two-story house with several bedrooms upstairs, but only one bathroom. There was a large kitchen downstairs that we were free to use. Also there was a large parlor for guests, but no visitors were allowed upstairs. The landlady was a shuffling little woman with a bad case of psoriasis. She scuffled up and down trying to make us safe and comfortable. There was also a front bedroom downstairs occupied by two wives of soldiers who were patients at the Kennedy Army Hospital. Each room upstairs had two women, most of whom minded their own business.

I soon made friends with two middle-aged residents across the hall. They were from Mississippi — one working at the Kennedy Army Hospital, and the other, a former school teacher turned office worker, at Fruehauf. After settling in, I began to prepare my meals in the handy kitchen. Trying to light the gas oven, I singed my eyebrows. But I was enjoying my freedom and independence. I could ride the streetcar for a nickel, and the room and board came out of the eighteen dollars weekly salary from Sears.

I became aware of a young man leaning against a column in the store, grinning and sizing me up. After a while he came closer and began to make conversation. I soon learned he was new in Memphis with a job with the fire department. Although a bit shy and bashful, a country boy from Dyersburg, it was obvious he was looking for a girl friend. He made a date to see me the next Sunday afternoon at my place. This Sunday morning I awoke with a splitting migraine headache. He came as planned, but I had to send my roommate to tell him I was sick and unable to see him. I never saw or heard from him again.

The cross-town streetcar route was now very familiar to me, but to get to other parts of the city, a transfer could be issued to city buses. I wanted to go to other parts of the city — mainly the movie theatre or to the fairgrounds. These routes would take me into unfamiliar territory or to the downtown area. When I reached a certain bus stop, I yanked the rope above the seat to alert the driver to open the exit door in the back of the bus. Many times I got off the bus and found myself at the wrong place. I did not want to seem rural and uninitiated to city life; therefore, I would not ask for directions. The next bus run would not be too long, so I would simply wait for the next one to continue on my way to my destination with aplomb, nevertheless.

Bus drivers and streetcar conductors gave me my sense of identity. As I paid my fare, they would smile flirtatiously and make some remark about my red hair. When I found my seat, they would find me in their rear view mirrors and continue to give interested glances. On one occasion, since I rode public conveyances almost every day, I forgot to drop my coin in the receptacle, walked right back and took my seat. The driver, grinning and glancing in the rear view mirror said, "Are you riding on your hair today?"

The conductor on the cross-town streetcar became very attentive to me, since I rode his run every day to Sears. He became very friendly, and I looked forward to this encounter even more. He asked for my telephone number, called and made a date on his day off from work for me to go with him to Mississippi, which was only a few miles to the state line. He picked me up at my place, and we took a short, leisurely trip for the day. He was somewhat older than I, having already served his time in the service, being one of the first ones to drop behind enemy lines in Europe. As he drove, we shared tidbits about ourselves. He seemed quite interested in my background and future. We had a pleasant trip, stopping for lunch, and back to Memphis. He was a perfect gentleman, treating me as his sister. He must have changed runs, as I did not see him for a while. Then one day, there he was at the controls of his trolley car on the usual run. He told me he was getting married to an old friend, a registered nurse. I never saw him again, but I still remember the warm feelings and respect I felt toward him.

Another driver told me of an amusing incident. The bus was almost empty of passengers, so he was free to chat. It seemed two ladies came on board and took their seats. The bus rolled along, making the usual stops. All of a sudden he heard a commotion in the back, glanced up to his rear view mirror and saw the ladies jumping up and standing in the seats, screaming. It seems that two days before, during inclement weather, they had worn boots to work. The weather improved during the day, so they went home, leaving their boots at the office. The following day, they were taking the boots home, when up and out of one of the boots came a frightened and scurrying mouse.

One Sunday during the summer, my father came to see me — out of curiosity, I suppose. He had heard, from the acquaintance of Cedar Grove, what an important job I had at Sears. I met him at the Greyhound bus station and took him out to my place by city bus. After a few hours, he was ready to return to the farm. Before leaving, his question was how much money I had put in the bank. I was making eighteen dollars a week, with carfare, meals and room rent; needless to say, the answer was "none."

With no work on Sundays, this was my day of leisure. I would sleep late, go down to the corner drugstore next door, and get the Sunday newspaper. In the afternoons, I sometimes took a city bus to the fairgrounds that stayed open all summer. After browsing along the main strip of the barkers' domain of games and freak shows, I would ride the ferris wheel and others — my favorite being the roller coaster. There were always soldiers from the Second Army base and sailors from the Millington Station doing the same thing. There were glances of interest, but only one sailor asked for my telephone number. He later called me, but the connection was broken and nothing came of it.

Usually, I went alone to the movies on Sunday night at a theatre near my place. Most of the films were wartime romances or Red Skelton flicks, with Gary Cooper or Humphrey Bogart, all ending with newsreels from the battle zones.

One mystery remains with me until this day: a young married sales lady in the adjoining men's department, took an interest in me, and we became good friends at work. Her husband and his brother ran a music store downtown. One Sunday she invited me to her home for lunch. It was a long way out, but the streetcar went that far, too. The visit was pleasant; the lunch was a great Sunday dinner enjoyed by all, including her husband and his single brother. After the visit, she dropped me as a friend and disappeared from the store. One day while downtown, I dropped by the music store to say "Hi" to the guys. Everything seemed okay, but later she called me to tell me that she and her husband were separating; the reason: he was smitten by me. I never heard or saw any of them again.

The drugstore at the corner adjacent to our big rooming house had a soda fountain. Since this was the intersection where riders from the cross-town trolley transferred to a city bus, commuters would occasionally drop in for a soda and a smoke, especially G.I.s on their way back to the army base or hospital. Most of the girls who were not working on Sundays found it very convenient to drop in at the friendly pharmacy for the Sunday paper, cosmetics, and other urgent items. With the slightest hint of invitation, some of the soldiers would drop into the parlor and adjoining sitting room for a chat. On one of these lazy Sundays, one of the G.I.s was clutching the front of his shirt and seemed to be at "unease" about something. A button had come loose, and his khaki shirt was gaping open. So I did my patriotic duty, and applying my domestic skills, took the shirt upstairs to my room and sewed the button back on. Soon, gratefully grinning, he was on his military way.

Sundays meant lots of free time for other adventures.

My new friend across the hall, Lillie by name, became like a big sister to me. Though some older in years, she was young and warm at heart. Sometimes she would join the younger crowd in the parlor and jest and joke with the jaunty G.I.s on their way back to their posts.

My "big sister" Lillie had a civil service job at the Kennedy General Hospital. Her duties were in the kitchen and dining room, and consequently, she worked most Sundays. She began asking me to come out on Sunday afternoons for short visits. While she was occupied with job duties, I would stroll through the halls of the hospital, peeking in the wards and waving to the patients. Most of them were in splints or casts, just returning from the war zones. Some pale and passive, would turn their faces toward the wall, no doubt embarrassed with their self-image of helplessness and limping masculinity.

I remember one very youthful soldier, whose chest was wrapped in bandages, listening to operatic music. He beckoned for me to come closer, and after a few words of greetings, told me he was from Massachusetts. He seemed quite contented in this period of healing and recovery. My heart was saddened to see this innocent and classic young man so brutalized by the evils of war. Others welcomed my brief visits. Perhaps I reminded them of a younger sister or friend back home.

I began pushing some of the immobiles down the long corridor in their wheelchairs to the PX. To a late seventeen year old, this was such a delight and privilege. I was bursting with pride and honor to be so near our country's fighting men and to share this short interval of fun and mobility with them. They were war-weary and homesick but such great boys and men.

My friend Lillie continued working at the hospital. The demands of the war were winding down. Some German prisoners-of-war were housed at the Army Depot and worked in the hospital kitchen under Lillie's command. They could speak very little or no English and carried a small book to aid in communicating with her. After the war was over and they were returned to their war-ravaged homeland, she continued corresponding with some of them, even sending them coffee, soap and other needy items. Later, she received pictures of

194

their newborns, and she, having a talent for crocheting, made a sent booties and little outfits to them.

One of the little ones of the German P.O.W.s continued to write her. These former prisoners-of-war were so grateful for the care and concern that Memphis had shown them that contacts continued with officials of the city. Later, a group of these men came back to Memphis for a commemoration and a book was written called *The Power of Memphis.*

In the late summer of 1945, we were still experiencing the aftermath of the German war which had ended in May. The United Nations had been formed, but through newspaper headlines, radio, and newsreels we were still much aware of the continuing conflict with Japan in the Pacific. The newsreels reported that the Battle of Okinawa was finally over after eighty-three days of the bloodiest land battles. Even the navy ships off shore came under desperate attacks by Japanese kamikaze pilots. But our country was winning the war. Super fortresses blasted Japanese industries in firebomb attacks. U.S. carrier planes bombed the main naval base, destroying the last of the Japanese navy. Even then, Japan turned down the Allied ultimatum to surrender.

Meanwhile, our country experienced a terrible tragedy. On July 28th, a B-25 bomber, lost in fog, ripped into the Empire State Building, killing thirteen people. Then, during the first days of August, our country dropped two atomic bombs, only four days apart, destroying the Japanese cities of Hiroshima and Nagasaki.

President Truman warned Japan, "Quit or be destroyed," and the "Land of the Rising Sun" offered to surrender. August 15th became the long-awaited V-J Day. No more war, victory was ours.

This particular day happened to be my day off from work. I first heard the good news by radio. This quiet city awoke with car horns honking and whistles blowing. Up until this time, there had been a city ordinance that horns could be blown only in an emergency. But not today! The city burst wide open with joy and jubilation. Soon the boarding house emptied, and I too left the premises and boarded a city bus for downtown. People were everywhere, mostly in the streets dancing and yelling whoops of victory.

Flags were waving, and hearts were fluttering including mine. And the greatest sight of all—numbers of servicemen making up the celebration, many wearing battle ribbons on their brave chests. The air was charged with a military band blaring forth patriotic tunes. Never did "Anchors Aweigh," "The Army Air Corps Song," or "The Marines' Hymn" seem so right.

The sailors from the nearby naval station were leading the crowds down Main Street, some swinging bottles of beer up in the air and grabbing and squeezing every available girl.

The soldiers seemed to be a little older, more sober and subdued, but nevertheless, a very important part of this tumultuous experience. What a privilege; I was right in the middle of this historic and unforgettable event.

After a while, as the crowds dwindled and the adrenalin drained, I caught a bus back to my place of abode. The house was still empty, except for the landlady in her usual hideaway, her bedroom. I climbed the stairs to my room and immediately spied a liquor bottle on the mantel. I assumed all the girls were out for the day. How did that bottle get there? Frantically, I ran back into the hall and there was a stumbling, mumbling, inebriated man going from room to room. Down the stairs I went, telling the landlady to call the police. While she was fumbling through the telephone directory for the police number, I ran back up the stairs yelling for this confused and seemingly harmless man to "get out," pointing to the front door. He managed to follow me down to the front door. I shoved him out, slammed the door, and turned the lock. The landlady was still muttering and shuffling through the pages of the telephone book. The poor, confused soul had been caught up in the revelry of the day and had wandered into the wrong house on his street.

It was late in the fall of 1945, and I was nearing my eighteenth birthday. My roommate had gotten a job with the telephone company and convinced me that I should apply. Certainly, there would be better pay, $28.00 weekly, plus benefits. I went to the main office of American Telephone and Telegraph Company, not knowing that this company was organized all the way back to 1885 to operate long distance lines. It was now the parent company of the whole Bell System. I made application, took a test, and was called in for an interview. The process was very thorough. Being an operator meant servicing not only local calls, but also all long distance calls for businesses, government, and military organizations. This was the time before Direct Distance Dialing (DDD). Each connection was made by a human voice and a switchboard.

When the interviewer realized that I had only an eighth grade education, she was concerned, but impressed by the results of the test. She kept saying, "You must further your education," implying that I had potential, which gave me confidence that I could do the job.

This was not the time or place to explain why I had not finished high school. I would have liked for her to know that my father would not allow me to do so. After graduating from the eighth grade at age thirteen, my father had jokingly said that was all that was needed to "rock the cradle."

Also, being the oldest of then, eight children, the four older ones being girls, I was needed as a farm hand on the farm. As a farm and field hand, I was milking cows, pulling a crosscut saw, and plowing crops with a horse- and mule-drawn plow and cultivator. These jobs I did not begrudge, but I took a measure of pride that I had the strength and maturity to be entrusted with these normally adult jobs.

But the world was opening up to me through a battery-powered radio. At this time, public electrification services had not come to our area. As I listened to news reports, public service programs and even soap operas, I knew my future was beyond the limiting boundaries of this farm and even this county.

Often, standing out in the cotton field, in the blazing sun, shaded by a broad-brim straw hat, wiping the sweat from my brow, leaning on a hoe handle, and dreaming of the day I would take wings and fly away, not literally, to that great big world out there.

Twenty-Three

So here I stood at the door of opportunity with a chance to prove myself. There were local, inward, and outward departments in this building. I was assigned to outward, which meant long distance. After giving notice of leaving Sears, I began a week of training with other trainees on a mock-up switchboard. This panel contained apparatus for controlling the operation of circuits with jacks, cords, and plugs. The headset was a listening device worn over the head with a tiny microphone in the mouthpiece for two-way connection with the customer. Each place called by Long Distance was recorded by hand on a card. Many codes and abbreviations were used. When the connection was made and the talking began, the operator stamped the time on the card. When the connection was finished, a light came on, and the card was stamped again, giving the length of time of the conversation for which the party was being charged.

While in training, we were plugged in to other operators to monitor their routine. Also, we were told that we would be monitored at random to evaluate our performance. We were instructed to use scripted words and phrases and were not to talk to the customer in an informal manner. Of course, clarity and a smiling voice were expected. Stress was put on diction, especially the numerals: five was "fiive" and nine was "nyun." We were not to get involved if the caller was angry or upset. If the first attempt to make a call could not be completed, it could be put on hold and tried later at the caller's request.

And most importantly, we took an oath that we would not divulge or disclose anything we heard of any connection or communication.

The position at the switchboard was an assigned revolving seat with back and footrests and a niche in the back for handbags. We were seated in a long line, elbow to elbow, to adjacent operators. Behind the operators, the chief operator sat in an elevated chair, also in headset, watching closely all operations. If there was any difficulty or problem with the customer or connection, she was right there to assist and over-rule if necessary.

At this time in the 1940s, all operators were of the feminine gender. But always around the perimeters of the switchboards, and sometimes above the panels, were men with Western Electric installing and repairing equipment. They were always quiet and focused on their own tasks at hand. Sometimes a few words might be said in passing in the elevator, but that was the extent of communication with them.

There were two kinds of long distance calls: station-to-station and person-to-person. Timing began when the connection was made on station-to-station calls. For person-to-person calls, no charges were made until the person called was there and ready to talk. Many times, the person called could be reached at another number. The operator would try the second number — sometimes to another city — before the called person could be reached. If the person called could not be reached at the immediate attempts, the call could be put on hold and tried later.

Long distance calls made from pay phones demanded extra care and attention. These were the days before the telephone credit or calling cards. The user must either pay for the call before the talking began or charge the call to the number being called. If paying on the spot, the operator consulted a rate book and quoted the charge for a three-minute call. The caller then deposited the amount by coins, quarters, dimes or nickels, into a slot and chute receptacle. As each coin hit a bell, it gave a ping that gave the operator the value of the coin. Then she would flip a tab on the board to release the coins into the repository of the phone. If the operator failed to secure the coins, the next operation of the phone would release the coins out through the return slot into the hands of a surprised caller.

Sometimes the user would talk beyond the three-minute prepaid; when he hung up, the operator would immediately ring the pay phone back and insist he deposit the amount he now owed the telephone company. Most of the time the caller complied, but other times he was long gone. If the party placed a collect call to the number called, the operator would say clearly and emphatically, "I have a collect call from 'John Doe.' Will you accept the charge?" The answer must be a definite "yes" before the connection was made.

Being a beginner with no seniority, I was put on a split shift with hours such as 9:00 a.m. to 1:00 p.m. and then back for hours 4:00 to 8:00 p.m. or 7:00 to 11:00 p.m. Needless to say I spent quite a bit of time on city conveyances going back and forth to work. The Telephone Company was there to serve the public seven days a week, which meant I worked most Sundays, usually having one Sunday off each month. There was a Toddle House near the telephone building where I ate most of my meals. Goose liver sandwiches became one of my favorite fast foods.

Even though the war was over, besides the personal calls, there were increasing business calls and frequent calls from military bases to other military posts, sometimes for a General. I can't remember having any calls to foreign countries, but there were ship-to-shore connections. There were calls to Hollywood. I especially remember a call to Deanna Durbin, an actress of renown and at that time, one of the most idolized young women in America. I remember making a call to Smiley Burnette, who was Gene Autry, America's singing cowboy's, sidekick.

I was amused many times when "Yankee" operators tried to pronounce some of the Southern towns—for instance Kosciusko, Mississippi or Obion, Tennessee. The local pronunciation was "Obine," but they called it "O-be-on," rightly so. I'm sure they were amused, bemused, and confused at the Southern bells' pronunciations of many places above the Mason-Dixon line. At this time, I became aware of the in-bred "Southern accent" and began to make an effort to shed this verbal image of a rural, unsophisticated country bump-kin. I took note of the precise enunciation and choice words of people of stature, such a radio news reporters and other media personnel. This mimicking must have had some effect, as over the years, some have expressed surprise that I was Southern-born and reared.

The adventure and diversity of this job was not work but fun and a challenge each day. I would leave from work as rested and relaxed as when I reported for duty. Even the mental exertion was stimulating. I learned and remembered most of the telephone numbers of the main businesses, hotels, and other organizations of the city, which gave more compe-tence and alacrity for my job.

It was now early December. I was pleased with my tract record on my new job and felt that my supervisors were too. Little did I realize that this month was going to be the most life-changing experience of my life. An article in *The Com-mercial Appeal* got my attention. It told of a new organization, The Memphis Union Mission, a church and civic-supported project sponsored by T. Walker Lewis and other businessmen of the city. The Rescue Mission had been in operation several months and was proving to be "the church in overalls down-town." Its energetic and dynamic director, Jimmy Stroud, saw the need to reach out to the young people also. In June, a weekly Saturday night rally called Youth for Christ had been started at the Mission and was soon moved to Character Build-ers Hall on South Claybrook Street. A picture along with the article showed young people singing and giving testimonies of their life in Jesus Christ. The reporter was impressed with the increasing attendance and the enthusiasm of the young people. As I read the words and scanned the picture, I had a warm, urgent feeling to know this source of joy and purpose for my life.

I had not attended church one time since coming to Memphis. I had no appetite for religion as I had observed it in my home and community. My father was a very self-righteous man, abhorring any vice like drinking strong drinks or cursing, but was totally lacking in affection or concern for my worth and future. He was strict to a fault, not allowing me to have any friends. The last year or so, he kept me from attending the yearly revival meeting at the local church, which served as a social occasion for the young people in that rural area. This restriction was to prevent the possibility that some interested boy might wish to escort me home. So when I left home for the big city and job, I had never had a date with the opposite sex.

Earlier, when I was about thirteen or fourteen, a Baptist preacher and two college girls from nearby Union University at Jackson came out on Sunday afternoons for services at the two-room schoolhouse where I attended school from third to eighth grades. As we sat at our school desks, the preacher would preach and tell us Bible truths. The college girls were aids and personal workers. One of the girls made a lasting impression on me. She was so pretty, friendly and concerned about us. In my tender emotions and imagination, I thought I would like to be like her when I grew up. As the preacher preached the Gospel and that all had sinned and Jesus Christ came to be our Savior, I knew I needed to heed his words for my life. But under the situation in my home — with constant threats, bickering, and quarrelling — I could not be a good Christian, so I would wait for a better time to begin my Christian life.

The article in the newspaper had also gotten the attention of my older friends across the hall. Even though they did not consider themselves of the younger crowd, they agreed that this is what I needed, and we made plans to attend the next rally. We went by city bus, as usual, and found the hall overflowing with enthusiastic young people singing and sharing their joy in the Lord. Three young men with trumpets filled the air with stirring music of Gospel hymns. The speaker, Dr. Merv Rosell, brought a rousing message from the Bible. I was overwhelmed. I had never experienced such a gathering of Christians before, with such warmth and love for each other and the Lord. This was what I needed and wanted. I did not go forward at the invitation, but determined in my heart that I would at the next meeting.

The following Saturday, I was scheduled to work and could not attend the rally. The next Saturday I was free and assumed my friends would go with me again. But they had made other plans to go downtown to the Convention Center for a Christmas Carol presentation. Still remembering my promise to myself, I got on the bus and went alone. Again I was thrilled and enthralled with the Spirit and seriousness of the event. The speaker brought a stirring but loving message I felt was just for me, presenting the claims of Jesus Christ on my life. I could hardly wait for the opportunity to go forward for salvation. As soon as the invitation song began:

> There is a fountain filled with blood,
> Drawn from Immanuels' vein's,
> And sinners plunged beneath that flood,
> Lose all their guilty stains.

I knew I was a guilty sinner, rising from my seat and making my way to the front. A young Christian lady led me aside and from her Bible read and showed to me John 1:12: "But as many as received him to them gave he power to become the sons of God, even to them that believe on His name." I knew I was believing and asking with all my heart for Jesus to forgive me of my sins and to become my Savior. The counselor later told me that she was from Minnesota. How she happened to be there, I do not know. I never saw her again. I went back to my place that night, not seeing anyone I knew, but knowing in my heart I had put my faith in the Lord Jesus Christ for salvation and that I wanted to live for Him.

The next morning when I awoke, I knew I was a new person in Christ Jesus. All my burdens had been lifted and my heart was overflowing with joy in my new found salvation. At the first opportunity, I humbly, but excitedly, told my friends across the hall of my experience at the rally. They were thrilled, but my roommate was very disinterested and seemed dubious about my attendance and experience at the rally. I was very puzzled; knowing she was a professing Christian, I assumed she would be happy for me.

Now that I was a new Christian, I wanted to know about the Bible and be with those who loved and served the Lord. There was a service at the Mission Chapel each evening with interesting speakers. The first night I was not scheduled to work, I went to the service, made up mostly guests of the Mission. This being all new to me, I quickly and quietly sat down in a secluded place. After an opening song or two, the director spied me from the pulpit and asked if I would tell everyone what the Lord had done for me at the Youth for Christ rally. Without hesitation, I was on my feet, nervous but eager to share with those, saved or unsaved, what the Lord had done for me and that my future was in His hands.

Twenty-Four

It was now the Christmas season. I would be working Christmas Eve and Christmas Day, as this was the busiest time of the year for the telephone company. Public communication systems and other public-servicing facilities would be on duty to connect the long-distanced families and friends.

I was looking forward to going home for a visit to share with my family my new experience as a Christian. In the meantime, I had written a letter to a former co-worker at the country store. This was an older man, with no family, who always seemed so lonely and was always very nice to me. I wanted him to know of my new experience, praying that he might find the Lord and know this peace and joy too.

When my schedule permitted enough time, I boarded that Greyhound bus to visit my family. Even though alone with my own thoughts on the one hundred-mile trip, I was rejoicing in my heart and anticipating sharing the good news with my parents. Even the whirring of those big Greyhound wheels seemed to be silently singing with me: "Thank you Lord for saving my soul, Thank you Lord for making me whole, Thank you Lord for giving to me, Thy great salvation so full and free." This being the first chorus I learned at Youth for Christ. Thinking my family would be thrilled about me being a new Christian, things were soon chilled. Mr. Chester, my older friend back at the country store, had shared with my father the letter I had written. He was irate and embarrassed and scolded me for sharing such personal things. My father, not only never talked of his own spiritual experience, but he certainly had an elongated list of "Thou shalt nots." This obsession of personal privacy was also true of his politics. He did vote in the general elections but never told anyone for whom he voted.

After returning back to Memphis and my job, I soon found a church home and family. My older friend was a member of the Kennedy Memorial Baptist Church. The congregation met in a modest bungalow right across the street from the expansive grounds of the Kennedy General Hospital. The combined living and dining room served as the sanctuary, the bedrooms for Sunday school rooms, and the kitchen as the nursery. The people and pastor received me with open arms. The pastor was a young man with beautiful wife and two young sons. My first step to becoming a member was to be baptized into the fellowship of the Church. Since this provisional building had no facilities for the mode of baptism required by Baptist Churches, the church requested, and was granted permission, to use the baptistry of a church nearby. I had never seen the performance of a baptism inside a church. In the country, all such religious rites were carried out in ponds, creeks, or rivers. All of the functions of this city church were new to me. I learned and claimed Philippians 4:13: " I can do all things through Christ who strengtheneth me." As a new member, I was given an offering envelope that had a designation "for tithes" I did not know the meaning of the word and quietly asked a nearby worshiper to explain. The hymns were new also. My exposure to church music had been the "Grand Ole Opry" style with morbid words and haunting tunes, or others with frivolous words set to syncopated rhythm and thumping beats. I was now learning the classic hymns of the church such as "Holy, Holy, Holy," "The Banner of the Cross," and "Footsteps of Jesus."

Not only was I learning new things at the church, I was learning the taste of new foods. My Sunday school teacher took our class home one day for lunch. She had prepared Italian spaghetti with red meaty sauce, hot airy rolls, and a tossed lettuce salad, which was all new to me.

During this time, many boarders, including me, were

becoming very discontented with circumstances at the boarding house on Lamar Avenue. The landlady was becoming more senile. Many of the residents began making other living arrangements, especially my roommate. Although she had helped me in finding a place to live and a better job, she remained detached and indifferent toward me. She found occasions to correct my grammar, which I accepted. For some reason she invited me to go with her to her home, a modest one, in Mississippi, one weekend. Although a responsible and prim and proper person, she bought her clothes at Woolworth's. Cotton housedresses, seemed to me, to be out of line with our kind of work. She was engaged to a soldier from Nebraska that she had met since coming to Memphis. Being preoccupied with plans for the future, she withdrew more and more and soon moved back to her married brother's home in another part of town. They eventually married and moved to California. In 1960, after I had married and had three children, we took a trip out west. I had her address and wrote that I would like to see her again. She immediately responded, indicating no interest in renewing our friendship.

After working several months at the telephone company, a job I dearly loved, it was time for my vacation. I had not made any plans. It was now early August, and one night the telephone rang. It was Mrs. Blagg from the Mission staff: "Want to go to Winona Lake Bible Conference with me this week?" That was it! So just a few hours before time for departure, I got an extra check, prepaid vacation pay from the telephone company.

Mr. Blagg took his wife and me to the train station. This would be my first train ride. We went in fine style—a sleeper Pullman, no less. Our ride overnight took us into Chicago, where we changed trains to Warsaw, Indiana. There, a member of the Memphis entourage, who was already there, met us at the train depot and took us to the conference center at Winona Lake. The site was located right on the lake where services were held at sunset. After a most palatable dinner, another service was held in the large Billy Sunday Tabernacle. During the day there were various Bible studies and displays.

A book store and small gift shop was owned and operated by Blanche and Virgil Brock, composers of the song "Beyond the Sunset." What a perfect setting for the inspiration of this beautiful song! It was at this bookstore I bought the classic devotional guide, *Streams in the Desert,* by Mrs. Charles Cowman.

Here, too, was the home of Mrs. Billy Sunday, the widow of the famous evangelist who used his baseball background and flamboyant manners to become the most popular evangelist of the time. He was supposed to have preached to over one hundred million people, a million having been converted to Christ in his campaigns. I assumed he had resided here until his death in 1935. One quiet afternoon Mrs. Sunday gave us a private tour of her home.

The famous singer and composer of gospel hymns, Homer Rodeheaver and his sister, Ruth Rodeheaver Thomas, also had a home here, situated on the lake. We were also invited to their home, which had an elevated deck that looked out over the lake. While we were viewing the beautiful surroundings, he jokingly called me his "Memphis sweetheart."

Those from Memphis included Jimmy Stroud, director of the Mission and Youth for Christ; his secretary, Mrs. Verla Pettit; and Dr. & Mrs. L. L. Carter, physician and friends of the Memphis ministries. There had been other weeks for youth groups, but this week, I was one of the few young people present.

It was a glorious week with chapel services, Bible studies, and beautiful music. Dr. Bob Jones, Jr., was the main speaker, but all the other board of directors were present, including Dr. J. Palmer Muntz, the director and pastor of the Dazenovia Park Baptist Church of Buffalo, New York; Mrs. Sunday; Mr. Rodeheaver; and R. G. LeTourneau, the inventor and industrialist and manufacturer of heavy equipment for road construction. Mr. LeTourneau was a giant of a man in many ways, a generous contributor to Christian causes, tall and stout of stature. As he sat on the platform one night with his legs crossed, the bottom of one shoe was exposed, revealing a big hole in the sole. This seemed to add to his humility and greatness.

After the main service in the tabernacle, things became more casual. Some would stroll around the grounds by the ice cream shop and take in the more informal gatherings such as missionary displays and presentations in smaller buildings on the compound. One night, as Mrs. Blagg and I were walking around, a large gathering on the outside of a hall got our attention. We came in closer to see what was attracting so many on-lookers in the doorway and those looking in the windows. We could hear music and laughter coming from the inside, so we edged inside to get a closer view. To our surprise, there were two of the main persons of the week upon the platform putting on a "Gay Nineties Revue," complete with costumes and songs of the period. As a young Christian I was rather taken back by this vaudeville rendition on the Bible Conference grounds. The two performers were, nonetheless, Homer Rodeheaver and Dr. Bob Jones, Jr.

But that did not deter me from the blessings of the week. On our last night as Dr. Paul W. Rood spoke on "Flaming Youth or Youth Aflame," the Lord spoke to my heart, and I answered the call to full-time Christian service, stepping out and down the sawdust trail of the Tabernacle, making my public vow: "Wherever He leads I'll go, Wherever He leads I'll go; I'll follow my Christ who loves me so, Wherever He leads I'll go."

The next morning, we were homeward bound, back to Chicago by train. In Chicago, we had a lengthy layover for our connection back to Memphis. Taking advantage of the free time, we walked along the Michigan lakefront to Soldier Field, the home of the professional football Chicago Bears. Mrs. Blagg captured the moment and place with her camera. She had been a wonderful traveling companion and tour guide for me. I had been blessed beyond measure with her friendship and spiritual guidance.

Down from the lake of inspiration to the plains of duty at Memphis, I resumed my position at the switchboard, attending the youth rallies and sharing my testimony as my work schedule permitted. I was asked to meet in the studio of a local radio station to give my testimony in a pre-segment of the daily radio program, "Above the Clouds." This was the theme song of the Youth for Christ rallies. The chorus was composed by Mervin E. Rosell, the noted author and speaker. His message and goal of the words were to entreat young people to aim high to avoid the pitfalls of life. "Seek those things which are above where Christ sitteth on the right hand of God." (Colossians 3:1) In a moment of meditation he wrote these words: "Above the clouds the sun is always shining. Above the clouds all tears are wiped away. Our loving God will lift you from sin's darkness. Above the clouds into eternal day."

Sometime later, Jimmy Stroud, the Youth for Christ director, and Mel Larson, editor of the national *Youth for Christ Magazine*, asked me to meet them at the Britling Cafeteria for breakfast and an interview concerning my conversion at YFC. They were also interested in my recent trip to Winona Lake Conference and my subsequent dedication to Christian service. The article appeared, along with my picture, in the March 1947 issue under the title, "She had the Wrong Number." The next article in the issue, "The Measure of Youth" was by Merve Rosell, none other than the one whose message had made such an impact at my conversion. A few pages over in the photographic section was a congenial pose of Cliff Barrows and Billy Graham at York, England, in the citywide youth crusade and another photo from Newcastle-on-the-Tyne where five hundred found Christ in the one-week campaign. A few pages on, there was youthful George Beverly Shea, announcing his own songbook, *Singing I Go*, and singing I go, praising the Lord.

Twenty-Five

My church family was my source of strength and belonging. I was at each service when not working. My schedule kept me from most of the mid-week services and the business meetings. Unknown to me, an incident had become known that shocked the church. One evening while at the switchboard, during a slow time, an operator who was attending the church whispered to me, "Do you know what has happened at church?" I answered, "No," anxious to know what she was leading up to. Her reply shocked my unbelieving and naïve ears. "Our pastor, Brother Daniel, has been caught in a very compromising situation with Johnny Doe on the grounds of Shelby High School. The deacons are asking him to leave the church." The other person involved was a handsome, stripling of a young man of the young peoples' group. The revelation shocked me beyond words. First of all, the pastor seemed to be the ideal man for the small but growing church. He had a beautiful wife and two young sons and everything seemed as it should be.

Secondly, this revolting behavior was new to me. I did not know such attractions existed between men. My country raising had not prepared me for such anomalies. I did know about hermaphrodites from freak shows at the county fair. Stunned with disbelief, I was very disappointed and puzzled. The pastor had been very supportive and helpful to me as a new Christian and had baptized me in a very meaningful service. I knew this rite had been performed as unto the Lord. Feeling confident in his position at the time, I felt no need for the baptism to be repeated. The church had to deal with the disturbing disclosure, and the pastor was dismissed.

The Union Mission continued to have an impact on the city of Memphis. More ministries were added which included the telephone outreach. Volunteers were needed to man the telephones. On my days free from work, I made myself available and enjoyed the contact with those who needed a kind voice and a word of encouragement.

Cards were placed in public places like telephone booths with a number to call for help and information. Each week a certain Scripture verse was chosen as a greeting to the curious caller and an invitation to the mission services. This encounter with a total stranger demanded discretion of any disclosure of personal information. On one occasion, after being at the post for a while, I returned to my place of abode. Unfortunately, the volunteer that took my place at the telephone was not as discreet as he or she should have been. A caller whom I had dealt with earlier, called again, being inquisitive about me, including a description of me. The volunteer disclosed more than was permissible and proper. This was a week of special meetings at the Mission chapel, and I had gone back for the service, since it was my day off from work. The structure of the chapel opened right onto the sidewalk, with a large glass window in the front. Before the beginning of the service, it became apparent to the director from the platform that someone was casing the crowd through the front window. He was able to determine that the person's interest was focused on me.

The director went outside and demanded that the interloper move on, but he continued to loiter the premises. After the service, I was warned to be careful that someone was stalking me. I had no alternative but to board the city bus, which fortunately stopped in front of the mission, to go to my place. A certain car hugged the bus all the way to my stop, which was clear across town. I had to walk two blocks from the bus stop to my place of residence. It was now about 9:00 p.m. and dark on the residential street. The bus turned at the corner at the stop, but the car continued slowly with dim lights right behind me. Walking briskly and praying hard, I was able to get to my place without harm.

At the time my work schedule on the split shift had me working until 11:00 p.m., after which I had to walk those two blocks from the bus stop each night. How and if this was the same stalker, a car continued to follow slowly behind me for the two blocks. At this time of night, all residents were inside, and the outside was dark and deserted. Then one night, a man figure was standing in a yard near the sidewalk. I became aware of him in the darkness, but I had nowhere to go and could do nothing but keep walking toward my place. How I prayed for the Lord's protection as I hurried by, pretending not to see him, as he stood motionless, staring at me. The Lord heard my prayer, and I made it safely inside for the night. The next day I went to the personnel office and requested the all-night shift, and it was granted to me immediately.

After the frightening experience of being stalked and the uncertain developments at the church, I decided I wanted to move from this area of the city. So again, I sought and found a new place of abode in South Memphis. It was a modest home in a quiet neighborhood. The man of the house was a fireman, and the wife was a stay-at-home mother with two small children. They were Christians but of another denomination. The wife was very austere in manner and appearance. She wore no make up and thought that even wearing a wedding band was a sin. In getting acquainted with me, one of the first questions to me was "Have you been sanctified?"

It was a new location, but I soon found a nearby church of like faith of my first church. After attending two services, I went forward for transfer of membership. The procedure was followed, but there was no further contact with me. No one reached out to me in fellowship or interest. Seemingly, I was a nobody to them. In the meantime, one of the local pastors, Rev. Milton Wright, taught a Personal Workers class on Monday nights at the Mission. He was also present at the Youth for Christ rallies, and I was aware of his interest and concern for the young people. He pastored a church of another denomination, the Cumberland Presbyterian Church, not far from my residence. I joined this church, made up mostly of older people, but they were loving and kind and made me feel special.

The ladies of the church had a Bible study on Thursday mornings. Oftentimes I would join them when free from work. I was especially intrigued and fascinated by the interpretation of the twelfth chapter of II Corinthians. From verses two through seven, the teacher told of how the Apostle Paul was caught up to the third heaven and when he descended back to earth, he landed on a thorn. Consequently, he had to endure the "thorn in the flesh" for the rest of his life.

It was now winter, not only cold outside, but cold inside. My room and bathroom were never comfortably warm. Even moreso, the atmosphere was cold also, and the family was very distant. Even though we did not share the same church beliefs, we were still Christians. There was only a wall between us, but they stayed in the back room of the house. I occupied the front bedroom and would go and come without seeing any of them.

I was working five nights a week, attending the youth rallies and church services on Sundays. I was lonely and seemed isolated from friends and former church family. Oftentimes at night, looking out from the city bus windows, I could see inside homes with warm lights and family members moving about or at the dinner table. How I longed for my own home with such love and security.

Then matters worsened. I became very sick and unable to report to work. Of course I called in and reported my illness. With a terrible headache, I was running a temperature and could hardly breathe. After two or three days, I called some friends, who in turn, found a doctor who made house calls. He came and gave me a shot; the diagnosis: acute sinusitis, my nasal passages being so small. I must have bed rest until recovery. Since I had been getting my meals on the outside or snacking in my room, I had no choice but to share in the family's meals, which were bland and stiffly served. But feeling so bad, I could eat but very little.

Rather than to be a burden to this family, I called my

father back home to come and get me until I was well. He came right away. A younger friend with a new car who knew the city of Memphis, graciously came with him and found my place without difficulty. I was home about a week, and feeling much better, ready to return to my job. Since I had missed several days of work and with some medical expense, I had to ask my father, for the first and only time, for financial assistance. So back to Memphis by Greyhound, I resumed my work with the telephone company.

When my friends learned I was back, they were surprised. My landlady had led them to believe that I was gone for good. Immediately, I began to make plans to find another place of lodging.

My life assumed a degree of normalcy at another place of abode. A few days later, while downtown, I went into a drugstore for some needed items. In those days, places to shop (like Woolworth's) were located in the downtown area. While in the store, a man approached me and began telling me of a special meeting at the Convention Center, the Association of Beauty Operators and Hairdressers of the Mid-South.

There had been a write-up in the Commercial Appeal telling of this special occasion. Manufacturers of beauty products were giving demonstrations of different hairstyles and styling products. The gentleman said he had noticed my hair and wondered if I would be interested in being a model for the convention. Of course, I was flattered, but was hesitant to make a commitment until I knew more of the working arrangements and compensations. He handed me his business card with his name and telephone number. Yes, I was interested, but I thought of the word "model," wondering what this could mean — perhaps even wearing a bathing suit. As a Christian young woman, I felt I would be very uncomfortable in this compromising situation. The next day, I called him and asked if the job might require me wearing a bathing suit and he answered "quite possibly so." My answer was "No, I'm not interested." A few weeks later, another short article appeared in the same newspaper. This same man had been questioned by the police as several questionable photos of young women had been found in his possession.

It was now April of 1947. Spring was dawning in this bustling city of which I had been a part for almost two years. The country seemed quieter, but grievances of workers of AT&T had not been settled, there being the threat of a walk-out in the nation's first phone strike. Thinking and hoping this would be a short-time stoppage. I was not too concerned, assuming I "could ride out the storm."

On the same day, April 7, the news media reported the death of Henry Ford at the age of eighty-three years. Every American, young and old, rich or poor, from the halls of aca-demia to the plains of the prairie, knew the name of this per-sonage and had been affected by the accomplishments of this great industrialist. His accomplishments were amazing: he was born on a farm near Detroit, a run-away at sixteen, and became a mechanic who tinkered with odd machines; but he had a dream. With much faith, a small investment and a vi-sion, came forth a Model T automobile, to a Model A, and before the war, he had sold twenty-nine million Fords. He became the father of the mass production system, built on the assembly and conveyor belt systems. His genius served America during the war as he directed production of Ford motored Liberator bombers, tanks, tank-destroyers, and jeeps. As master of this massive industry, he believed in high wages and short hours. From the early days of his endeavors, his workers were paid well.

Could this not be a rebuke to such giant companies as AT&T, as an incentive for its workers to demand a small in-crease in wages, improved working conditions, and better benefits?

For the first, time women hit the picket lines en masse—two hundred thirty thousand—the largest number of the fair sex to ever participate in a strike. Placards proclaimed "The Girl with the Smile is Gone for Awhile." We were gone from the switchboard, but we were present at the union meetings to plan and plot the course of action to win this battle. Some of the meetings were a little raucous, but determination and

216

dedication to the cause over-ruled.

We were assigned hours to walk the picket lines, wearing sandwich boards. These were two boards hung from the shoulders, one on the front and one on the back, carrying concise words to convey our cause and rights. As six of us in stride marched sedately back and forth in front of the main building, a passerby came in very close and blurted out, "strong back, weak brain."

As we filled in our hours of duty for our cause, we were disgusted to see a few of our fellow-workers cross the picket line and enter the building to cover the many empty spaces on the switchboards. Some of the picketers called them "scabs," a term given to those who refused to strike. One of my friends from Youth for Christ fell into this category, believing it was sin to partake in this aggressive action. I believed otherwise: that we were doing this for the benefit of all, even for those who refused to extend themselves for this cause. When we won, they would benefit also. Other incidents happened on the picket line, one in particular, the Orkin Pest Control truck parked in front of the main building and two men jumped out with their pest-fighting apparatus and crossed the picket line. The picketers heckled them, "Go on in; there are pests in there."

Picket lines were at other small branch offices scattered across the city. The strike was now going into days, and we were desperate for this fractious stalemate to be resolved. A special meeting was called to gather at a branch office clear across town. From there a cadre of strikers, including myself, marched back across the city to the main office with placards, singing and chanting, making our cause and determination known to pedestrians on the streets, passengers in cars, and all who would listen and support us.

The strike was going into the third week. It seemed some of my friends were becoming concerned about me. My pastor, the Reverend Milton Wright, and his wife invited my friend and me (the one who refused to strike) to their home for supper. When we had finished eating, the pastor reached for his Bible and began sharing a devotional thought with us. The passage he had chosen was I Timothy 3:1-7. He emphatically read verse three: "Not given to wine, no striker, not guilty of filthy lucre, but patient, not a brawler, not covetous. My friend, the non-striker, dropped her head, glanced my way, knowing the Scripture verse was meant for me. The subtle, open rebuke did not bother me, so I made no comment, thanked them for their hospitality and made my departure.

There was still no sign that the strike was going to be settled soon. Even though long distance and toll calls had been cut to 20% of the normal volume of the Bell system, AT&T refused the offer for the half, the union originally demanded. I was running out of money for food, bus fare, and room rent. Since my Christian friends were not in favor of my participation in this labor union action, I was getting no sympathy from them. I had no recourse but to pack my suitcase, head for the Greyhound bus station, and buy a ticket with the little money remaining and go back to the farm. A cloud of uncertainty settled over me and on me. I did not have a job, and if and when the strike was over, would I be able to reclaim it?

When I arrived home, my family did not seem surprised, so I had little explaining to do. It was now late spring and the weather was perfect. I began cleaning and dusting the back bedrooms, not knowing where I was going from here. On the third day after working inside all morning and having lunch, I sat down on the edge of the front porch for a break. Shortly thereafter, a car came slowly down the road and turned into the yard. At first I did not recognize the strange car, but out stepped Mr. and Mrs. Blagg, workers at the Memphis Union Mission. They had driven one hundred miles and inquired at the country store the direction to my father's farm. The strike had been settled, and I must be back to report to my job on the night shift tonight or I would lose my job. I knew the Lord had intervened and sent these precious people to retrieve me and get me back in His way.

Not only was I back on the job, but a new place to live was available. The Mission had secured a large three-story house on Popular Avenue for the director and his family. The second floor was for guest speakers and the third floor quarters served as a refuge for girls and women with various needs. Behind this commodious and classic home was a large garage with space overhead for an apartment for working girls. So this was my new home, adequate for me and two other girls who worked during the day. The location was right on the city bus line and not far from the telephone company. The Lord was providing my every need.

Although I had worked the night shift for some time, the daytime temperature in the top floor apartment, without air-conditioning, made it difficult to sleep in the day. So going in to work at 11:00 p.m., without adequate sleep, found me about 3:00 a.m. almost falling asleep on the switchboard. Things were quiet and calls were few, but we must be alert for those who were awake and needed a connection with a friend or family member. Sometimes after the connection was made and the talking began between the two parties, I would pull the key back to hear them and doze off a bit. When the conversation stopped, I would snap out of my nap and stamp the timing of the call.

Many of the persons calling in the wee hours of morning were lonely, distraught, or slightly inebriated. I remember one certain call made by a desperate man to another party in a fractured relationship who was threatening to shoot himself. Obligingly, he would get off the carpet before he pulled the trigger.

At times when business was very slow and only one or two operators were needed to man the switchboard, the chief operator would pull the other operators off the board to help with filing the cards. A large table held a filing system with cards of cities called during the day. Each city was alphabetized and recorded. An interesting fact came from this procedure; there were more places in the U.S. that began with the letter "C" than any other.

Sometimes when the board was silent, a light for service was welcomed. Oftentimes, it was a lonely person who could not sleep and would ask us frivolous or personal questions, which we could not answer. I used poor judgment when one male caller began asking the color of my hair. "Are you a blond?" "No." "Is it black?" "No" "Is it red?" "Yes." He called again in a few minutes and another operator picked up the call and he asked for the red-headed operator. She embarrassed me and taught me a lesson as she called down the line, "Somebody wants to speak to that red-headed operator." I did not respond, but busied myself with other duties. Sure enough, that morning at 7:00 a.m. when I exited the elevator into the corridor to the front entrance, there was a man waiting for me. He appeared to be about thirty-something and in some type of service job. He walked alongside of me to the bus stop and wanted me to go with him for breakfast. I said "No, thank you," and got on the bus and never saw or heard from him again.

A young man, Calvin by name, of the Youth for Christ rallies, invited me to a Bible class on Thursday mornings, to be taught by Mrs. Eugene Jones at her home on Madison Avenue. I was very much impressed by her knowledge of the Word. She had developed a course, covering the entire scope of the Bible from Genesis 1 to Revelation 22. This class was for young people. She also taught an adult class one evening each week and a teachers' training class for child evangelism workers.

Besides her depth and method for teaching the Bible, Mrs. Jones had a burden and concern for young people, that they might find the Lord's will for their lives. Already she had helped and directed several young people into Bible colleges—some were at Moody Bible Institute in Chicago; others were in Columbia Bible College in South Carolina; and still others were in other parts of the country. In her office, she had pictures on the wall of those already in training, which she jokingly, but proudly, called her "Rogues Gallery."

Eventually I found out that she had an initial interest and influence in the work of the Union Mission and Youth for Christ, but early on, she and the director had a disagreement and came to a parting of the ways. It had been her idea and project to decorate the walls of the youth lounge with musical scores of gospel songs and choruses. This alienation remained a mystery to me.

It was now early summer. Mrs. Jones had trained teachers and sponsored a Child Evangelism Vacation Bible School in a church located in a black section of Memphis. Since I had mornings free, she sent another Bible class member and me over to assist in the Vacation Bible School. The church was filled and bubbling over with eager youngsters. When they sang "Onward Christian Soldiers," the rafters would almost rise with their volume and enthusiasm. The other helper had red hair also, and she, being in the ebony midst, was a sight to behold. I, in turn, knew I was appearing likewise on my side of the aisle of the church.

My main responsibility was to help with the games on the outside. I had never been close to black people in any situation. As I held these small, sweaty, grimy hands and we played "ring around the roses," and "drop the handkerchief," I realized that their warm, squeezing little fingers were as human as any little white hand. This was my first experience in any Christian work, and I knew I wanted to be more involved in other meaningful things.

The urge to serve the Lord grew more, but I knew there must be training, and I did not have the means to pursue a college education. Furthermore, I had only an eighth grade education, which was an obstacle in itself. Later, in a private moment with Mrs. Jones, I confided in her my desire and determination to get training for the Lord's work. The following week she called, asking me to come to her home. Not knowing the reason for the visit, she told me she was impressed with my faith and dedication and that she had a special school in mind for me. If I were willing to step out on faith, she would see that I had the means to attend school. An application was made and I was accepted for the fall semester. I would continue working at my job until the first of September.

Twenty-Six

With the second year at the telephone company, I had already made plans for my vacation the second week of August. This had been the time for the yearly revival at my parents' home church for years. Through the year, the church held services once a month, but the revival week was the most important event of the year. August was about the only time the families were relieved of field work, as the crops were laid by until harvest time in the fall.

Becoming more burdened for my family's spiritual status, I wanted to be with them during this special time. Since I was being nurtured in a scripturally sound and well-ordered church, I longed for my family, especially my younger sisters and brothers, to have this same experience and opportunity. I wanted to share with them the reality and job of knowing the Lord and living for Him.

As my vacation time drew near, I shopped for some cool summer frocks. Besides being a confident, mature Christian, I wanted to appear as a composed, competent young businesswoman. But knowing the folkways and mindset of this isolated area, I expected some skepticism. No doubt, I would appear as a spectacle to some: who does she think she is? On an earlier visit home, I had attended church for one service. As usual, I took my Bible. As I started up the steps, one curious cousin seeing my Bible tauntingly said, "Are you going to preach today?"

So on a hot day in August, I arrived at my homeplace with suitcase in hand and a heart full of hope and concern for my family and others whom I might encounter. As always, everyone looked forward to revival time—the highlight of the church year. It was a time of re-gathering of friends and neighbors and a refilling of the Spirit to their souls. There would be rapturous singing, shouting, and probably, scorching sermons. Even moreso, there were silent burdens for family members and friends who needed to get right with the Lord. Even some of the deacons who had been lax in attending the once-a-month meetings would be present each night, pleading and prodding penitent sinners to come to the alter to pray through for salvation.

The pastor, who was also the evangelist, was loved by all the people and highly respected by all who knew him. At the first service, it was obvious that he realized the responsibility that was his for the coming week. He not only must preach the Word in gentle tones about the love of Jesus, but must also exhort and warn in stern words of the coming judgment, to those who would not repent of their sins and make heaven their home. He must make them see, through the power of the Holy Spirit, that this is the time to seek the Lord. The singers were assembled and smiling as the pianist's warm and eager fingers hit the first chord. The amen corner was filled with the older men, and the women and children filled the wooden pews. On the back rows were the young people, squirming and squiggling with the songbooks. The open windows breathed in the night air, and fluttering moths flitted in, being attracted to the naked light bulbs. On the outside, lightning bugs twinkled in the darkness, along with the smoldering, burning ends of cigarettes being puffed by the curious, wayward prodigals leaning on parked cars and pickup trucks.

When the momentum moved on up to high tempo on the inside, those on the outside couldn't resist coming closer, some peeking in; their peering eyes could be seen by the devout and proper ones who were gently sweeping the charged air with funeral home fans. The preacher preached with a throbbing tongue from a gasping throat, energized by a burning heart. His whole body lurched up and down on his tiptoes, stomping his heels, his arms flinging through the air, and his fists pounding the pulpit. With sweat dripping from his bold and furrowed brow, he took time out to pull from his pocket a snow white twisted handkerchief to mop up the fervent perspiration and take a deep breath. He felt himself a firebrand burning with a message from the King of Kings, the Lord of heaven, to ignite the cold hearts of men, women and young people and to save their souls from that place where the fire is never quenched.

Now it was the critical time, from preaching to pleading to praying through at the altar. The invitation number was announced. How many hearts had been pricked with conviction of their sins? How many wanted the sin problem settled tonight? The hymn began, "O Why Not Tonight?"

> O do not let the Word depart
> And close thine eyes against the light
> Poor sinner, harden not your heart,
> Be saved, oh tonight.
> Oh, why not tnight?
> Oh, why not tonight?
> Wilt thou be saved,
> Then why not tonight?

As the song continued into the second verse, no one had responded to the altar call. Then out stepped two or three deacons from the amen corner and scanned the waiting crowd. Who was going to make the move tonight? Then the men zeroed in on certain ones whom they felt needed to make a move for salvation. They pled with them to make this the night to get right with the Lord. For some, this personal prod was all they needed, as they almost ran to the altar where older Christians had fallen on their knees to pray for any seekers. For others, the prodding and pleading was of no avail, as they stood stiffer and hardened their hearts even more.

As the responses slackened, so did the singing, and quietly, the crowd dispersed with those seeking salvation still kneeling at the mourner's bench. Some remained there for some time before things were settled in their souls.

So at the beginning of the revival week, I quietly and prayerfully merged in with my homefolks. Since I had not been a regular attendee at the church services, my presence must have been a curiosity for most of them. It was probably known by some of them that I had left home and gone to Memphis for work. Now I was in the midst of the people and this special week. Since my father was so reticent about personal and spiritual matters, I'm sure he had not shared with any of them of my conversion experience.

The pastor soon became aware of my presence and came the following afternoon to the home of my folks. There on the front porch of the farmhouse, he fervently prayed for my sisters and brothers and for the continuing week of revival.

The next evening, as the crowd gathered for the service, one of the deacons, an older man, came close for some casual remarks. Our talk gave me an opportunity to tell him of my new-found salvation. His response: "Huh! I didn't think they preached enough grace in Memphis for anyone to be saved." By now I felt my presence was more warmly received, so I joined other praying Christians at the altar each night.

At home during the day, I was much aware of my unsaved sisters and the brother who was at the age of accountability. The next day, while drawing water from the backyard well, my nine-year-old sister, Maria, came up to me, shy, but wanting my attention. I asked her how old she was, to impress upon her, the need, even at this age, to be saved. I stressed to her that she needed to invite Jesus into her heart as her Savior. That evening, during the invitation, she went forward for salvation, and she has been a steadfast and joyful Christian ever since. I could only pray that the seed of truth for conviction had been sown in the hearts of the rest of the family.

My father had made a confession of faith during his earlier illness and had been baptized in 1939. My mother, a devout Christian woman coming from another denomination, had never been baptized. During the week of services, three of my sisters, including the nine-year-old, made professions of saving faith in Christ, and along with my mother, were baptized with other converts at a nearby farm pond.

The week was over; church members had been revived, and souls had been saved. I had been blessed by the fervent (fervid) sermons of the dedicated pastor-preacher and the love and concern he had for his flock, the people of the Church. My heart had been stirred as I witnessed lost souls coming to the saving Christ of Calvary. My own faith had been renewed, and my prayers would be for all of them.

The week had been a time of rest and relaxation from city life. The country air and quietness had been so refreshing. Even the August heat inside my folks' home had been cooled by electric fans. This was the first year to have the services of electricity. TVA had finally reached this part of the country. No more need for kerosene lamps, wood-burning cook stoves, ice boxes, and tubs with scrub boards.

For many it was a new frontier, both spiritually and practically. I was facing a new frontier also. In two weeks I would be leaving my telephone company job to enter a Bible Institute for training in Christian service. I had casually shared this with the pastor in the presence of my father. As I disclosed more details of this venture of faith and of a dear Christian woman in Memphis making this possible, my father smirked and scowled as he remarked, "You are going to be living on charity." The pastor came to my defense, rebuking my father, saying if that was true, he had been living on charity for many years.

So with suitcase again in hand and a little sadness in my heart, I boarded the bus back to Memphis. The one hundred miles gave me a quiet time to reflect back on the blessings of the past week. The touch of home had been good for me in more ways than one; platters of fried chicken, Crowder peas picked fresh from the field, and bountiful banana pudding prepared by my mother's tender heart and serving hands. To be back again with my younger brothers and sisters was a delight. Seeing them in their youthful innocence and natural energy brought joy and a prayer to my heart. My father had no words for me, but I was sure he was pleased with my chosen plan for my life. I did appreciate my family, but I had never been homesick or had any thought of returning permanently back to this familiar place. I knew my life belonged to the Lord, and He was leading one step at a time.

I was soon back in the halls of AT&T for a few days. Soon, I would submit my intent to leave my job by a certain day. It was a somber time. I had enjoyed the work and had so many interesting experiences. But I knew in my heart even greater things were waiting for me as I obeyed the Lord's leading. In just a few days, Mrs. Jones, my benefactor, called and asked me to meet her downtown at a certain department store. We shopped for school-wear, underwear, sleepwear, and hosiery. She knew more of what a student living in a dormitory would need than I, which meant sheets, pillowcases, blankets, and towels. Together, we chose the items I would need. Then she paid the total amount for the purchases.

Later, somewhere, she found a second-hand wardrobe trunk. On the day of my departure, she and her willing husband came to my place and loaded up all my belongings and drove me to the train station. They then purchased my ticket to Pikeville, Kentucky, the site of the Southland Bible Institute, where I would be an eager and studious student in days to come.

All aboard with the wardrobe trunk in the baggage car and a bag in hand stuffed with crackers and cookies to tide me over the night, I was ready for the ride across the long state of Tennessee. I had two coach buddies, a young man and a lady, also students sponsored by Mrs. Jones. We only knew each other slightly, but the long ride would give us time to chit and chat, stretch and squirm, as we faced each other on the reversible seats. The unknown place and untried future gave us the fidgets, but not fear, as we had faith and confidence that we were following the Lord's leading.

The young man, abounding with nervous energy, was full of quips and tricks. The other passengers gave us glances, and some were obviously laughing at us. As the rails rumbled and the lights were lowered, our fatigued bodies and boggled minds drooped into a doze.

The early morning hours brought us to our first destination, Johnson City. Here we disembarked to take another train to Elkhorn City, Kentucky, a few hours later. The long layover gave us time for breakfast and a time to freshen up inside the train station. This being Sunday morning and a church nearby, we made our way there for the morning worship service.

By early afternoon and having had a sandwich, we were ready to board the second train for our final destination. We were now entering the mountains and scenic byways. This train was not only a passenger train but included some freight cars, stopping at most of the village towns, dropping off goods and commodities for local businesses.

To stretch my legs from the restricted coach seats and the slow travel, I strolled down the narrow aisle and out onto the open deck of our car. The moving air and the wide-open valleys were so refreshing. Soon, I was joined by the brakeman, a youthful looking gentleman of interest and query. Our quick chit-chat let him know where I was going. It was a moment of delight and thrill for me. But my traveling buddies were curious of my absence and soon became aware of my time-out and visit by the brakeman on the deck. Their silent grimace and head-bobbing was an accusation to this innocent moment of flirtation.

Slowly and finally, we arrived at the small town of Elkhorn City. There, an older student, also from Memphis, was waiting for us. He loaded our belongings into the school president's car, which he was privileged to drive. Now the curving roads were dark, with only the light from the moon peeking over the mountains. We, too, were peeking over the horizon of tomorrow.

In a few minutes and miles, we turned from the main highway on to a large steel bridge, scooted around two stiff curves, then made a steep ascent up a narrow road to a large, classic, two-story house encased with many windows, twinkling with soft, gentle lights. The groan of the second gear and the car's beaming lights alerted those inside that the expected students from Memphis had arrived. From the warm lights of the opened door came the president's wife, a tall stately matron. Behind her was the school secretary, a slender, lanky woman with a wide smile and red hair. They greeted us with open arms and a prepared meal in the president's private kitchen. We were famished and exhausted by the long tiresome day. Subdued and in silence, we consumed good filling food, eager to see our new place of abode.

We two women students had been assigned to two different dormitories. My placement was in a long barracks-like room with bunk beds for nine girls. My assigned bed was a lower bunk in the far corner. The lighting was from bulbs dangling from the ceiling. There was one bathroom with one shower stall and two closets to be shared by all the dormmates. As soon as my bed was readied and nighttime duties taken care of, I slipped into slumber even before the pull chain extinguished the light.

The next morning, dawn was broken, not by sunlight, but by a humble bell. The sun slowly made its way over the towering mountains. The president's home and the two girls' dormitories were nestled up against a tree-shrouded mountainous hill. An older student, who served as dorm monitor, hustled the drowsy new students from bed to bath to breakfast. Breakfast and the other meals were prepared and served downstairs in a kitchen and large dining area. As we descended the clunky steps, we were met by looks from curious eyes and silent scrutiny. We were, likewise, sizing up the new place and new faces.

An announcement was made from the faculty table that there would be an orientation meeting at the administration building at 10:00 a.m. All returning and new students must attend. This building and the chapel were on a lower level beside the main highway.

The president of the school, Mr. Joseph S. Otteson, presided over the meeting. He was a strong, stalwart man, six feet of statue, of Norwegian extraction. He had broad shoulders, a bold brow, strong jaw line and keen eyes. His resonant strong voice conveyed resolute and forthright convictions. His presence and demeanor denoted leadership and authority. He had been well prepared for the role of training young people for Christian service. A graduate of Moody Bible Institute of Chicago and of the Biblical seminary of New York, he, along with his wife, served as missionaries to India for fourteen years. He knew the need for dedication, training, and experience for the Lord's work. He was a gifted song leader and avid Bible teacher with a sense of practicality in all things.

After an appropriate song and a prayer for discernment and dedication, he laid down the laws and regulations for the coming school year. First, he dealt with personal and practical matters. There were rules for attitude, attire, grooming, and personal interactions. More importantly, he expounded the requirements of academia. There were certain courses required for first year students. In addition to the afternoon study hall, there would be an hour of study hall in the library each weekday evening. There would be no excuses for absences of classes except for emergencies.

Thirdly, there were policies for the premises. No single student was to leave the campus without permission — checking out and in on return. Single students did not leave campus together unless properly chaperoned. Other possible problems were covered and regulations propounded for the good of each student and the public image of the Institute.

The next meeting would be with Mrs. Otteson, the Dean of Women, with the female students in the small parlor in Severance Hall that afternoon. This was the name given to the large house on the hill, which included the president's residence, the school kitchen and dining area and the dispensary. Mr. Rollin Severance, owner of the Severance Tool Company of Saginaw, Michigan, had given a generous contribution to purchase the property for the school.

At the appointed time, the "freshwomen" filed into the elegant sitting room with a comfortable sofa and chairs. Mrs. Otteson made her appearance with the bearing of a queen. She was regal in manner and gracious of spirit. After a greeting and warm welcome, she led in prayer and praise for the gathered group of students for the coming school year. With note pad, she had a list of work assignments. It was the known policy of the school that each student would perform one hour of domestic duties each day. For the girl students, this would be dusting and sweeping, helping with the food preparation, setting and clearing tables, washing and drying dishes. Some of the older students were privileged to work in the school library. I was assigned the job of washing and rinsing the cream separator two times a day. This dairy apparatus was in the basement of the first girls' dorm. Yes, there were cows that provided milk for the school. The barn for the cows and some chickens was on the lower level of the campus beyond the administration building. Two farm boys, one from North Dakota and the other one from Michigan, did the milking and gathering of eggs. This was a duty performed morning and evening and the "out-pull and in-put" was delivered to the creamery room by the two gangling gauchos in a little red pickup truck. So my domestic duty had a degree of delight and amusement, sharing my task with the "buttermilk boys."

The most important task was registering for classes. The freshman courses were Bible Synthesis, Doctrines of the Bible, Personal Evangelism, Bible Basis of Missions, Fundamentals of Music and Personal Hygiene. Unfortunately, but fortunately for my good, I was required to take Remedial English since I had not finished High School. I was aware that some of the more sophisticated students noticed this and minimized my worth. The course was taught by Miss Beth Bromley, from Wisconsin, a dedicated and able teacher. There were several others, mostly fellows, taking the class. Supposedly, English is a dull and boring subject, but the class was very beneficial and interesting and made us more competent and qualified for our calling and future work.

The following week, the school secretary conveyed to me that a gentleman from the railroad had called, looking for me. I assumed it was the brakeman of the brief encounter on the deck of the run from Johnson City to Elkhorn City. It was merely ships that "pass in the night." (1) Supposedly, when he found that I was really a student destined for Christian service his interest came to "the end of the line."

Twenty-Seven

Usually the fellows were the first in line at mealtime. They had to walk from the lower level of the campus up a steep hill of steps to Severance Hall. Instead of meditating they were salivating for the daily portions of some goodly morsels. But their patience overruled as each descended the steps to the dining area forming a line against the wall, and waiting to be seated at the bountiful tables of filling foods. This waiting time was a time of quiet chatter and palaver before the prayer of blessing on the provisions for the physical strength. As the students, both boys and girls, were in close proximity, there were guarded glances and spontaneous grins. A few moments of harmless jest and levity served as a cohesive bond for the students.

We had been orientated, familiarized, and categorized of abilities and possibilities. We were adjusting to the routine of work and study and the schedule of classes and chapel. The newness of our surroundings and others was wearing off, and we were relaxing and accepting others as Christian brothers and sisters. I had one encounter with an older student of the senior class that brought me down a notch or two. We were gathering around the entrance to Severance Hall, waiting for the dinner bell. The school mascot, a big, black hound, "Tammy," stepped up on the steps going into the dispensary. Being nearby and thinking this was no place an animal, I stepped over and kicked at the massive canine, telling it to "git." From the top of the steps came this tall woman student with broom in hand scolding me, "If you kick Tammy, you have me to deal with."

By now, we had had a trial run of all our responsibilities. The Sunday services were over except the evening service, which was informal and flexible. After two selected songs from the school hymnal, the students were asked for their favorites. Then there was a time for testimonies. This had been one of the normal and spontaneous things of my Christian experience. I had been so blessed and impacted by these times of sharing at Youth for Christ ministries. After two or three fellows had shared their thoughts, I stood to my feet. With heart fluttering, I gave thanks and praise to the Lord for saving me, giving me Christian friends and leading me to this place of training and service. Instead of smiles of joy, I got stares and glares of consternation as if saying, "Are you going to preach?" Needless to say, I suppressed any further inclination to speak out and confirm my faith and calling.

Music and singing were an integral part of the ministry of Biblical endeavors. The music and choir director was eager to meet the new students and evaluate the possibility and potential of an organized choir. At the appointed time, the students assembled for practice, which was in reality an audition for each one. Mr. Cal Beukema was a gentle man and a gifted director. Not only was he skilled in vocal tones, but also an accomplished musician in piano and the trombone.

I did not pretend to know anything musical or "note worthy," but all students were required to be present. The language of music: notes, bars, scores, parts, key and time was foreign to me. What I knew I had learned through osmosis from country music from the Grand Old Opry, Nashville and the country church. I had learned and enjoyed the simple choruses at Youth for Christ by note.

The director chose two very familiar hymns from the school hymnal, *The Voice of Thanksgiving*, to warm up the vocal chords and each other. Then he chose one that was new to the group, having definite parts from the high soprano notes to the low bass and the alto and tenor in between. As the novices screeched and reached for the high notes, others dropped down, singing the melody an octave low. The maestro was subtly scanning each student, listening with discerning ear,

233

and carefully sizing up each participant. As I reached for the high sustaining note, I knew I had missed the mark. He looked askew, astounded, and confounded as he endured this rookie rendition of this classic hymn.

Needless to say, there was no encore; the dedicated instructor knew his work was eminent and urgent. The course in Fundamentals of Music would begin tomorrow.

The minutes of each day were pre-scheduled, beginning from the time of rising in the morning until lights out at 10:30 p.m. From breakfast, work, chapel, classes, lunch, physical exercises, supper, study hall, quiet time, and bed, we kept our pace as duty demanded. Some classes required more preparation than others. Synthesis, the study of a particular book of the Bible, meant two hours of reading for each class session which met three times each week. There was much memorization of appropriate and designated Scriptural verses for Personal Evangelism.

The class that was most fun and challenging was Fundamentals of Music. We were exposed and taught the many various elements of notes, melody, harmony, and rhythm. After the basic introduction to the rudiments of composition of chords and keys, we were required to stand before the class and lead a song. This meant beating out the time with hand and arm, punching the timorous air. The one I chose to lead was "Work for the Night Is Coming," being in a simple four four time. Braver souls attempted the more complicated, convoluted six-eight time of "Faith is the Victory." For instance, if the number of the song was announced as two-hundred and eighty-five, part of the class would turn to page two hundred and start singing and others would turn to page eighty-five and do likewise. We learned quickly and rightly to say two hundred eighty five.

Our teacher and director was Mr. Beukema, affectionately called " Uncle Cal." He was the embodiment of all the virtues and beauty of sacred music and was truly a virtuoso in ability and spirit.

After being assigned to a dorm, a domestic duty, and classes of study, one other remained—that being the practicum. Here the students would have the practical experience of applying what was learned in the classroom. Since this was a Bible Institute, all activities would be involved in Christian services. Various opportunities were that of teaching Sunday School classes, hospital visitation, and jail services.

My practical work assignment was teaching a Sunday School class at Greasy Creek Grade School on Sunday afternoons. The work was under the supervision of an older student and his wife. The first day of this assignment was quite an experience. Since it was Sunday, I dressed in my Sunday-best, that being a black crepe dress with white collar and matching pumps, my Sunday shoes. Our conveyance was a vintage red pickup with seats on the back covered by a shell. The way took us over a small mountain and into a valley, crossing through a creek before reaching the school. There had been a heavy rain the night before, washing the bed of the creek into potholes, making it unwise to ford with the truck. So with fellow students, I tiptoed from rock to rock of the creek bed in my high-heel shoes, to drier bank and "higher ground."

I was given a class of boys and girls of primary age, that of six to nine years old. Our classroom was on one side of this two-room schoolhouse. We would be going over to this area each Saturday afternoon for visitation, letting the people know who we were and inviting them to Sunday School. Eventually, there would be a week of special meetings for all, children and adults.

This would be my first experience of teaching and reaching out to the needy and un-churched. Back in the dorm, we shared our experiences and prayer requests for our new endeavors. Others had more heart-rending experiences. Some of the girl students visited the very sick in the hospital, sharing the Word and praying with them. The men students were taken in the school bus to the county jail. The guards swung open the locked doors and gave the students, with Bibles in hand, free rein to preach and reach the wayward and sobering inmates. To many of these aspiring and budding preacher boys, these would be their first sermons.

The school grounds were situated on two levels of terrain. The girls' dorms were on the higher level connected to the lower campus by a well-worn footpath. The incline was quite steep with rocky and rutted places which we, jokingly, called the "cow path." Consequently, we girls had to descend and ascend this trail three times a day: in the morning for chapel and classes, in the afternoon for P.E. and study hall, and in the evening for study hall in the library. The fellow students were forbidden to use this shortcut since it came around the girls' dorms with open windows. I welcomed the walk and exercise, but I did not have suitable shoes for this rough path and other work assignments. Having a former semi-professional job, my wardrobe was casual but not heavy duty. I needed some heavier shoes to tread the rough path but did not have the money to purchase them. I had nowhere to go but to the Lord, and this I did in earnest prayer for this need. In a few days, a letter with a check came from a ladies group at Bellevue Baptist Church. They had attended a special Youth for Christ service on Court Avenue. Dr. Bob Jones, Sr. was the featured speaker. Since this event was to promote the work of YFC in Memphis, I was one of the young people that gave my testimony of how the Lord had reached and saved me through this ministry and outreach. I have never met these ladies before or after this event, but the letter expressed how the Lord had laid me on their hearts. Through Mrs. Jones, my sponsor, they obtained my name and address. The Lord had answered my prayer and met my need. The amount of the check more than exceeded the price of a pair of saddle oxfords, which I secured right away. With renewed faith and trust, I knew the Lord would take care of my needs and guide my life into the future. I claimed my special verses even more: "I can do all things through Christ which strengtheneth me." (Phil. 4:13) and "My God shall supply all my need according to His riches in glory." (Phil 4:19)

My school expenses were underwritten, including room and board and textbooks, by Mrs. Jones, my sponsor and benefactor. But there were no provisions for spending money such as toiletries and incidentals. Consequently, I must find work at the school for these needs. There were some small and odd jobs that would give me credit at the school store. These I readily accepted to do on Saturday, the more unstructured day. I could make a few coins by ironing the fellows' dress shirts for ten cents each. There was an ironing board and iron handy in the laundry room in the basement of the girls' dorm. At other times, there were floors to be scrubbed and baseboards to be wiped in various rooms and the baths in Serverance Hall. Under the direction of Mrs. Otteson, I scrubbed with buckets of soapy water, brushes and rags. Mops were not a part of my cleaning tools.

Since I was country bred and fed, it was assumed that I was accustomed to not only eating beans and cornbread, but also cooking these country victuals. Since I had been mostly an outdoor girl on the farm, cooking had not been my forte. The school cook, Mrs. "Cookie" King, was relieved of kitchen duties on Wednesday afternoons. I was given the task of preparing the day's supper of dried beans and cornbread—these being full of fiber, wholesome, filling, and inexpensive. So at three o'clock this Wednesday, I descended the steep steps to the kitchen and applied my life's verse, "I can do all things through Christ which strengtheneth me." I literally knelt down by the counter and asked for wisdom and know-how. I did know that dry beans needed to be soaked in water a few hours before cooking, and this I had done at breakfast time. The cook's cookbooks were always handy in the corner cabinet. Soon, thumbing through the splattered pages, I found the directions for cooking pinto beans. Four cups of beans with six cups of water needed to be cooked for one and one-half hours. With strips of bacon and mental math I determined how much and how long to cook a pot of these soup beans.

While the beans were simmering and softening, I found the recipe for cornbread, which called for yellow cornmeal, some flour, sugar, eggs, and milk. The sugar I deleted, knowing sweet cornbread was not suitable to a southern palate. In greased iron skillets and a hot oven, the batter turned into solid, crispy corn pones. Finding some pickle relish in the refrigerator and chopping small bowls of onions for each table, the feast was ready for hearty appetites of these rustic Bible recruits.

The lowly legumes were not to be served at the faculty table. Their refined digestive systems could not tolerate this mountain grub. So a casserole of milder sustenance had been prepared earlier for them. The students' eyes gleamed and their mouths watered as they gulped down hefty portions of this country cuisine. Their palatable performance proved to me that the meal had been well prepared, well seasoned, and well received. Again the Lord had helped me through a moment of culinary learning.

The freshman course load was not too demanding. Some of the students were involved in musical groups or private piano lessons. I did consider piano lessons, but an introductory session with the teacher convinced me that I was not ready, and she readily agreed.

Twenty-Eight

My academic, social, and domestic lives had taken on different dimensions. I was enjoying and thriving with my studies. My social life, interacting with the female students, was okay. But there was marginal interacting and "outer-acting" with the male populace. With my domestic duties and classes, everything was on an even keel. My life now had three levels — literally. The lower level was the library in the basement of the administration building, where I browsed through books, read *The Courier Journal*, the daily newspaper from Louisville, and studied for my classes. The dormitory and Severance Hall were on the middle level where I slept, ate my meals, and worked.

The upper level was the high hill or mini mountain behind Severance Hall. Most of my free time was on Saturday afternoons after I had done my weekly laundry and assigned housekeeping duties. I would ascend this high hill with a book of interest. There was not a defined path, but I enjoyed the climb through low bushes, under twining vines, around trees, and sometimes across logs on the ground. Occasionally a squirrel would scamper up a tree and on to a limb. At the top, the ground was level, and there was an open sky with wisps of feathery clouds. There was such a sense of peace and serenity. Even though I had climbed a steep hill, I felt like standing on my tiptoes to see more. I did not know then that John Keats had experienced this same emotion: "I stood on tiptoe upon a little hill (big hill). The air was cooling and so very still. I knew and felt in my heart: God's in his Heaven,

All's right with the world."(2)

There was a big tree surrounded by a plush carpet of moss. Here I sat on the ground and leaned against the sturdy trunk, reflecting on my life and contemplating my future. After meditating upon the goodness of my Lord and pondering over current incidentals, I was ready to descend the mountain, back to regular routine of student life. The cushion of moss had been so comforting . On second thought, I would take some of these velvety clusters with me. Since moss has no real roots, it was easy to pull it from the ground. So carefully I was able to get a large piece for a prayer mat for the side of my bed. Needless to say, my dorm sisters were curious and exasperated when they saw this chunk of wild stuff with strands of dirt clinging to it. Moreso, the one assigned to housekeeping for the week was very perturbed, but I promised to sweep around my area and keep the dust and dirt under control.

From the mountaintop to the valley below and the rocky foot paths in between, we were all tenderfeet in training for life's goals and scouting for the gold of truth. Sometimes hidden fears took on the faces of fun and frivolity. Since I always loved nature and the outdoors, I gravitated toward any wriggling thing, especially frogs. I spied a big, fat one by the waterspout that came out of the hillside. With both hands I scooped up the knobby green creature and took it inside my dorm. Its presence inside the girls' domicile drew shrieks of disgust and fear. I whispered to a nearby bunkmate, "Whose bed shall I put it in?" "NO! NO!, NOT MINE!" At bedtime the girls could be seen peeking under the covers. Of course, the friendly frog was long gone.

Another time I came upon a long king snake on the sidewalk beside our dorm. There was a large lump ballooning from its upper body. It was obvious that it had swallowed a rat. I called for the residents to come and see the harmless reptile with its recent meal. Needless to say, there was a lot of screeching and squealing as the frightened females scampered back inside, and the gorged snake crawled off into the tall, shady grass.

One of the dorm-mates was a quiet, reserved handmaiden of the Lord. She was a very devout and solitary soul. Even before quiet time for devotions, often she would be down on her knees beside her bed in prayer. On one occasion, the toilet overflowed and was flooding the floor through the door and around her bed that was adjacent to the bathroom. Although we were running for mops and a plunger, she remained on her knees as the water touched her toes. The dorm big-sister had to disturb her prayer by calling her name and shaking her by her shoulders.

Another time I needed to go down in the basement for some urgent reason and did not turn on the lights. In the darkness I stumbled over a warm clump. It was this same girl kneeling in prayer. With apology and admiration, I turned on the lights and helped her to her feet. She accepted the interruption as an accident and lingered behind to continue in her prostrated position and prolonged petitions, but with the lights on.

Pent-up concerns for grades, family, friends, and finances sometimes erupted into moments of jest and joking. The most apt place for this harmless flummery was the dinner line while waiting for the serving bell. A degree of formality was present for the evening meals. The male students were required to wear jackets and ties for supper except on Saturdays; slacks or pants of any sort were not acceptable for the girls, even on Saturdays.

The members of the faculty, Mr. & Mrs. Otteson and single staff members, did not take their places at their table until the last minute, so there was no figure of restraint present. Preoccupied bodies and minds began to relax and loosen up to things more mundane. Quibbles and quirky remarks were exchanged back and forth, most in fun, but some too focused for comfort.

One of the preacher-plebes, down from the northern climes, was trying to impress his fraternal dorm brothers with his social boldness and worldly wit. Flexing his sagging, flagging, mindless, masculine-challenged muscles, he blurted out, "Ninety percent of the girls in the world are good-looking and the other ten percent are here at Southland." His male counterparts dropped their eyes to the floor. The branded ten percent stared and grinned at their Christian brother. No one dreamed that there would and could be anyone in their midst, who could bring forth such hare-brained humor. If they only knew that Disraili labeled this irresponsible chatter many years ago; (3) "The hare-brained chatter of irresponsibility and frivolity."

The student body was made up of young people from various states and cultures. Some were privileged; some were deprived, having no social underpinning. Primarily the school was planned for young people of the Appalachian area. After two or three years in operation, interested ones from other areas heard of this unique Bible Institute and sought training and experience here. Some of the applicants were children of pastors and missionaries; others were influenced and encouraged by mountain missionaries or pastors.

In my case, a Bible teacher and matron directed and made it possible for me to be here. The Lord led each one of us to this place of training. The male students were aspiring to become pastors, evangelists, or youth leaders and most necessary vibrant song leaders. Their idealism was obvious and prevailing. The conception of these roles meant having a prim and proper helpmeet (helpmate) to augment their image more perfectly. Their wives must be talented — that is able to play the piano and sing alto.

The female students were more realistic, seeing themselves as missionaries or children workers. The present practical matters helped them to face the fact that they might pursue the Lord's calling alone. Consequently, the girls sensed the subliminal requirements of the male counterparts. Those who qualified became the elite and the "cream of the crop." Those who did not "fill the bill" withdrew emotionally and compensated with an indifferent air and attitude.

As the pre-meal chatter continued, the verbal shadow-boxing served as a warm-up for the day. The content could be amazing, amusing, and bemusing. One evening, the fellows seemed to be unusually quiet which made the girls more self-conscious. So we girls stirred the air with some shuffles and remarks. I personally felt that I had been "weighed in the balances and found wanting." I could not play the piano or sing alto; I could just barely follow the melody of a song. Refusing to accept this evaluation, I perked up and spouted a coquettish quip. "I'm going up to Alaska where there is six months of darkness." Yes, I had entertained the idea of transferring there when I worked for the telephone company. The girls grimaced and almost shuddered as they thought of the extreme cold conditions, but the fellows' eyes fluttered and probably their toes twitched. Some seemed to be saying "I'm going too."

From the fledgling flock of eager preacher-boys was a student from Ned, Kentucky. He came from a dysfunctional family and had been mentored and influenced by a mountain missionary. He arrived on campus with his meager belongings in two paper bags. In one of the bags was a pair of boxing gloves, ready for battle in the boys' barracks, and moreso, symbolically, with the Devil as he later expressed in the school yearbook: "I thank God for His gift of eternal life to me. I owe everything to Him and nothing to the Devil, but the best fight I can give him."

He enthusiastically became a learner of the Word and a buddy to his fellow-students. Having a natural knack for trimming hair and with a stool and clippers in hand, he became the school barber for thirty cents a head. Sometimes his eagerness for drastic cuts brought down the ire of the school president.

He had a proclivity for mimicking well-known evangelists, namely one John R. Rice. Next to the Bible, he treasured the writer's book of sermons. One of his favorites was "Bobbed Hair, Bossy Wives, and Women Preachers." As a cub exhorter, he took great delight in proclaiming this topic in the presence of the female bystanders.

From his rural roots, he would take on the guttural articulation of country preachers, propounding such profound truths as "Where a hen scratches, she is sure to find a worm." Even with his sense of humor and levity, he was serious about his calling for the Lord's work. His role model and example was Coy Turner, an area evangelist. In years to come, he would pursue and complete more levels of education and be a camp director for many years.

Mrs. Esther Otteson, the wife of the school president and the Dean of Women, was a constant force of inspiration and purpose. Her compassion and composure permeated the Campus, the classroom, the chapel and the residences. Her presence and aura of grandeur impressed upon me a desire to learn from her and achieve the same level of confidence and social skills. She was both a gentle and strong woman, one possessed with grace and charm. She had good taste in dress and in the décor of her home. Gestures and a natural ease of manners set all at ease. There was beauty of soul and insight, a mental alertness and a tender heart. She was the perfect hostess, and in a moment's time, she could greet visitors and guests and make them comfortable situated with a cup of coffee, a slice of cake or a crunchy muffin.

The students knew that she and her husband, Mr. Joseph Otteson, had been missionaries to India for several years, which meant training and competence for such a responsibility. But particulars of their early lives were not well known. She was the daughter of Norwegian immigrants, which made her an ideal companion for Mr. Otteson who had the same heritage, even though he came from Minnesota and she from New Jersey. Brought up in a Christian home, at the age of twelve she accepted the Lord and grew up helping in her church by doing secretarial work, playing the piano and singing. She had held two business jobs, first working for the chief inspector of the Maryland Casualty Company in New York. Later, she became an assistant purchasing agent for the General Chemical Company in New York City. Although she enjoyed her work and made good money, she felt the Lord wanted more for her. One Sunday afternoon she attended a young people's meeting at a church in Brooklyn. The guest speaker was a missionary from India who spoke of the great need for women to minister to women in India. She had always wanted to be a nurse, and when this need was made known, she went forward, surrendering to the call and task of reaching those souls in this faraway land. She gave up her job and found a school near home, enrolling at the Union Bible Training school, which later became the National Bible Institute. She also enrolled for nurse's training at the Deaconess Hospital in Brooklyn.

During this time, at a meeting at a church in Jersey City, she met the man who would later become her husband. She thought this young man was on his way to Africa, and she had already committed her life to service in India. Many months later, circumstances brought them together, and their lives coincided perfectly. She continued with her nurse's training and he went on to India. Three years later, he became seriously ill and needed medical care. An urgent plea from the mission board cut short her training, and she joined Joe in India in 1921. There in Amalner, Mahawashtra State in India, they were married and continued their mission work together. Two children were born to them. After five years on the field, they returned to America for needed rest and medical care.

In 1932 the family returned to India for their second term of service. Mr. Otteson was named field chairman where he organized conferences and helped new missionaries learn the language and become acclimated to the culture. More importantly, he conducted evangelistic meetings and taught Bible classes. Mrs. Otteson taught the Bible to the women and served as the hostess for the mission compound. She also organized weddings and attended to births and deaths and took care of the general medical needs of the compound and district. The people responded to their warm and caring personalities. They even entertained many government officials including the American Counselor General.

In the meantime, Mr. Otteson had developed a Bible course to train lay workers to win their own people to the Lord, which proved to be the surest and fastest way to evangelize India. In 1939, the Ottesons returned to America. Their daughter had returned three years earlier to begin high school. The family moved into a mission house in Chicago.

Mr. Otteson traveled for the Mission (The Evangelical Alliance Mission-TEAM) during the winter and directed the Gull Lake Bible Conference in Michigan through the summer.

During a meeting in Chicago, a Christian worker from the Kentucky mountains heard Mr. Otteson speak of the Bible course that had been successfully used by his Indian converts in winning their own people to the Lord. The Christian worker was convinced that this type of training was needed in the mountains where young people, now growing up, needed this same type of Bible training and challenge for their own people.

After returning to the mountains, the missionary shared the possibility of this training with other Christian workers. They began to pray about the matter and invited Mr. Otteson to come and speak at a regional conference. The workers prevailed upon the Ottesons to seriously consider coming to the Appalachians and permanently establishing a training center instead of going back to India. In the meantime, while all were praying about this undertaking, one of the interested parties found property at Wolfpit, Kentucky, which would be the future campus of the Southland Bible Institute.

While this undertaking was being considered, Mr. Otteson was asked by a Christian businessman, George Headberg, the general manager of the Severance Tool Company to speak at a Christian Business Men's meeting at Saginaw, Michigan. After the meeting these men gave a sizable donation to help purchase the property at Wolfpit. By the end of the week, another businessman, Mr. A. W. Beckstron from Pittsburg, gave the sum for the balance.

It was a difficult decision for the Ottesons to make — leaving foreign missions which had been their life's work. All variables pointed to the Lord's leading, and they answered the call to the Kentucky Mountains and the ultimate establishment of the Southland Bible Institute.

The Southland Evangelistic Center was established in 1942. The grounds were made ready for use, providing a place for Bible conferences. Intensive Bible study courses were offered during the summer months for the young people of the area. The first conference held on the grounds drew one hundred missionaries and a well-known Bible teacher. After three years of progress and promise, Mr. Otteson began considering a three-year Bible Institute, and he was urged to pursue the project by the Christian workers of the region.

By September 1945, a staff had been acquired and the Institute was incorporated in the state of Kentucky and approved for study under the G.I. Bill. There were only fourteen full-time students the first year. For the second year, the enrollment doubled, and the third year it doubled again, this being the first year of the graduating class.

It was my first year (1947) to arrive at the foot of this mountain, to view its heights and to climb its craggy sides under the care and encouragement of this remarkable guide, Mrs. Otteson.

From the pious to the practical, I had much to learn. Being country raised, I was now under the tutelage of a city-bred lady of refinement. There was never any hint of condescension or superiority, for I felt confident in her presence. There were gaps of culture from my upbringing — one of the obvious being that of food. I knew all about fried chicken and chicken and dumplings but had never heard of chicken fricassee, which was chicken cut-up, fried or stewed and served in a sauce of its own gravy. Then there was chicken a la king, the same procedure but using chopped or cubed chicken, served over hot biscuits or mashed potatoes. These chicken dishes were our usual Sunday noon fare. Most of the meals were planned and supervised (overseen) by Mrs. Otteson. Most fascinating of all was Swedish coffee prepared especially for guests. Mrs. Otteson would crack an egg and crumble shell and all and put into the coffee grounds before pouring on the water for boiling. It made a strong brew of coffee and was delicious to the taste buds of Scandinavians, who were coffee aficionados.

One dish most of the students loved and looked forward to was Indian curry and rice, a dish from the mission field prepared by Mrs. Otteson. It was a combination of cubed beef and potatoes cooked in a sauce of sautéed onions and curry powder and served over rice. Mrs. Otteson even mixed her own curry powder from tumeric, cumin and cayenne pepper. The side dish was always chutney, a relish made of fruits such as apples, pears, pineapple or prunes cooked with onions in vinegar, and spiced with cinnamon and ginger.

No doubt, I was being acculturated and motivated to higher heights and wider horizons.

Twenty-Nine

It was an honor and privilege to be under the commanding influence of this devout and distinguished lady, Mrs. Otteson. She was, indeed, a queen of all Christian graces in the eyes of the students and in the heart of her husband, Mr. Otteson. The most moving influence was the example of love, honor, and respect she had for him. Indeed, "her husband was known in the gates." Her countenance glowed in his presence, and her voice bathed his name as she lovingly called him "Joe," and at informal times spoke to us students as "Poppy Joe."

Even though she was a tall woman, she seemed to be taller as she stood by his side, prompted by pride. He, in turn, took great delight in her and realized fully her worth to his ministry. She was most assuredly "a virtuous and worthy wife, earnest and strong in character, a crowning joy to her husband." (Proverbs 12:4, Amplified Bible) She was a woman of strength and dignity. (Verse 25). A sage of old penned these words: "The perfect woman nobly planned is one who thinks, loves, and acts with the large heart of a woman." Tributes from Proverbs 31 aptly describe her:

"A wife of noble character who can find? She is worth far more than rubies. Her husband has full confidence in her and lacks nothing of value. She brings him good and not harm all the days of her life. Her husband called her blessed and he praises her. Many women do noble things but you surpass them all." (NIV)

Although her husband, Mr. Otteson, was an imposing

male figure with a strong authoritative force, when he spoke her name — Esther — there was a gentle tenderness and his eyes softened with love and devotion. Sometimes they would sing a duet for chapel and the blending of love and tone spoke of their life and service together. Certainly that which crowned her life and service was confirmed in Proverbs 31:30: "A woman that fears the Lord, she shall be praised." This sense of the Lord reigning in her heart gave beauty to the soul. From the Living Bible: "these good deeds of hers shall bring her honor and recognition, which she rightly deserves."

To we, the uninitiated young singles with "stars in our eyes" and dreams in our hearts, this union of love and service gave us assurance that the Lord would also direct and lead our lives unto service and His glory.

As the days of fall rolled into the early days of winter, I was becoming more acclimated to my schedule of work and study. I was learning through my practical work assignments, that of teaching Sunday school at Greasy Creek Grade School. The leader gave me an assignment to teach a Bible story for all the students. To make it more visual and focused, I chose to use the flannel graph method. With easel set up and flannel figures ready on deck, I stood beside the board with Bible in hand and told the whole story. Then I looked down and the flannel figures were still lying flat on the deck. I plopped down on the front seat, dropped my head in disappointment and left the hearers to wonder why the board was empty.

The year was coming down to the end and I had no plans or money for the free days of the Christmas break. Then came a letter with a check for transportation from Youth for Christ, inviting me to be a special guest at Ellis Auditorium. Since the trip up by train had been rather awkward and besetting, I made plans to travel back to Memphis by Greyhound bus. The routing would take me from Pikeville to Cincinnati and down to Nashville. I had been able to ride with another student into Pikeville. The longer trip was quiet and uneventful which gave me time to ponder over the last few months and to pray about the immediate future, that of giving my testimony before a large audience. While in the Nashville terminal, waiting for a bus to Memphis, a curious bystander asked me if I was a sister (nun). No doubt my dour appearance gave that impression. We were not permitted to wear makeup, and I had chosen simple clothes to travel including black shoes. I arrived in Memphis and caught the city bus to my temporary quarters, which was the mission director's residence at 1084 Poplar Street. His home now was a spacious three-story building, the former Henry Halle home. I would be staying in the girls' shelter on the third floor. This was a large area with ten beds, the dormitory for girls who needed economic, physical or spiritual aid. Thank the Lord, I had been spared these dilemmas and prayerfully hoped I could be of help during my brief stay.

Right away I reported to the telephone company for temporary work during the holidays. On Christmas morning before daybreak and time for me to rise for work, I was awakened by the sound of the most beautiful singing of Christmas carols coming from the street below. I assumed it came from a local Catholic church at early mass, proclaiming the joyous tidings, treading the thoroughfare of the city.

At the YFC rally I blended in with the other participants, one being Doris Doe, a former prima dona of opera. She, in voice of splendor and attire of the elite, gave beautiful renditions of two gospel songs. Here I was—a peasant girl from the cotton fields of west Tennessee—sharing the same platform. "I sought the Lord and He heard me and delivered me from all my fears. He set my feet upon a rock and established my goings and He hath put a new song in my heart, even praises unto our God." (Psalm 40)

With the old year behind me, I was back from switchboard and city friends and ready for the new year, all settled in for the second semester of studies. The most challenging class had been Synthesis, a study of the books of the Old Testament. This course was a birdseye view of the scope of the Bible in which we read and scanned the books, the parts that made the whole.

Now for the second semester we were assigned one major book of the Old Testament, Isaiah. The study was called

Analysis, in which we separated the whole into parts. In other words, we would dissect the chapter and verses, focusing on the details and determining the function and place in the Holy Scriptures. The teacher was a very demanding instructor and very knowledgeable of the Bible. We students stood in awe of him. His lectures to the class were powerful and so convincing that Isaiah was the greatest of the prophets and the most comprehensive in range of the eternal counsels of God, the creation of the Universe, and the redemptive work of Christ.

Our written assignment for the course was to outline the book of Isaiah. I had not been taught the steps of outlining but was aware of its purpose. By observing the table of contents of history and reference books, I could see the systematic listing of the most important parts. The main headings were defined by Roman numerals; the subheadings were shown by capital letters, followed by regular numbers and small letters. It was very obvious that the first words of each topic and subtopic were capitalized. By analyzing and separating into parts, we were to determine the main thought of each paragraph and then choose a word or phrase that covered the contents. Most of our teachers were also preachers, and their sermons were mostly expository in form. There was detailed explanation of a portion of the Scriptures, usually with the points tied together with alliteration. This form often used the repetition of sounds or words that began with the same letter. This method was very effective and pleasing to the ear and also a mnemonic, that is, an aid to helping the memory, even to the hearer.

As I read and scanned the book of Isaiah, I was amazed at the lucid words and pattern of phrases in the text. I found many combinations of thoughts and sounds that made the reading so interesting and alive. Here are some of the phrases:

Blood of the bullocks
Ragged rocks
The stay and the staff
Wheels like a whirlwind
Smooth stones of the stream.

And some couplets were so illustrative:

> Swords into plowshares
> Spears into pruning hooks
> The haughty shall be humbled
> The high ones hewn down.

In chapter 11:2 there was a ready-made outline:

A. The Spirit of the Lord
1. The Spirit of wisdom and understanding
2. The Spirit of counsel and might
3. The Spirit of knowledge and of the fear of the Lord.

I had always been fascinated with words and their sounds and meanings. Now I had found a pattern and purpose, the outline. My brain had been primed. With dictionary in hand, I began to mine the rich ore of words of same sounds and letters.

After many days of digging and dangling words for fit and sound, I turned in my super-alliterated paper to the professor. He was not impressed, giving me a marginal grade, saying I had over-embellished the work.

Perhaps I had, but the experience and sense of achievement and discovery gave me high marks to myself.

Thirty

After another summer at the switchboard in Memphis, I was back at Southland in the fall of 1948 for my second year. My daily hour of domestic duty continued as before, that of washing the cream separator twice each day following the morning and late afternoon milking. I had been elevated from odd jobs to a regular job as the maid-in-residence. I was solely responsible for the care and upkeep of the president's home. The basement of the house was the area for students' dining and the school kitchen and storage. The main floor contained one large living room and a large parlor with grand piano and expansive fireplace, framed with a handsome mantelpiece and ornate andirons. There was a dining room, with cabinet of fine china, and a private kitchen. Also there was a dispensary, an office and a half bath. Surrounding the front side of the house was a large sunroom, and fronting the house was a large veranda enclosed with copper wire screening.

An elegant winding staircase led to the second floor. Here was an extended hall lined with linen closets. The master bedroom was tastefully decorated with elaborate tapestries. There was a spacious bathroom with ceramic tile floor and walls. An imposing seven-foot bathtub lined the wall to a free-standing porcelain wash basin. Even more commanding was the shower stall with seven heads — one large one at the top and three on either side. The guest bedroom was at the other end of the hall. Here, Mrs. Otteson gave me implicit instructions to every detail to make this room comfortable and inviting for guests. The bathroom must be sparkling clean and water faucets in working order. There must be plenty of bath towels, face towels and washcloths, a fresh bath mat and a new cake of soap. Also there must be a clean wastebasket and an ample supply of toilet and facial tissues at hand. I was taught how to properly make a bed, making sure the sheets were long enough and properly tucked in with the top sheet turned back about six inches with the rough edge of the hem turned outside away from the face of the occupant. Nearby there were to be extra blankets or covers. Mrs. Otteson remembered, with regret, an embarrassment of a previous incident when there were no blankets for the beds of some guests, and the night was very cold.

In between these two main bedrooms were two others — one for the maid and a bath. Here also was a private stair and a built-in call bell for maid service.

I was honored to be entrusted with the care and upkeep of this honored residence which meant dusting furniture, making beds, cleaning windows and scrubbing the floors and baseboards. No mop was ever used, but with bucket, brush and cloth the work was done at close range.

This classic and commodious residence had originally been the home of the superintendent of a mining company that encompassed this area. Several hundred men were employed by this operation, and most of their homes were built and owned by the coal company. The centerpiece had been this large house situated on the side of the mountain overlooking the smaller dwellings below. At this time, the coal had been mined and the company and the ruling regime had moved on, leaving many buildings vacant and for sale to the locals. It was at this time when Christian workers of this region became aware of this ideal property for a Christian training place. The building was well designed, and the structure was substantial and permanent with gutters and downspouts of copper. No expense had been spared for the amenities; even the receptacles and outlet covers were of solid brass. All the faucet handles were of porcelain.

When the Ottesons arrived, there was only this building on the premises. There had been a church on the lower level built by the coal company, but when the organization moved on, the building was demolished, leaving only the foundation filled with ashes and debris. When the summer school began, this hard surface served as a skating rink for the students.

The increasing interest and enrollment demanded more space. By this time, two older experienced carpenters had joined the staff. One of the fellow students had worked with the Seabees, the construction wing of the U.S. Navy. In a matter of months, with the experienced workers and fellow students pushing wheel barrows and mixing cement, work in earnest was underway. An administration building was taking shape, constructed on the former foundation of the church. The ground floor became the library, the bookstore, a snack shop, and the printing area. The main floor became the chapel, offices and classrooms. The second floor gave more space for the balcony, more offices and classrooms.

The lower campus became the location for married couples' residences, called G.I. Cottages. An Army barrack was brought in and re-erected on the site and divided into rooms for the boys' dorm, and in close proximity, a residence for the dean of men was added. Some of the former coal company foremen houses in the village were secured for faculty residences.

The faculty, staff, students and volunteers had been faithful to their calling; the Lord provided every need and blessed the work beyond all expectation.

My practical work assignment continued at the grade school at Greasy Creek. This area was isolated due to the rough terrain and culturally insulated from the outside world. Their patterns of religion and social life were frozen in time. The church leaders were theologically illiterate. They did not promote Sunday School and met only once a month for church meetings. Any newcomers or new ideas were looked on with scorn and suspicion. But the Institute considered these hollows and settlements as frontiers to be reached with the Gospel. We were now doing more visitations on Saturday afternoons. After reaching the schoolhouse, we went in pairs up and down the creek inviting the families, and especially the children, to Sunday School.

One afternoon, my partner and I walked into a family emergency. The father and mother and their little girl about eight or nine years of age were rushing out the door on the way to the hospital. The child was very sick and writhing in pain. She had eaten or chewed on some poisonous weed or tree sprout and had vomited all over the floor. We were helpless to the situation and after they were gone, we found a bucket and mop on the back porch and cleaned up the floor.

Another time, we were on visitation after a flash flood which had occurred the day before. This was quite prevalent down the hollows and creeks. One of the persons we called on excitedly told us of an incident which happened to one of their neighbors. The turbulent waters had come rushing down the creek, and up on a bank above the creek was situated an outhouse. The rushing water swept the privy off the bank and into the stream below. Unfortunately, there was an occupant inside that escaped through the porthole.

We saw and heard many interesting things. I remember seeing a grandmotherly figure walking around in her kitchen kneading bread in a dough bowl and smoking a corncob pipe. Another time we were leaving the area in late afternoon and were sitting in the back of the pickup truck shielded by the shell, when rocks pelted the side of the truck, bidding us an unwelcome goodbye.

We continued the work and held a week of evangelistic meetings with Coy Turner, an area evangelist, who was well known and well liked by the mountain people. Also our conveyance was upgraded from the vintage pickup to a G.M. carry-all.

Thirty-One

In the second semester of my second year, I took the required course of Public Speaking. Through lectures and instruction we were shown proper platform mannerisms and positive posture and given drills in enunciation (that is, pronouncing words clearly and distinctly). To finish the course, we were assigned to choose a famous speech and give it forth with enthusiasm and command before the class.

At this time in my young life, I had not chosen my political identity. As a teenager I had experienced the throes of victory of WWII and remembered vividly the death of FDR. I was aware that Vice President Truman took the rightful office of President and seemingly calmed our country by furthering the Fair Deal and continued the fight for freedom for all nations known as the Truman Doctrine. But when his time came to win the office of President from ground zero, it seemed certain that the Republicans would grab the victory for the 1948 election. Being able to peek and browse through the daily newspaper in the school library during study hall time, I was aware of the political fury and the almost certain victory of Thomas E. Dewey, the Republican candidate.

In our dorm was an older student, having been a school teacher before coming to the Bible Institute, her first year. She was more sophisticated and worldly-wise and an avid Republican. Freely and frequently, she vented her political opinions to we politically uninitiated students. Noting her subdued defeat when President Truman won one of the biggest upsets in political history, I chose to give Truman's inaugural address to the class. Of course, it was done in fun and harmless teasing. But certainly, the substance of the address was not trivial but very serious. Here are some opening and closing remarks of the speech.

"I accept with humility the honor which the American people have conferred upon me. I accept it with a deep resolve to do all that I can for the welfare of this nation and for the peace of the world.

In performing the duties of my office, I need the help and prayers of every one of you. I ask for your encouragement and your support. The tasks we face are difficult, and we can accomplish them only if we work together.

The American people stand firm in the faith which has inspired this nation from the beginning. We believe that all men have a right to equal justice under the law and equal opportunity to share in the common good. We believe that all men have the right to freedom of thought and expression. We believe that all men are created in the image of God.

From this faith we will not be moved."

Knowing President Truman's courage and imagination, he would have been proud of me, and I did get an A- for the course.

Spring had come to the mountains. The hillsides were decked out with dark pink blossoms of the Eastern Redbud trees. The school planned an Easter Sunrise service some distance away at a state park. All were dressed in our Easter attire, and the students were transported to the site by the school bus. Since I was involved closely with the going and coming of the Ottesons, I was invited to ride with them. It so happened that their son Ted, now gainfully employed as a translator and living elsewhere, was home for a visit. He was driving the family car and Mr. and Mrs. Otteson were seated in the back and I up front with their handsome gallant son.

When we arrived for the outdoor service, did I get the stares and silent heave-hoes from the pusillanimous preacher boys.

At this time, for the nearly two years I had concentrated on my studies and work, resolved not to pine and wilt over some possibly-remote romance. In fact, in defense of my stance, I had written my mother saying not to worry about me getting married while here, as there was not one guy I would consider worthy. But things would soon change. There was one student also free from any noticeable romantic inclination. He could have been because two of the girl students were obvious admirers of his ability and could have become very interested in knowing more of him. He was president of the senior class, editor of *The Torch*, the school's yearbook, and sang bass with the Ambassadors, the school quartet. While the quartet was on an extended trip through the mid-south and the east coast, I received a letter from him. They were on an engagement at a college in Tennessee and it seems that the bright moonlight and fragrant honeysuckles reminded him of me.

I was astounded and surprised that he saw any merit in me. There I was, the maid-in-waiting, considering myself of no talent and of limited education. He was a class leader, chosen for Mr. Intellectuality, a budding theologian and future pastor and teacher.

Returning to campus with a grinning interest, he asked if he could sit with me in chapel, of which a rule had recently been made. I humbly accepted the invitation and shared the short time with him until the school term was ended.

He graduated and returned to his home church in West Virginia as an assistant pastor; I returned to Memphis to work for the summer.

In parting, my interested friend had pronounced a prophetic utterance that the Lord had more in store for me than being a telephone operator. Arriving back in Memphis, I assumed that I would again work for the telephone company. But working conditions and the economy had stabilized, and the company was not hiring anyone at this time. I immediately scanned the classified ads in the newspaper and found that General Electric was hiring at the local light bulb plant. I applied and was sent to downtown Memphis for a placement test, which was a written test and dexterity evaluation. I was assigned as an inspector on an assembly line for small bulbs, mostly Christmas ones. The belt was about four feet in width, of which the bulbs came tumbling down the line. If any were defective, they flashed blue when they made contact with a certain part of the belt. It was my job to observe closely and snatch the faulty ones before they tumbled into the next section for packaging. I sat on an elevated metal stool that enabled me a wide swath over the moving belt. I heartily accepted my assignment because I needed a job and earnestly tried to adapt myself to the task at hand. But frequently, when making contact with the apparatus around me, I would receive an electrical shock. My supervisor was indifferent to my predicament. With increasing apprehension, I became more tense until one day, in much pain, I had to report to first aid, but still no attention was given to the cause.

I had no recourse but to look for another job. Again I went to the Sears retail store, applied and was given a job in the toy department. In the meantime, letters were coming more frequently from my preacher-boyfriend in West Virginia. Our correspondence was becoming more chummy and cuddlesome. Certainly the distance and "the absence were making our hearts grow fonder." Soon a letter came asking if I would accept an engagement ring. My reply must have been in the affirmative, as in a few days a notice came from the post office that I was to pick up a registered package.

At this time, one of the department stores ran a sale on wedding gowns, and I was able to select a style at a price I could afford on my limited income. In September my fiancé came to Memphis for a brief visit. One of his classmates was from the area, so he stayed at his mother's place. We were able to have some intimate moments together and to make plans for our wedding. Together we agreed that by the end of the year we could have our affairs in hand and ready for the day. I would work through the Christmas season and we would be married New Year's Eve.

Since he was assistant pastor of the First Baptist Church, he was busy, now doing most of the Sunday services and the mid-week meetings. The senior pastor was away most of the time, taking advantage of his stand-in. Besides the church duties, he was going into two coal camp communities, Tuesday and Thursday nights for Bible classes. Twice each week, he conducted chapel services in two of the area schools. There were funerals to conduct and two weddings to officiate — one in particular that was a novelty and surprise. He had just presided over a formal wedding, the church being decorated with flowers and candles. The wedding party had departed, but the chapel was still in formal array. He had just walked into his mother's house when the telephone rang. Someone from the church was calling to inform him that another couple was there, wanting to get married. Putting back on his formal jacket he dashed back to the church, and after minutes of consultation with the young couple from the hills, he led them into the church for the vows. Naively, they thought the decorations were just for them. Hopefully, they had happy memories for years to come.

As Christmas time drew near, it was a turbulent time for the miners and their families. The workers were on strike against the coal companies. The church chose to hold a series of revival meetings to under gird and strengthen their faith during this time of uncertainty. The meetings went into the second week with much response and interest. The two pastors, the older and the young one, alternated the speaking each night. By the end of the two weeks, both were exhausted and down with colds, and the wedding day was drawing near. Christmas Day was on Sunday, and plans were made to leave the next day by Greyhound for Memphis.

Tired but eager, he boarded the bus and headed west toward the long state of Tennessee. Being winter, the heater on the bus was on high and passengers became restless and opened windows that brought in cold air on the travelers. Already in a weakened condition and wracked with a cold, his sickness worsened. When the bus arrived at the station in Bristol, he could go no further. Putting his luggage in a locker, he took a taxi to a hospital. Since this was Christmas week, no doctor was on duty. Desperate for medical attention, he took another taxi to another hospital where he had to wait some time for a doctor to see him. Then medicated with a powerful pill the doctor called a "yellow jacket," he was put to bed for two days.

In the meantime, I am in Memphis wondering and worrying about him as he had not arrived as scheduled. Finally, a call came through explaining his delay. I had friends waiting at the bus station upon his arrival. Apologetically, he tried to explain, but his paleness proved his plight. We had to go to the courthouse to secure our marriage license. While downtown, we dropped into a shoe store where one of our former classmates was working. While there, his nose started bleeding profusely. It was urgent that he receive immediate medical attention. We called a cab and went to the emergency room at the Baptist Hospital where they contained the bleeding with a nasal pack. Back with friends, we discovered we had lost our marriage license during the hustle and confusion. The friends went back to the hospital and found the important permit in the emergency room.

We were wearied and worn, but the rehearsal for the wedding ceremony was before us. We hoped the worst was over, and it was, as friends gathered around us expressing joy and delight in the occasion. I had asked the pastor of my childhood church to perform the ceremony. He had driven one hundred miles and seemed honored to be a part of this very important venture of my life. I listened closely to his procedure, taking clues for each part where I was to respond, especially when we were to seal our vows with a kiss. Now somewhat rested and relaxed, I felt confident that I was ready for the most important day in my life beyond the day of salvation when I found the Lord.

Our friends dropped me off at my place of abode, a lonely room that I rented along with other working girls in a spacious house on a side street. Along with my thoughts, I realized that this was my last night of "singlehood." I thanked the Lord for Christian friends who had encouraged, nurtured, and sheltered me, and were now proving their love and concern even more in so many ways. The friends from my first church were providing the flowers and ornaments for my wedding, even the aisle runner for my entrance for the ceremony.

The Youth for Christ director, Jimmy Stroud and his wife Dorothea were having the reception at their elegant home after the wedding. I had already taken my wedding gown to their residence for last-minute dressing before leaving for the church.

Thirty-Two

After a short night's sleep, I quickly packed my belongings in two suitcases, freshened my face, fixed my hair, and boarded a city bus to the director's residence. I knew my father and two sisters were coming to the wedding, but my father declined any part in the wedding ceremony, so I had asked the YFC director to give me away in the ceremony. From his home, he and his wife drove me to the church. My maid of honor, Peggy Ellis, a friend from the telephone company and Youth for Christ, was waiting for me in her emerald green satin dress with a beautiful bouquet of red roses. We had chosen the colors to continue with the Christmas season. The best man, Raymond Childress, a former classmate and the groom's roommate, brought in the handsome six-foot groom. Robert Deline and Albert Miller, also former classmates, were the ushers. Sherrill Cranfield, the pianist of YFC was playing a beautiful medley of wedding music. The soloist, Robert Festress, sang, "I Love You Truly Dear." Reverend W.A. Moody officiated in a stately fashion but did not follow the same phrasing as in the previous night's rehearsal. I was listening closely for clues for the vow finality for the kiss, but there was none, and consequently, no kiss. My new husband turned me around, and we proudly but humbly traipsed down the aisle facing the guests and the world together as the soloist sang:

O Jesus I have promised, to serve Thee to the end.
Be thou forever near me, my master and my friend
I shall not fear the battle, if Thou art by my side.
Nor wander from the pathway, if Thou wilt be my guide.

We were back in the stately home of the Strouds for the reception and some pictures. The presence of our family members gave a special touch to the occasion. They had traveled many miles for this event. Mrs. Cook had traveled alone by Greyhound bus from West Virginia to see her preacher-son claim a girl from Tennessee as his bride. It was my first time to meet her and I felt that I had gained her approval. After we had enjoyed bites of a delicious and beautiful wedding cake and sipped sparkling punch, tearful goodbyes were said and each went on their own way.

From a nearby room, I donned my going-away suit of vibrant green. The best man took us to the Claridge Hotel in downtown Memphis. No reservations had been made, but there were rooms available. Keys were given to us for room 716. This was Saturday, New Year's Eve 1949, and at the stroke of midnight, horns were blowing, fireworks were popping, and revelers from the street below were whooping and celebrating just for us, so we pretended.

The next morning being Sunday, our friends came by and took us to the Bellevue Baptist Church where the honorable and well-known pastor, Robert G. Lee, brought the morning message, "The High Cost of Low Living." Here we filled out the visitors' card, "Rev. and Mrs. Arnold B. Cook" for the first time. A few days later, our visit was acknowledged by a card from the church, signed by Mrs. Herbert Smith.

The next day, leaving dear friends behind but with their prayer following us, we boarded a train to West Virginia. Around midnight we arrived at the station at Charleston where my husband's mother and a friend, Millie Thompson, were waiting for us. There were still thirty-nine miles to go over mountainous roads on a cold, snowy night, but our hearts were warmed with delight, for we at last were in Whitesville and home.

The next morning, the sun was delayed because of the mountain to the east. Whitesville was an elongated town with two streets parallel to Coal River, and sandwiched between two mountains. The leafless trees and craggy hillsides wore snatches of fallen snow.

We spent our first few days with my new husband's mother who lived in a duplex right across the street from the Moose Lodge where there was much coming and going. Mrs. Cook's floral shop was one block over, sharing the corner of the building with the drug store. The church was in walking distance on the street by the river.

My first visit to the church was a reception and shower hosted by the senior pastor and his wife, Mr. and Mrs. O.E. Stump. We received many durable and practical gifts, among them a set of stainless Revere Ware given by Alvin Miller. These pots and pans we used for fifty years. Another gift was a set of Fostoria sandwich plates given by Mr. and Mrs. George Branham, he being a mine superintendent. There were many other needed and practical gifts to set up housekeeping.

For the first service at the church, I wore my green "going-away" suit for my "coming-in" to this community and church family. Obviously, there was much peeking and peering from curious on-lookers as I made my debut into their midst. Perhaps there were mothers with eligible daughters who felt jilted. The nerve of this hometown boy to bring in a bride from a far country, and a redhead at that!

Right away, we moved into an apartment across the alley from the church. It was a three-room and bath triangular arrangement with the tip end adjoining a clinic where sometimes mothers could be heard in labor.

Furniture was our next need. Mr. Alvin Miller, owner of a hardware and appliance store, took us to Charleston to select a couch and chairs, bedroom suite, and from his store we chose a Hotpoint range and dinette set.

Since the miners were on strike, the men of the church were free to visit and loaf around. The day our furniture came, they were there to unload it and place it in the apartment. Not only did they unload the new stove but stayed around to observe my first operation of it and to partake of my first meal prepared on it. There was one young man, who had been converted in the recent revival, who stayed close by each day and sometimes into the early night hours.

As we did not have our own car, friends and church

members transported us around for business and church visitation. In the immediate town we walked since everything was so compacted at hand. The community of about one thousand people had almost every kind of business and service. Besides the floral shop, drugstore and clinic, and hardware store already noted, there was a bank and state police post. There were three grocery stores, several restaurants, two theatres, two funeral homes, two department stores, a jewelry store, a shoe shop, a hotel, and of course, the post office. Also two dentists, six doctors, and an attorney there to serve, heal, and protect the people. Most importantly, there was one school and only one church, the First Baptist Church of two hundred members, and the pastor, the Rev. Stump, who had been the pastor for twenty years.

The busy, bustling town was the commercial center for an area of large coal mines and a C&O Railroad yard. A transit bus system served the outlying areas, bringing in shoppers on weekends. The women shopped for food and necessities, the children went to the shows, and the men furthered their fellowship and brotherhood at the beer joints.

There was an interesting mixture of cultures and blood-lines. This Appalachian area was predominately Scotch-Irish, but there were remnants of the Cherokee and Mingo tribes of the American Indian lineage. Later, immigrants from Eastern Europe found their way into the mountains and found their flair in restaurants and cafes. Second and third generations of these foreign-born people moved on into the field of medicine and education.

William Elsworth Cook and his wife Bida had been a part of this thriving community, having reared a family of seven children—three daughters and four sons—losing one son in infancy. The father was an engineer with the C&O Railroad, running the trains loaded with coal from the mines and bound for Russell, Kentucky, to be loaded on barges on the Ohio River. Mr. Cook came to an untimely death at age fifty-five, when my husband was only fourteen years old. Mrs. Cook, the mother, had to resort to a menial, low paying work of making soft, wood-fiber flowers to sustain her family of three children still in school. The following year another tragedy befell the family: my husband, then fifteen years old and in the tenth grade in high school, had a shooting accident while squirrel hunting with a buddy up in the mountains. Being a boy scout and knowing first aid, he was able to control the bleeding by making a tourniquet out of his undershirt until he was rescued and carried to the hospital, thirty-nine miles away at Charleston. There, he spent two months, gangrene having set in, and his right leg had to be amputated above the knee.

Needless to say the family were survivors with strength and determination, Mrs. Cook now owned the floral shop she once worked for and was a respected and proven business woman. Her middle son, my husband, was a graduate of a School of biblical studies and the assistant pastor of the First Baptist Church. Needless to say, this hometown boy had made this town and his mother very proud.

We were happy and so blessed by our Lord. Our family loved us, and we were accepted by the community and appreciated by the church. Our future was before us, knowing the Lord would lead in his paths of service.

Addendum

The events in the life of Carmelene after the account of her marriage would be material for another book. She and her husband and daughters travelled all over America, and to several foreign countries. Their three daughers married and settled down in North Carolina. The parents did likewise.

Carmelene was a regular patron of the public library at Eden. The annual book fair witnessed her faithful attendance. The following occured at one of those yearly events and is a fitting closure to *My Heart Knows* . . .

It was Monday, the last day of the book fair. A bag of books of one's choosing could be bought for one dollar. I had been one of the first-comers on Friday, the first day of the fair. The price had been one dollar for hard backs and twenty-five cents for paperbacks. With no interest in the paperbacks, I soon found five hard backs to add to the crowded shelves of my own library, but the fun of seek and search for serendipities brought me back to the final day. Knowing there were boxes of books underneath the tables yet to be displayed, I armed myself with a shopping bag with sturdy handles and headed again to the public library. The tables were still heaving with volumes of classics, fiction, science fiction, and may other categories, neatly labeled by the volunteers.

Eagerly, I scanned the rows of books on the long, laden tables looking for Louis L'Amour westerns for my husband, to justify this second day of book mania. Although not finding any L'Amours, my paper book satchel was soon filled with other acceptables. During this time of thumbing book backs, the area around the religious books was crowded with curious seekers. I, too, was looking for a certain book for a friend. The browsers were now thinning out, except one acquaintance I had not seen for a while, until the previous Friday. We were both amused that we were here again, neither one really needing any more reading materials. I quickly glanced at the remaining tomes of sermons by T.V. evangelists and Sunday School study books, but saw nothing of personal interest, but then noticed there were some books under the table, half-hidden from view. Not wishing to overlook any gem, I dropped to my knees and reached into the cardboard box. The first book my fingers grasped, froze in my hand. The book *Skidrow Stopgap- The Memphis story"* stared at me. I breathlessly gasped to my nearby friend, "I bet I am in the book." She looked puzzled as I quickly turned the pages to the first pictures. There was the "Story in Pictures," pictures of Jimmy Stroud and the Memphis Union Mission. I did not want to appear too presumptuous, closing the book, putting it in my bulging bag of bargains. Feeling confident of my emotional instinct, I followed my somewhat bemused book-sister to the paymaster, joyfully paying the one dollar.

Trudging home with my treasure-trove, I still did not know for sure what I had surmised. Since it was lunchtime, I quietly placed the bag of books near the recliner at my husband's feet. With suppressed anticipation, I put on the teapot and opened a can of soup, meekly suggesting to him that my story might be in one of the books. Quickly, he scanned the Memphis book: "Yes, beginning on page eighty-eight, there are three pages about you."

After a quick lunch, I tiptoed to my bedroom, propped my head on three pillows and almost reverently opened the book again. Memories actually preceded the contents of pictures and narrative. I did not know that this book had been written. The account of the impact of the Memphis Union Mission and Youth for Christ upon my life had appeared in previous publications. A monthly magazine, *Down to Earth* (June 1946), had featured an article of my exodus from a Tennessee cotton farm to the bustling city of Memphis, where Youth for Christ gave me a new focus and meaning for life. The following year, March 1947, another article was written by Mel Larson in the national *Youth for Christ Magazine,* none other than by the same author of the book I was now holding fifty-five years later. The book had the copyright date of 1950. I had married and left Memphis in 1949, not knowing the book was being written.

On the mellowing pages were the black and white photos of capsulized memories of these precious people and familiar places. There were Mrs. Jimmy Stroud with the three Stroud youngsters; Mrs. Verla Pettit, secretary-bookkeeper for the Mission; and T. Walker Lewis, key lay leader in the Memphis Project. I remembered anew the great speakers that came to speak in chapel, and the Youth for Christ rallies. Dr. Charles E. Fuller and pianist Rudy Atwood, Rev. James McGinlay, Dr. Bob Jones Sr., Dr. Vincent Bennett, Dr. Merv Roselle and many others. The pages also reminded me again of other girls who had come to the big city, seeking adventure and a future. Now their lives were shattered and wrecked—one in particular, thrice married, a heavy drinker and suicidal. The girls' shelter provided by the Mission had been a refuge for unwed, pregnant girls, some led astray by married men.

As I closed the book, I shuddered at the words "skid row-stopgap" which this had been for these girls and many men, young and old, who had fallen through the cracks of life. But thanks to the good Lord, there had been Memphis Union Mission with its many ministries that had rescued them from failure and despair and gave them a new start and purpose for the future.

I was humbled and yet overjoyed, as I, too, had been impacted by this great organization but had been spared the scars and regrets of most of these persons.

It may have been a stopgap to bad choices and poor judgment in my future if I had not been reached by the message and ministry of these caring people of the Mission. But there are three pages about me in this newfound book and I must tell you why I am there. On a late spring day in the middle of May 1945, just after dark, I was on a Greyhound bus entering the perimeter of Memphis, Tennessee.

Notes

(1) "Ships that Pass in the Night." and speak to each other in passing, only a signal shown and a distant voice in the darkness; so on the ocean of life, we pass and speak to one another; only a look and a voice; then darkness again and a silence. (Henry Wadsworth Longfellow) p. 233.

(2) "Pippa Passes." (Robert Browning) p. 242.

(3) Benjamin Disraili, "Speech Guidhall, London November 9, 1878. p. 244.

ORDER FORM

Additional Copies of *My Heart Knows . . .* may be ordered directly from the author. The following prices apply:

Cost per book	$16.00
Add 6.75% sales tax for North Carolina residents	_____
Shipping and handling per book	3.00
Total Amount:	_____

To place an order by mail, send check made payable to:

Mrs. Ethel Cook
600 Whetstone Creek Road
Stoneville, NC 27048
(336) 432-0069

With all orders, include the following:

Name _____

Address _____

City _____ State _____ Zip _____

Phone Number _____